About the Author

DUBRAVKA UGREŠIĆ is the author of several works of fiction, including *The Museum of Unconditional Surrender*, and several essay collections, most recently *Thank You for Not Reading*. She has received several international prizes for her writing. She has held positions at Harvard University, the University of North Carolina, Wesleyan University, and the University of California, Los Angeles. Born and raised in the former Yugoslavia, she left her homeland in 1993 for political reasons and lives in Amsterdam.

About the Translator

MICHAEL HENRY HEIM is a professor of Slavic languages and literatures and comparative literature at the University of California, Los Angeles. His many translations include Chekhov's *Essential Plays*, Milan Kundera's *The Unbearable Lightness of Being*, and Thomas Mann's *Death in Venice*, for which he won the 2005 Helen and Kurt Wolff Translator's Prize. He also has translated Dubravka Ugrešić's *Fording the Stream of Consciousness*.

THE MINISTRY
OF PAIN

THE MINISTRY
OF PAIN

Dubravka Ugrešić

Translated by Michael Henry Heim

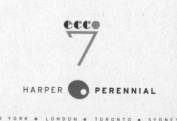

ecco

HARPER PERENNIAL

NEW YORK • LONDON • TORONTO • SYDNEY

HARPER ● PERENNIAL

Revisions to the Croatian edition of *Ministarstvo boli* originate with the author.

A hardcover edition of this book was published in 2006 by Ecco, an imprint of HarperCollins Publishers.

FIRST HARPER PERENNIAL EDITION PUBLISHED 2007.

Designed by Cassandra J. Pappas

Title page photo © Peter Tumley/CORBIS

The Library of Congress has catalogued the hardcover edition as follows:

Ugrešić, Dubravka.
  [Ministarstvo boli. English]
  The ministry of pain / Dubravka Ugrešić ; translated by Michael Henry Heim.
      p. cm.
    ISBN-10: 0-06-082584-7
    ISBN-13: 978-0-06-082584-3
    I. Heim, Michael Henry. II. Title.
    PG1619.31.G7M5613   2006
    891.8'2354—dc22

                                                2005048837

ISBN: 978-0-06-082585-0 (pbk.)
ISBN-10: 0-06-082585-5 (pbk.)

07 08 09 10 11 ❖/RRD 10 9 8 7 6 5 4 3 2 1

NOTE

The narrator, her story, the characters and their situation in the novel you are about to read are all fictional. Not even the city of Amsterdam is wholly real.

D. U.

Those pangs of homesickness!
That long since detected upheaval!
I am altogether indifferent
As to where to be altogether

Alone or how to drag my tote
From bazaar to house and home,
A home that is mine no more
Than a hospital or garrison;

Indifferent to what sort of people
Will see me, the caged lion, bristle
And from what sort of world I will—
As I must—be banished into

Myself and my own feelings.
Like a Kamchatka bear with no ice floe,
I don't care where not to fit in
(I don't try to) and where to eat crow.

Nor am I charmed by my mother
Tongue's call, cajoling and creamy:
I set no great store by the tongue that others
Use to misconstrue me

(Readers solely intent upon
Milking the press of its bletherings),
For they're of this twentieth century,
And I precede the centuries.

I am stunned like a log left to lie
On a path with trees. Everyone's the same
To me, it's all the same to me,
And what is all the more the same

And closest of all, perhaps, is the past.
All my features, all traces, all dates
Have vanished into its morass:
I am merely a soul born—somewhere.

My country has so let me down
That should a sharp-eyed sleuth
Search that soul inside out
It would fail to sleuth forth native roots.

Every house is alien, every temple empty,
All the same, all one, all mere trash.
But if by the road there's a tree
That chances to be moutain ash . . .

                                    Marina Tsvetaeva

PART 1

The northern landscape like the desert makes for absolutism. Except that in the north the desert is green and full of water. And there are no temptations, no roundnesses or curves. The land is flat, which makes people extremely visible, and that in turn is visible in their behavior. The Dutch are not much for contact; they are for confrontation. They bore their luminous eyes into those of another and weigh his soul. They have no hiding places. Not even their houses. They leave their curtains open and consider it a virtue. Cees Nooteboom

I don't remember when I first noticed it. I'd be standing at a tram stop waiting for a tram, staring at the map of the city in the glass case, at the color-coded bus and tram routes that I didn't understand and that were of little or no interest to me at the time, standing there without a thought in the world when suddenly, out of the blue, I'd be overcome by a desire to bash my head into the glass and do myself harm. And each time I'd come closer to it. Here I go, any second now, and then . . .

"Come now, Comrade," he would say in a slightly mocking tone, laying a hand on my shoulder. "You're not really going to . . . ?"

It's all my imagination, of course, but the picture it creates can be so real that I actually think I'm hearing his voice and feeling his hand on my shoulder.

People say that the Dutch speak only when they have something to say. In this city, where I'm surrounded by Dutch and communicate in English, I often perceive my native language as alien. Not until I found myself abroad did I notice that my fellow countrymen communicate in a kind of half language, half swallowing their words, so to speak, and uttering semi-sounds. I experience my native language as an attempt by a linguistic invalid to convey even the simplest thought through gestures, grimaces, and intonations. Conversations among my compatriots seem long, exhausting, and devoid of content. Instead of talking, they seem to be stroking each other with words, spreading a soothing, sonorous saliva over one another.

That's why I have the feeling I'm learning to speak from scratch here. And it's not easy. I'm constantly on the lookout for breathing spaces to deal with the fact that I can't express what I have in mind. And there's the larger question of whether a language that hasn't learned to depict reality, complex as the inner experience of that reality may be, is capable of doing anything at all—telling stories, for instance.

And I was a literature teacher.

After going to Germany, Goran and I settled in Berlin. Germany had been Goran's choice: Germany did not require visas. We'd saved up quite a bit, enough for a year. I quickly found my feet: I landed a job as a nanny for an American family. The Americans paid me more than a decent wage and proved to be decent people. I also found a part-time job at the National Library, shelving books in the Slavic Division one day a week. Since I knew a thing or two about libraries, spoke Russian in addition to "our language," and could make sense out of the other Slavic tongues, the work came easy to me. I lacked the proper work permit, however, so they had to pay me under the counter. As for Goran, who'd taught mathematics at the University of Zagreb, he soon found employment in a computer firm, but he resigned after a few months: a colleague of his had been hired as a lecturer at a university in Tokyo and was trying to lure Goran there, assuring him he would get a better job forthwith. Goran in turn tried to persuade me to leave, but I held out: I was a West European, I said by way of self-justification, and I wanted to be close to my mother and his parents. Which was true. But there was another truth.

Goran could not make his peace with what had happened. He was a fine mathematician and much loved by his students, and even though his was a "neutral" field he'd been removed from his post overnight. Much as people assured him that it was all perfectly "normal"—in times of war your average human specimen always acted like that, the same thing had happened to many people, it happened not only to Serbs in Croatia but to Croats in Serbia, it happened to Muslims, Croats, and Serbs in Bosnia; it happened to Jews, Albanians, and Roma; it happened to everybody everywhere in that unfortunate former country of ours—they failed to make a dent in his combined bitterness and self-pity.

Had Goran really wanted to, we could have put down roots in Germany. There were thousands upon thousands like us. People would begin by taking any job they could muster, but they eventually rose to their own level and life went on and their children adapted. We had no children, which probably made our decision easier. My mother and Goran's parents lived in Zagreb. After we left, our Zagreb flat—mine and Goran's—was requisitioned by the Croatian army and the family of a Croatian officer took it over.

Goran's father had tried to move our things out, the books at least, but failed. Goran was a Serb, after all, which I suppose made me "that Serbian bitch." It was a time of fierce revenge for the general misfortune, and people took their revenge where they could find it, more often than not on the innocent.

And yet the war settled our affairs far better than we could have done on our own. Goran, who had left Zagreb in the firm resolve "to get as far away as possible," had in fact ended up on the other side of the world, and very soon after his departure I received a letter from a friend, Ines Kadić, offering me a two-semester appointment as lecturer in *servo-kroatisch* at the University of Amsterdam. Her husband, Cees Draaisma, was chair of the Department of Slavic Languages and Literatures and needed someone to take over on the spur of the moment. I accepted the offer without hesitation.

The Department found a flat for me on the Oudezijds Kolk. It was a small canal with only a few houses, one end opening onto Amsterdam's Central Station, the other, like the sections of a palm frond, branching into the Zeedijk, a street known for its Chinese population, and the Oudezijds Voorburgwal and Oudezijds Achterburgwal, two canals running through the red-light district. It was a basement flat and small, like a room in a cheap hotel. Apartments were very hard to come by in Amsterdam, or so said the departmental secretary, and I resigned myself to it. I liked the neighborhood. In the morning I would take the Zeedijk in the direction of the Nieuwmarkt, stopping off at the Jolly Joker, Theo, or Chao Phraya, the cafés overlooking the old De Waag. Sipping my morning coffee, I would observe the people stopping at stalls displaying herring, vegetables, wheels of Dutch cheese, and mounds of freshly baked pastries. It was the part of town with the greatest concentration of eccentrics, and since it was also where the red-light district started it was a hangout for small-time pushers, prostitutes, Chinese housewives, pimps, drug addicts, drunks, leftover hippies, shopkeepers, peddlers and delivery boys, tourists, petty criminals, and the jobless and homeless. Even when the sky (that famous Dutch sky) descended and spread its pallor over the city, I would revel in the leisurely rhythm of the various passersby. Everything looked slightly squalid, the worse for wear, as if the sound were down or the picture in slow motion, as if there were something illegitimate about it all, yet it all seemed to hold together in the name of a higher wisdom. The departmental office was located in Spuistraat, a ten-minute walk from my flat. Everything was in perfect proportion, at least so I thought at first. Besides, that year there was an Indian summer that lasted all the way to December, and Amsterdam, mild and slow-moving as it was, reminded me of the towns along the Adriatic during the off season.

I'd heard the story about the Bosnian woman before coming here, while I was in Berlin. Her whole family was in exile—her husband, their children, the husband's parents—and one day she heard rumors to the effect that the German authorities were going to deport all Bosnian refugees, repatriate them. Because she was afraid of going back to Bosnia, she asked a doctor to give her a false referral to a psychiatric hospital. Her two-week stay there was like a breath of fresh air, so bracing, so redolent of freedom, that she decided not to return. And so she vanished, disappeared, changed her identity. Nobody knew what had happened to her, and she never went back to her family.

I'd heard dozens of similar stories. The war meant great losses for many, but it could also be a reason to slough off an old life and start from scratch. In any case, it radically altered human destinies. Even mental institutions, prisons, and courtrooms became everyday elements of existence.

I wasn't the least bit certain where I stood in all that. Perhaps I was looking for an alibi. I didn't have refugee status, but like the refugees, I had nowhere to go back to. At least that was how I felt. Maybe like so many others I subconsciously turned the misfortune of others into an excuse not to return. Though weren't the breakup of the country and the ensuing war my misfortune, too, and reason enough to leave? I don't know. All I know is that I'd set off in what seemed the distant past, and hadn't yet reached a destination. When Goran left, I felt relief combined with a more intense feeling of loss and fear: suddenly I was completely alone with a professional capital of little value and an economic capital good for no more than a few months. I had a degree in Slavic languages and literatures; I had written a dissertation on the use of Kajkavian dialect in the works of Croatian writers; I had a few years' teaching experience at the Zagreb Teachers Training College. Amsterdam was a paid breathing space. What I would do or where I would go after Amsterdam I had no idea.

They called me Professor Lucić at first, but once we'd settled into our topic for the first semester they switched to Comrade, *drugarice*, affectedly drawing out the final *e* and raising it at the end like a verbal tail, just as I had done in my day. The word "comrade" became a kind of intimate password between my new students and me, linking us, one and all, to the school benches we had long since abandoned, to times long past and a country no longer in existence: "comrade" was the word used by Yugoslav children in the fifties and early sixties to address their teachers. Here in Holland it was not so much a word as the tinkle of a Pavlovian bell. And although I addressed them with the formal "you," I referred to them as my "pupils" or "kids." It was all a humorous bit of make-believe: I wasn't and never had been a "comrade"; they weren't pupils. Nor were they kids, most of them ranging between twenty and thirty, which made me only a few years older. Meliha was my age, and Johanneke and Laki were older than I was. The only thing reminiscent of the rules of the game, therefore, was my use of the formal "you."

They'd come with the war. Some had acquired refugee status, others had not. Most of the guys, the ones from Serbia and Croatia, had left to avoid military service; some had come from the war zones; others had gone along for the ride and stayed on. There were also those who had heard that the Dutch authorities were generous with welfare and accommodations for Yugoslav refugees and came to exchange the dicey currency of their lives for the hard stuff. And there were those who had happened on Dutch partners.

Mario had met a Dutch girl in Austria—where his parents had sent him, fearing he'd be conscripted into the Croatian army— and she took him back to Holland with her. "Maybe I married her for the passport and fell in love with her after the fact," he once told me with a smile. "Or maybe I was in love with her to begin with and made it official because of the passport. I can't remember."

Boban had gone to India on a package deal with a group of Belgrade matrons, followers of Sai Baba. The trip had been engi- neered and financed by his mother, whose only concern was to save him temporarily from the army. In India he'd ditched the tour and wandered about for two months, but then he picked up dysentery and boarded the first plane out. He landed in Amsterdam, where he was to change planes for Belgrade, but somewhere on the way from one toilet to another in Schiphol he'd had a brilliant epiphany and asked for political asylum. It was still a possibility back then. For a year or two the Dutch author- ities were lenient: anyone coming from the former Yugoslavia could use the war as a credible motivation. But in time things changed and the gate slammed shut.

Johanneke was Dutch. She spoke "our language" fluently and with a Bosnian accent. Her parents were Dutch leftists who had built roads and railway tracks with international youth brigades after World War II. Later they went to the Dalmatian coast as tourists. During one of their stays Johanneke visited Sarajevo, fell in love with a Bosnian, and was stranded there for a while. Now, divorced and the mother of two little girls, she had made up her mind to get a degree in Slavic languages. She was an accredited court interpreter from "our language" to Dutch, which turned out to be highly useful: she would translate and authenticate any document our kids needed.

There were those who showed up once or twice and quietly disappeared. Laki was from Zagreb. He remained in my memory because he was the only one who called me Mrs.: Mrs. Lucić. He clearly considered "comrade" to be "Yugoslav," "Communist," and therefore "Anti-Croat." He had a Zagreb way of talking that got on my nerves—the la-di-da stress on the last syllable, the constant use of reflexives, verbal forms referring to the self, that made him sound intimately related to everything on earth. . . . Like so many others, Laki had come to Amsterdam for the cheap pot. He had come before the war and studied Slavic languages and literatures for years, living on welfare and in heavily subsidized public housing. The kids all said that he was a paid police informer, that he bragged about translating the bugged telephone conversations between Yugoslav mafia members the Dutch police had under surveillance. The kids called him Laki the Linguist because he claimed to be working on a Dutch-Croatian dictionary for which he could never find a grant. He refused to acknowledge the existing Dutch–Serbo-Croatian dictionary.

Then there was Zole, who had set up house with a Dutch gay partner to qualify for a residence permit, and Darko, from Opatija, who really was gay. The Dutch authorities were particularly generous about granting asylum to those who claimed they had been discriminated against in their home countries for "sexual difference," more generous than to the war's rape victims. As soon as word got around, people climbed on the bandwagon in droves. The war was a fig leaf for everything. It was something like the national lottery: while many tried their luck out of genuine misfortune, others did it simply because the opportunity presented itself. And under such aberrant circumstances, winners and losers had to be judged by new criteria.

They studied *servo-kroatisch* because it was easy. If you didn't have a refugee visa, you could prolong your stay legally by enrolling in a university program. Some had begun or even completed programs at home, but they meant next to nothing here. *Servo-kroatisch* was the fastest and easiest way to come by a Dutch diploma, not that even a Dutch diploma would get you very far. If, like Ana, you had another language as your "major," you could pick up a few effortless credits with *servo-kroatisch,* but if what you were really after was student loans and scholarships, then *servo-kroatisch* was your ticket.

They coped. Most of them "played tennis," playing tennis in their group slang meaning housecleaning. It paid fifteen guilders an hour. Some worked as dishwashers or waiters in restaurants. Ante picked up small change playing the accordion in the Noordermarkt. Ana sorted mail in the post office every morning. "It's not so bad," she would say. "I feel like the dwarf in Čapek's 'Postman's Tale.' "

But the best-paying job you could get without a work permit was a job at "the Ministry." One of "our people" found work at a place where they made clothes for sex shops and soon the whole gang was working there. It wasn't strenuous: all you had to do was assemble items of sadomasochistic clothing out of leather, rubber, and plastic. Three times a week Igor, Nevena, and Selim went to Regulateurstraat in Amsterdam Nord where the Atelier Demask, purveyor to the many-faceted Dutch porno industry, was located. There was an S/M porno club in The Hague called the Ministry of Pain, and my students took to calling their porno sweatshop "the Ministry." "Those S/M types,

Comrade, they're real snappy dressers," Igor would joke. "They don't think the most beautiful body is a naked body. I wouldn't forget that if I were a Gucci or Armani."

The kids did a good job of coping—considering where they came from. They dragged their former country behind them like a train. People said the Yugomafia was responsible for a third of the criminal activities in Amsterdam. The papers were full of its thefts, prostitute trafficking, black marketeering, murders, and vendettas.

Nor did they know what to make of the country's current status. If they mentioned Croatia and Bosnia, it was with great caution. If they mentioned Yugoslavia, which was now the name for Serbia and Montenegro, it was with great agony. They couldn't deal with the names the media kept throwing out. Rump Yugoslavia, for instance. ("Where'd they get that one from, for Christ's sake," Meliha would cry. "Is it 'cause they hacked it up like a steak?")

Yugoslavia, the country where they'd been born, where they'd come from, no longer existed. They did their best to deal with it by steering clear of the name, shortening it to Yuga (as the *Gastarbeiter*, the migrant workers in Germany, had done before them) and thus "the former Yugoslavia" to "the former Yuga" or playfully transforming it into Titoland or the Titanic. As for its inhabitants, they became Yugos or, more often, simply "our people." The possessive pronoun also came in handy when referring to the language they spoke together (none of them being Slovenian, Macedonian, or Albanian): to avoid its former, now politically incorrect name of Serbo-Croatian, they called it simply "our language."

CHAPTER 3

It is not photogenic
And it takes years.
All the cameras have gone off
To other battlefields.

Wisława Szymborska

The first time I entered the classroom I could tell what made them "our people." "Our people" had an invisible slap on their faces. They had that sideways, rabbitlike look, that special tension in the body, that animal instinct of sniffing the air to tell which direction danger is coming from. The "ourness" came through in a certain strained melancholy in their features, a slight cloud on their brows, a barely visible, almost internal stoop. "Our people prowl the city as if it were a jungle, terror-stricken," Selim would say. And we were all "ours."

We had scampered out of the country like rats deserting a sinking ship. We were everywhere. Many had scurried about within the borders of the former country, taking cover for a time, thinking the war would soon be over, as if it were a rainstorm rather than a conflagration. They would hole up with relatives, friends, or friends of friends, who did their best to help. They would go to the improvised refugee camps, abandoned tourist colonies, hotels willing to put them up temporarily, mostly hotels on the Adriatic coast, but "only in winter, when there weren't any tourists and then they'd have to take care of themselves, then they'd go back home, the war wouldn't last forever, no war lasts forever, war wears people down and when they're tired enough it stops." Some stayed on for a year or two or three—the tourists didn't come back after all—others moved on. And they all had stories to tell.

A woman from Belgrade, "seeing where things were heading" and horrified at the hatred she perceived in her fellow Serbs, sold her house and, just before the war broke out, moved to "peaceful" Croatia. She bought a flat in Rovinj. But when the Croats started showing their fangs, she sold the flat in Rovinj and moved to Sarajevo. The very first Serbian grenades thcy might have been following the lines in her palm to bring about the fate awaiting her and her family—split her Sarajevo flat down the middle. "Thank God she wasn't at home when they hit," said a friend of hers in her artless version of the woman's story. "And now she's just fine," she writes in her latest letter. "Who'd have thought that of all the cities in the world she'd end up in Caracas!"

Refugees from Slovenia—Croats—made for Zagreb, for Istria, for the sea. Refugees from Bosnia went south, to Croatia, or east, to Serbia. The Croatian Serbs beat a quiet retreat from Croatia until they were chased out en masse. The Vojvodina Hungarians slipped noiselessly into Hungary, followed after a while by a number of Serbs as well. And soon the Kosovo Albanians were on the move. . . .

We fled from wherever we could to wherever we could. The

price paid depended on the circumstances. Some thought only about their own, some about their own and others', and some never bothered to ask who was who. Some Bosnian Muslims went to Turkey, Iran, Iraq, even as far as Pakistan; many rued the day. Some Bosnian Jews went to Israel; many of *them* rued the day. People changed their names, given and sur; they bought cheap passports when they could. What had till recently meant everything to them—their faith, their nationality—was suddenly worthless currency. Survival took over. And once survival was assured, once they had landed on a safe shore, heaved a sigh and pinched themselves to make certain they were alive, many of them again hung out their flags, put up their icons and escutcheons, and lit their candles.

We were everywhere. Those who scrambled got the best places: America, Canada; others hesitated and were lost, relegated to whatever was left open to them with tourist visas for a month, for two months, then returning home and gearing up to start again. In the general confusion many used rumors as their sole compass, rumors about where you could go without papers and where you could not, where life was better and where life was worse, where they were welcome and where they were not. Some found themselves in countries they would otherwise never have seen. Passports from the first two breakaway countries of Slovenia and Croatia quickly soared in value. A Croatian passport could get you to Great Britain for a while—until the Brits caught on and shut the gate. A few of the more naive fell for obsolete rumors—like the open arms with which whites were greeted in South Africa—and followed suit. The Serbs were a pushover for Greece, as tourists and prostitutes, as war profiteers, launderers of dirty money, and thieves. Some acquired three passports—Croatian, Bosnian, and "Yugoslav"—in the hope of hitting the jackpot with at least one; others decided to wait, following the war as if it were a tempest about to die down. And people with children were more concerned for the children than themselves: it was the children's safety that mattered.

Europe was teeming with former Yugos. The wave of war émigrés numbered in the hundreds of thousands. Hundreds of thousands of recorded names, names of people with legal refugee status. Sweden had accepted some seventy thousand, Germany three hundred thousand, Holland fifty thousand. As for the illegals, their number was legion. We were everywhere. And nobody's story was personal enough or shattering enough. Because death itself had lost its power to shatter. There had been too many deaths.

I soon learned to pick out my fellow countrymen in a crowd. The men, especially the older men, stood out the most. The main railway stations and the flea markets were their cult gathering places. They would appear in formations of three or four, like dolphins, wearing windbreakers, leather by preference, their hands thrust into their pockets. They would stand together for a while—shifting from one foot to the other, exhaling cigarette smoke, exorcising their fear—and disperse.

In the Berlin neighborhood where Goran and I had lived, I would stop in front of the large window of a refugee "club." Through the glass I could see "our people" mutely playing cards, staring at the television screen and taking occasional swigs of beer straight from the bottle. The hand-drawn map on the wall was festooned with postcards. It had a geography all its own. The places they came from—Brčko or Bijeljina—stood at the center of the world: they were the only country the men had left. Surrounded by smoke rings, they looked as "former" as their onetime nationality; they looked like corpses that had risen from the grave for a bottle of beer and a round of cards but ended up in the wrong place.

On the street I often caught snatches of their language. It was all numbers. They couldn't stop talking numbers. Marks, five hundred marks, three hundred marks, a thousand marks. . . . Here in Amsterdam it was *guće,* this or that number of *guće.* . . . They would draw out their vowels as if babbling, and it was in fact more babble than talk, their endless computations of existing or imaginary funds.

They all had derogatory terms for the inhabitants of the countries where they had landed: *Švabo* for the Germans, *Dačer* for the Dutch, *Šved* for the Swedes. It made them feel important. They peppered their conversations with "Like I say" and "Take it from me," emphasizing their role in the matter at hand, as insignificant as the matter was and as piddling as their role was in it. Sticking to your guns was all. "I can make it from Oostdorp to the Leidseplein in eleven minutes." "How can you make it in eleven minutes? It takes fifteen at the very least. Have you timed it? Well, I have, man. Fifteen minutes on the nose. From the second you get on the tram." They totally did the men in, those conversations. Each word was calculated to postpone the encounter with humiliation, to exorcise the fear.

The manner in which they moved and the places where they came together betrayed their loss of personal space: the bench in front of the house, where they could watch the world pass by, or on the waterfront, where they could see what ships came in and who came down the gangplank; the town square, where they could walk with their friends; the café, where they could sit at their table and have their drink. In the cities of Europe they vainly sought the coordinates of space they had left behind them, their spatial coordinates.

———

They also sought human coordinates. Goran was often prey to Yugonostalgia, and when it was on him he was wont to pick up the first "compatriot" he ran across and drag him home for a drink. I'd soon heard my fill of stories about German refugee centers and their experiences there. "Our people" would stick like glue to every Russian, Ukrainian, Pole, or Bulgarian they met, feeling an our-like bond with them. A Bosnian told us the story of some Polish women who would come to Berlin on one-day bus tours to give "our people" good prices on Polish cheese and sausages and occasionally on a "roll in the hay." With the money thus earned they'd do their Berlin shopping for the week and take the bus back home. They could always sniff out one another on the street: it was their common misfortune that did the trick. The same Bosnian told us about a Berlin brothel (he used the German slang word *Puff*) where he spent all his refugee allowance. The girl he went there for, Masha by name, would "take him for all he was worth" and "give him zilch in return," but that was fine with him. "Because she's a Russian, one of us. I wouldn't throw my dough away on a German girl. Those German girls have no soul. Not like ours." And by "ours" he meant his Russian Masha.

The men complained more than anyone; they were eternally complaining: about the weather, about the war, about their fate and the injustices done them. They complained about conditions in the camps if they lived in one; they complained about conditions in the camps if they didn't. They complained about welfare; they complained about the humiliation of having to accept welfare; they complained about not receiving welfare. They complained all the time and about everything with the same intensity. It was as if life itself were a punishment: everything chafed, everything itched, everything pinched; nothing was enough for them and everything much too much.

Women were much less visible than men. They remained in the background, but kept life going: they darned the holes to stop it from flowing out; they took it on as a daily assignment. Men seemed to have no assignments; for them being a refugee was like being an invalid.

Here in Amsterdam I occasionally looked in on a Bosnian café called Bella, the hangout for a gloomy, tight-lipped crew of card-players and TV watchers. Each time I entered, I'd be met by long looks expressing nothing—not even surprise or indignation—at the sight of a female invading male space. I'd take a seat at the bar, order "our" (Turkish) coffee and sit there for a while, as if doing penance, instinctively drooping my shoulders a bit to fit in. I felt the invisible slap on their faces invading my own. I had no idea what I went there for. Out of an obscure desire to sniff out my "herd," perhaps, not that I was ever certain it was mine— or ever had been, for that matter.

My pupils too consented to being "our people" part of the time, though none of us quite knew what it meant, and refused part of the time, as if it entailed some real, concrete danger. And when we refused, we refused to belong to either "our people down there" or "our people up here." There were times when we accepted our fuzzy collective identity and times when we rejected it in disgust. Over and over I heard people say, "It's not my war!" And it wasn't our war. But it was our war, too. Because if it hadn't been our war, too, we wouldn't have been here now. Because if it had been our war, we wouldn't have been here, either.

CHAPTER 4

Our language, our souls' only treasure,
We stuffed in the suitcase
Next to the family album,
And off we went to tilt at the windmills
Beating the chilly Dutch air.

Ferida Duraković

The first thing I required of them was to write out the answers to a few questions. I asked them what they expected to get out of the course, whether, given that Yugoslavia no longer existed, they thought the literatures of the country should be treated separately or as a unit, which writers and works they admired, and so on. Then I had them compose thumbnail autobiographies. In English.

"Why English?"

"To make it easier on you," I said.

And I meant it. I was afraid (though I was wrong) that using "our language" would lead them to adopt a confessional mode, and that I didn't want. Not yet.

"Whatever," somebody mumbled.

"Well, do as you like."

"You want our full names?"

"The first name will do."

"What do you want us to put into it?"

"Whatever comes to mind."

"We did this in elementary school," grumbled somebody else.

I read them at home. I was touched by how naive their responses were. ("Literature is a painting of the mind, a song of the soul.") The writers and works they listed as their favorites were disappointingly predictable. Hermann Hesse, of course, represented by several novels: *Siddhartha, Magister Ludi, Steppenwolf.* Then Meša Selimović (the students, who read literature for its "powerful message about life," rightly or wrongly thought of Selimović as Hesse's Yugoslav counterpart) and his classic *Death and the Dervish.* I am certain they could all reel off two passages from the book, one that encouraged them to bolt from their provincial existence ("Man is not made of wood; his greatest tragedy is to be tied down") and another that infused them with the sweet nihilism of the provinces ("For death is as nonsensical as life"). Another popular item was *The Zoo Station Kids,* a cult teenage book their generation identified with. There was also the inevitable Bukowski, who had wowed several generations with his rebellious outsider status. They called him "cool," "hip," "in"; he represented "what literature is all about," "literature with balls."

Their responses called up a long-forgotten image of Yugoslav provincial towns: the sole bookshop, which sold more stationery than books; the sole cinema, where they saw—once if not twice—every new film; the few smoke-filled cafés, where they gathered regularly; the *korzo,* that Mediterranean institution of public square cruising, sniffing out one another like puppy dogs. Their taste had been formed by lackluster provincial towns like Bjelovar and Vitez and Bela Palanka plus a dollop of Castañeda, who had come their way along with their first joint, a little third-hand Buddhism, a little New Age fashion, a little vegetarianism, a little Bukowski, a lot of rock, a little required reading (just enough to keep the prof at bay), loads of comic strips (read under the school desk), loads of movies and bits of English, which derived more from the movies than from their English teachers. It was a bittersweet patchwork, one that kindled a desire to make a run for it, take the first opportunity to head for Zagreb, Belgrade, Sarajevo—or beyond.

In the end, what my little exercise demonstrated was that they couldn't care less about literature. It bored them. Even if they'd had a literary education—Meliha had a degree in Yugoslav lit from the University of Sarajevo—the war had altered more than their priorities; it had altered their taste:

My taste began to change the moment the war began [Meliha wrote]. By now I can scarcely recognize myself. Things I despised before the war, ridiculed as sickeningly sweet, I now shed tears over. I can't tear myself away from old movies that end with justice triumphant. They may be about cowboys or Robin Hood or Cinderella or *Walter Defends Sarajevo*. I might as well have forgotten everything I learned at the university. I put down any book that doesn't pull on my heartstrings. I have no patience with artistic folderol and the swagger of literary devices or irony—the very things I used to set great store by. Now I go for simplicity, for plot stripped to parable. My favorite genre is the fairy tale. I love the romanticism of justice, valor, kindness, and sincerity. I love literary heroes who are brave when ordinary people are cowardly, strong when ordinary people are weak, noble and good when ordinary people are mean and ignominious. I admit that the war has infantilized my taste: I weep when I read my old children's books—*The Strange Adventures of*

Hlapić the Apprentice, The Pál Street Boys, The Train in the Snow. And if anyone had told me I'd go wild over tales of partisan exploits in Bosnia—the stuff of Branko Ćopić, say—I'd have thought he was off his rocker.

Most of them answered the question about whether Croatian, Serbian, and Bosnian literatures should be treated as a unit in the affirmative. ("Of course it should. We speak the same language, don't we? But then why not go all the way and include the Slovenes and Macedonians and Albanians. The more the merrier," wrote Mario.)

When it came to the thumbnail autobiographies, they all wrote two or three sentences in stilted English ("I was born in 1969 in Sarajevo, Bosnia, where I lived all my life . . ."; "I was born in 1974 in Zagreb of a Catholic mother and a Jewish father . . ."; "I was born in 1972 in Zvornik. My father was a Serb, my mother a Muslim . . ."; "I was born in Leskovac in 1972. . . .") The more I read, the clearer it became that writing in a foreign language had provided an excuse for being dry and brief. I myself wouldn't have been able to squeeze out much more than that I was born in 1962 in Zagreb in the former Yugoslavia, so I was all the more gratified by Igor's *"Shit. I don't have any biography,"* and burst out laughing.

My own biography struck me as empty as my empty apartment, and I didn't know whether somebody had removed the furniture when I wasn't looking or whether it had always been like that. Confronting the recent past was pure torture, looking into an unknown future—discomforting. (What future anyway? The future there? The future here? Or a future awaiting you somewhere else?) That's why we found the standard thumbnail autobiography so tough a genre. Even the most basic questions gave me pause. Where was I born? In Yugoslavia? In the former Yugoslavia? In Croatia? Shit! Do I have any biography?

I was also a bit nonplussed by their dates of birth: their mental development lagged far behind their age in years. Maybe exile was a kind of regression. At their age they might well have been gainfully employed and bringing up children, yet here they were, hiding behind school desks. The state of exile had brought all kinds of deeply suppressed childish fears to the surface. Suddenly the sight and touch of Mother were no more. It was like a nightmare. We would be in the street, in the market, on the beach, and, whether through our fault or hers, our hands would disengage and Mother would vanish into thin air. Suddenly we faced a world that seemed terrifyingly large and hostile. Gigantic shoes advanced menacingly toward us as we made our way through a jungle of human legs, our panic growing . . .

I often had the impression of seeing a kind of hologram of that fear in the shadows flitting over my students' faces. "In emigration you are prematurely old and eternally young—at the same time," Ana once said, and therein, to my mind, lay a profound truth.

In response to the question about what they expected to get out of the course, Uroš wrote, "To come to," which, given the way he used it, seemed to mean not only "recover from a shock," "regain consciousness," "come back to life" but also "come back to oneself," as if it presupposed a space and an individual floundering in that space and searching for the road home. I was first unnerved, then frightened by Uroš's response. Was I prepared to deal with that kind of need?

CHAPTER 5

The lay of Holland's land is horizontal;
It tapers off, when all is said and done,
Into the sea, the which, when all is said
And done, is also Holland.... In Holland
One cannot mountain-climb or die of thirst,
Let alone leave behind a clear-cut trace
By leaving home astride one's bicycle
Or yet by setting sail. Our memories
Are but another Holland. And no dyke
Can hold them back. Which means that I've
Been living here in Holland a lot longer
Than all the local waves that roll on with
No landing. Like these lines.

                                             Joseph Brodsky

Occasionally, when confronting my own image in the bathroom mirror, I felt a fleeting desire to know where I actually was. I had never asked questions like that as long as Goran and I were together; I had never asked questions at all: there seemed to be no time for it. Suddenly I had time to spare, and it made me very anxious. It was as if there were too much time and too little me. More and more often I was overcome by an unpleasant sensation, a numbness I'd never known before. I kept examining myself, the way one examines one's mouth with one's tongue, hoping to get my feeling back, but the self-induced anesthesia was powerful and refused to yield. I had no idea where it had come from or when it had come on.

Very soon after I moved in, the flat started making me nervous. The poky, windowless bathroom with its shower, white tiles, and concrete floor had a nightmarish feel to it; it was like a quotation from an old black-and-white movie. I kept trying to spruce it up; I bought little gewgaws—a nice soap-dish, an expensive towel with a hand-embroidered lace border; I redid the lighting. The new lights revealed thin accumulations of dirt in the indentations between the tiles, and one night I spent hours removing the dirt with an old toothbrush in a headstrong attempt at transfiguring the looscape by brute strength. The wall of the tiny hallway was painted a gray-green halfway up from the floor and divided from the other half by an ugly green line. The floor was covered with black linoleum, which gave the flat the aura of a hospital or penitentiary. I did everything I could—I bought a vase, a lamp, a black-and-white poster of the skyline of New York—but their presence merely pointed up the anxiety of absence. The absence of what? I had no answer. I wondered whether another space would have made me feel better. I wasn't too sure. At night, wound round with darkness and a woolen blanket, I would sit at the window in my armchair and stare out through the bars on the qui vive for noises and voices, for a pair of shoes or a cat darting past. The space was definitely not me. But then again I wasn't me, either.

My angst in the basement flat grew with tropic alacrity, like a passionflower, a *passiebloem,* the creeper that decorated house walls and garden gates in many parts of town. I kept finding myself grabbing my bag, flinging a coat over my shoulders and racing out of the place, not knowing where I was off to.

The city, which was like a snail, a shell, a spider's web, a piece of fine lace, a novel with an unusually circular plot and hence no end, never ceased to baffle me. I was constantly getting lost and had the greatest trouble remembering street names, to say nothing of where the streets themselves started and stopped. It was like drowning in a glass of water. I had the feeling I might well— if like Alice I should lose my footing and fall into a hole—end up in a third or fourth parallel world, because Amsterdam itself was my own parallel world. I experienced it as a dream, which meant it resonated with my reality. I tried to puzzle it out just as I tried to interpret my dreams.

The most fascinating thing about it was the sand. I would stand next to a house that was being demolished and watch the rotten beams coming down and the water spurting up out of the invisible depths through an ugly hole in the sand. I would watch workers repairing the Amsterdam cobblestones, prizing them up out of and setting them back into the sand. Sand provided the city with a metaphorical as well as literal foundation and provoked an almost physical reaction in me: I constantly felt it in my mouth, hair, and nostrils.

I couldn't get over the number of signs and signals—"fingerprints"—by which the inhabitants of the city made it clear that they belonged. I thought the signals childlike and consequently touching, like the breadcrumbs Hansel and Gretel sprinkle behind them to guide their way home. Every one of them—the figurines of cats climbing the fronts of old houses, the flags hanging out of the windows, the posters and even family photos, especially of newborn babes, inscriptions and slogans, tiny sculptures, toys, teddy bears, African masks, Indonesian vajang dolls, models of ships, miniature replicas of typical Amsterdam houses—had one and only one message: "I live here. Look! I live here." I had the feeling that all the "still lifes," the *ikebanas,* the "installations"—even the simple window decoration of a cheap Ikea vase housing an inspired two-guilder Xeno "shipwreck"— bore witness to the inhabitants' subconscious fear of evanescence. The doll's houses embedded in doll's houses, the infantile urban exhibitionism, the imprints left willfully in the sand—on some level they all resonated with my own angst, whose name and source I was unable to put my finger on.

I lived very close to the railway station and found myself increasingly drawn to the main hall, where I would stand staring at the timetable, as if the display of arrivals and departures could provide the key to my angst. Once, on an impulse, I took a train to The Hague, walked through the city, and returned a few hours later. From then on, I made a habit of taking trains to places not particularly meaningful to me. I would go north, to Groningen and Leeuwarden, or south to Rotterdam, Nijmegen and Eindhoven, east to Enschede; I would go to the nearby cities of Haarlem, Leiden, and Utrecht; I would go to places simply because the sound of their names appealed to me: Apeldoorn and Amersfoort; Breda, Tilburg and Hoorn; Hengelo and Almelo; or Lelystad, whose name reminded me of a lullaby. The Netherlands was poignantly small. Often I simply got out, walked up and down the platform, and took the next train back to Amsterdam. The journey alone calmed my nerves. I would gaze out of the window, my mind blank, the Dutch lowlands tempering my angst. I took pleasure in the absolute, undisturbed constant of the horizontal in motion. I also came to appreciate the signs and would read out their words flashing past in the rhythm of a children's counting rhyme: *Sony, Praxis, Vodafone; Nikon, Enco, JVC; Randstad, Philips, Shell; Dobbe, Ninders, Ben* . . . And just as we seem to fancy people more for their faults than for their virtues, so I gradually developed a sympathy for that landscape of absence, the straight, light green line of the horizon, the cold nocturnal vistas with their full moons and flocks of large white geese shining in the dark, or the frozen shadows of cows idling in the road like friendly ghosts.

In the trains and stations I mastered the language of loneliness. I, the aimless wanderer, soon discovered I was not alone. Standing on the platform, I would turn to a fellow traveler, who could see the computerized timetable as well as I, and ask, "Excuse me, but the next train is going to Rotterdam, isn't it?"

"Sorry, I couldn't say."

"And where are *you* going?"

"Me? Rotterdam."

I would watch the people in the trains, listen in on their conversations even though I didn't understand the language, sniff their smells. I would project their faces onto a computer screen and scroll down, registering one detail after the other, the chance images taking hold for longer or shorter periods of time, and I often had the feeling that someone other than myself had opened the door to them.

The image of a young girl sitting opposite me in a train. There is a tiny speaker in her ear. It is attached to a wire. The wire ends up in a half-open handbag with an Esprit label on it. The train is packed, but the girl is oblivious to her surroundings: she is talking loudly, staring expressionless at a point straight ahead of her. On and on she talks, her voice strident, like a machine, and she sits bolt upright, her bag in her lap, afraid perhaps it will fall and break. The handles of the bag are upright, too, and nearly reach her mouth, which gives the impression that the words are pouring out of her mouth into the bag. When the conversation is over, she removes the plug from her ear, takes the mobile phone out of the bag, turns it off, sticks it into the invisible sand of words that has just poured out of her, and zips up the bag.

The image of a dark-skinned young man poring over a text-book of Dutch for foreigners and chewing on the eraser of a pencil as if it were a gumdrop. He lays the book down in his lap for a moment, turns toward the window, mumbles a few words to himself, fixing them in his mind, then goes back to the book.

The image of a young Chinese couple chewing gum in synchronized motion, their faces gray and mouselike. She is wearing a thin, open, none-too-clean blouse with no bra, her small breasts showing through. He, still chewing, puts his arm around her, slips his hand into the blouse, and tugs with lazy satisfaction at a breast as if adjusting the nipple of a bottle. She too goes on chewing and blinks her pupilless eyes.

The image of a tired Moroccan madonna with a boy child in her lap. He is no more than two. He has thick black hair, parted on the side like a grown-up's. His face has the terrifying absence of all children's faces, the kind seen in icons and early paintings.

During one of my trips the train came to a sudden halt. The train coming in the opposite direction had stopped, too. The seat corresponding to mine in the other train was occupied by a man holding a sheet of music with one hand and conducting with the other. He was completely absorbed in the music inside him and conducted with brief, delicate, restrained strokes of the hand. I was spellbound. His face was illuminated with exaltation from within. The external world did not exist: he was surrounded by the silent music as by an impenetrable capsule; nothing could touch him. But then the trains started up, his and mine, and the man's face disappeared. I felt a twinge, as if I'd been watching myself in the glass, as if I'd seen myself but couldn't hear myself. I felt my own reflection had gone off in the opposite direction.

Wandering through the city, I was sometimes overcome by a sudden, almost uncontrollable impulse traceable to an innocent detail. Crushed on a tram next to a bare, smooth, male muscle, I would feel an urge to press my lips to that golden region of alien skin. Or confronting an earring in the ear of a man squeezed in next to me, I would itch to tear it off with my teeth. The force of these unexpected attacks terrified me, yet gave me a feeling of release. Release from what? I couldn't say.

My internal city map took shape of its own accord. Images would come and go, take hold for a while or dissipate like sand. It was like making my way through a mist or a dream. I drew my internal map on the finest of tracing paper, but the moment I separated it from the real map I saw to my surprise that it was blank. It had nothing on it. Not a thing. I'd be moved by a line advancing in high spirits, and all at once it would stop and break off. Sometimes my internal map looked like a clumsy children's drawing. A city that in fact looked like a snail, a shell, a spiderweb, a labyrinth, a piece of lace, a novel full of mysterious tributaries, would, on my internal map, turn into a series of blanks, gaps, snippets, and dead ends. My internal map was the outcome of an amnesiac's attempt to plot his coordinates, of a flâneur's attempt to leave his tracks on the sand. My map was a dreamer's guide. Virtually nothing on it coincided with reality.

But there was one thing I knew for certain. No matter where I went, my students provided the direction. They were my internal center, my public square, my main street, my jugular. I mean that literally.

CHAPTER 6

Thus we see that life was preserved here, but at a price dearer than the value of life itself, for the strength to defend and maintain it was borrowed from the coming generations, which were thus born into debt and servitude. What survived in the struggle was the sheer instinct to defend life, while life itself lost so much that precious little more than the name itself remained. What has lasted and lives on is stunted or warped; what comes into the world and survives is poisoned in the bud and sick at heart. The thoughts and words of the people are unfinished, cut off as they are at the root.   Ivo Andrić

I told them they had nothing to worry about: they would all get high grades. I told them I realized that most of them were studying *servo-kroatisch* for practical reasons so I had no intention of being a pain in the neck.

"I'm here as a guest lecturer for two semesters only. It would make no sense on my part to play 'teacher,' so you too are absolved of playacting."

"Then what are we going to do?" someone asked.

"Nothing," I said

"Nothing?" they asked, tittering.

"Oh, we'll keep busy somehow," I said.

I felt their eyes on me. They were obviously intrigued.

"Well, I can't come to class anyway," a young woman said. "I've got a baby."

"No problem," I said.

"Thanks," the young woman said, and, picking up her things, she left the room.

The others laughed and looked back at me, wondering what was to come. It was Meliha who took care of that.

"The first thing they did when we came was to put us in refugee camps and—you know the ways of the *Dačer* folk by now—give us psychiatrists. Well, our psychiatrist turned out to be one of 'ours', a refugee like us. And you know what she told us? 'Do me a favor, will you, everybody? Find a little crazy streak in you. Think up a trauma or two if need be. I don't want to lose my job. . . .' "

We all laughed. The ball was rolling.

I was naturally well aware of the absurdity of my situation: I was to teach a subject that officially no longer existed. What we once called *jugoslavistika* at the university—that is, Slovenian, Croatian, Bosnian, Serbian, Montenegrin, and Macedonian literature—had disappeared as a discipline together with its country of origin. Besides, the students I was assigned had no particular interest in literature; they were interested in their Dutch papers. I was hired to teach the literature of a country (or the literatures of countries) from which my students had fled or been expelled. The house was in ruins, and it was my job to clear a path through the rubble.

My main tool, I decided, would be language: "our" language, *servo-kroatisch*. But the language that had been spoken in Croatia, Serbia, Bosnia, and Montenegro had now, like the country in which it had been spoken, been divided into discrete units; it had become three official languages: Croatian, Serbian, and Bosnian. True, Croatian and Serbian had enjoyed a certain official autonomy even in Yugoslav times, but there was something new: the erection of checkpoints to highlight the differences between them. I was not much concerned with the "new" languages and had no interest in dividing them up according to the fifty or so words that distinguished them. What concerned me more was a certain rigidity in the language as such, a rigidity that made my students unwilling and unable to use it: their questionable mother tongue was being taken over by a half-baked English and, more recently, half-baked Dutch.

I told them I firmly believed that Croatian, Serbian, and Bosnian were variants of a single language. "A language is a dialect backed by an army. Croatian, Serbian, and Bosnian are backed by paramilitary forces. You're not going to let semiliterate criminals advise you in matters linguistic, are you?" But I was also aware that I belonged to the last generation whose primary and secondary school literature textbooks had been speckled with readings in Slovenian, Macedonian, Serbian, and Croatian, duly printed in the Roman or Cyrillic alphabet, and that the fact of the very existence of such textbooks would soon be forgotten.

But things weren't quite so simple. My students knew all too well that I wasn't speaking metaphorically when I brought in the military; they knew that "our" languages were backed by actual troops, the "our" languages were used to curse, humiliate, kill, rape, and expel. They were languages that had gone to war in the belief that they were incompatible, perhaps precisely because they were inseparable.

The papers abounded in language columns. The butcher, the baker, everyone was an instant linguist. The war gave rise to "differential dictionaries." Serbs, who had for the most part converted to the Roman alphabet, started going back to Cyrillic; Croats, eager to make Croatia as Croatian as possible, introduced a few awkward constructions borrowed from the Russian and a few even more awkward lexical items in circulation during World War II. It was a divorce full of sound and fury. Language was a weapon, after all: it branded, it betrayed, it separated and united. Croats would eat their *kruh,* while Serbs would eat their *hleb,* Bosnians their *hljeb:* the word for bread in the three languages was different. *Smrt,* the word for death, was the same.

Not that the language as it was before the divorce—Serbo-Croatian or Croato-Serbian or Croatian and Serbian—represented a better, more acceptable linguistic construct that the war had then destroyed. No, it, too, had performed a political function; it, too, had been backed by an army; it, too, had been manipulated, polluted by a heavily ideologized Yugospeak. But the history of melding the linguistic variants into a single construct involved a much longer and more meaningful process than the overnight divorce, just as the history of building bridges and roads involved a much longer and more meaningful process than their overnight destruction.

Boban told us of a recurrent dream of his. He was looking for a street in Zagreb, but was afraid to ask for directions, because people would hear that he was from Belgrade.

"And what if they did?" I asked.

"Then they'd know I'm a Serb. They might spit at me or send me away."

"So what?"

"Then I'd never find the street I was after."

"Who were you looking for?"

"A girlfriend of mine. Maja was her name."

Somebody sniggered.

"Where did she live, your Maja?"

"You turn right off Moša Pijade. One of those streets."

"Moša Pijade has a new name," I said.

"What is it?"

"Medveščak."

"Oh, thanks," he said seriously, as if he would be using the information that night.

"Could Maja's street possibly have been Novakova?" I asked.

"That's it!" he cried, his face beaming with relief. "Novakova!"

"Good thing you didn't dream about Bosnia, man," said Selim. "If our guys got their hands on you, you'd sweat bullets."

The room was still. Selim had tossed a mine into it.

"From now on you will keep all such comments to yourself, Selim. I will not have the classroom turned into a battlefield."

Selim couldn't stand Boban's Serbianisms, that was plain: when Boban talked in class, Selim would roll his eyes, take loud breaths, and cough into his hand, and when Selim talked in class he went heavier on the Bosnianisms—I was sure of it—than he did "on the outside."

Nevena was completely different. Her speech was characterized by a sort of linguistic schizophrenia: she stuttered and used all kinds of regionalisms and accents indiscriminately; she'd start a sentence in a South Serbian dialect, move on to an imitation of Zagreb speech, launch into the Bosnian drawl, and finally make such capricious use of the tonal system that she sounded like an autistic child. She later explained to me that her Serbian father and Croatian mother had constantly been at each other's throats and separated at long last just before the war broke out. We all had our ethnic burdens to bear. Nevena had moved in with her grandmother in Bosnia and made her way from there to Amsterdam as a refugee.

"I feel more comfortable in Dutch," she told me, as if Dutch were a sleeping bag.

Uroš mumbled so much of the time we could hardly understand him. His speech was also marked by an inordinate number of diminutives. Like the servants in nineteenth-century Russian novels he seemed to be using them to placate the people around him. It was as if he were afraid the person he was talking to was going to punch him in the nose and the nice little diminutives would shield him. The rest of the class made fun of Uroš's diminutives as they did of the tendency of the Dutch to use them. Talking in class became such a trial to Uroš that I mostly left him alone.

Igor spoke fluent Dutch. Dutch meant freedom to him; his mother tongue had become a burden.

"When I speak 'our language,' I feel like a character in a provincial play, *if you know what I mean*," he said. The "if you know what I mean" was in English. He always peppered "our language" with Anglicisms: it made it more tolerable for him.

"All 'our' languages are trying to establish their own literary norm, but the only variant that sounds natural is the impure, bastardized variant. Or a dialect. When I hear Dalmatians talk Croatian, I think, 'Hey, that's *cool*.' When I hear officials talk Croatian, I think airs and graces and rape. There's something unnatural about the lot of them—Croatian, Serbian, Bosnian. . . . Look, I'm a rocker, a musician. I've got a hell of an ear. *I know what I'm talking about*."

The version of "our language" Igor was talking about, standard Croatian, had grown even stuffier since he'd left. Not a day went by without some mention of the language in the media. The pressure to change was enormous. Some took to the newspeak with amazing docility; others shied away in horror. Some saw it as the only way to affirm their loyalty; others saw it as the very nightmare they were experiencing. Stiff, dry platitudes made life easy, made long stories short. Platitudes were a coded language: they depersonalized the speaker, put a shield around him. Platitudes were a language about something that couldn't be put into language anyway. There seemed to be only two options: to keep an honest silence or to speak and thereby lie.

The young took spontaneous shelter in dialects, which they had once despised as "bumpkinese," or retreated into more personal speech, the parlance of their playmates or schoolmates, for instance. These were their temporary refuges from the official language that had come with the war, spreading everywhere, polluting everything. They were like the secret languages we use as children to keep grown-ups from understanding us. *I-ay ust-may el-tay u-yay um-say ing-thay*.

Language was our common trauma, and it could take the most perverted of shapes. I am haunted by the case of a Bosnian woman who is said to have memorized the story of her rape and repeated it whenever prompted to do so. Then rape as a form of warfare became international news, and she turned out to be the only victim capable of giving a coherent account of it. Soon she was in great demand by foreign journalists and women's organizations, one of which invited her to America. There she traveled from city to city, spinning the tale of her humiliation and eventually even memorizing an English version of it. On and on she went—reciting a story by now several times removed from its content—like the keeners peasants hire to lament the deceased at funerals. Reeling off the painful tale like a machine was her way of deadening the pain.

I often wondered whether my Croatian, too, wasn't starting to sound dry and colorless. There were times I felt like a student of Croatian as a foreign language. I would catch myself saying something so formulaic, so cold that my mouth might have been filled with ice cubes.

"Remember the samurai in those Japanese movies we used to watch?" Boban said one day. "Samurai don't talk; they make faces and roll their eyes. I was always afraid they'd burst from those words they couldn't spit out. Well, we're like them, the samurai. We turn bright red, our eyes pop, the veins in our temples swell to bursting, and no words come out. So out comes the sword."

The class broke into a round of applause.

"Well, well, well!" said Igor. "Didn't know you had it in you! You beat Milošević in eloquence hands down!"

"Right on!" cried Meliha. "And I'm a Sarajevo samurai."

I could always count on Meliha. We never got enough of her stories about Sarajevo—the fear, the dark, the humiliation, the madness, the hatred, the living and the dead. . . . Meliha was a master of detail, even when describing the impenetrable darkness in the shelters during an alarm. And the stories she told. Of a woman who had gone mad when a grenade blew up her child, and spent hours rubbing her cheeks against the stucco facade of her house until her face was one live wound; of her own life before the war and the refugee camp where she was first interned and the fine old Dutchman who paid her to keep him company; of her mother, who was learning Dutch by taking care of a neighbor's three-year-old, and was using the child's babble to ease her way into a world without pain, to erase the recent past she so longed to forget.

We hung on her every word. No one else was willing to open up the way she was. Some were still too scared, others too ashamed; some were stymied by the guilt of not having experienced the war, others by the horror of the experience.

In the end, the hue and cry back home over the "national substance" of language was both a pack of lies and the gospel truth; in the end, my students had an easier time saying what they had to say in languages not their own—English and Dutch—even though their command of both left much to be desired. The mother tongue—the "tongue of the clan," the language that, as the Croatian poet's ecstatic verse would have it,

> Rustles, rings, resounds, and rumbles
> Thunders, roars, reverberates—

the mother tongue had suddenly appeared to them in an entirely new light. From here the "substance" was more like linguistic anemia, verbal exhaustion, a tic, a stammer, a curse, an oath, or just plain phrasemongering.

"Hey, everybody!" Meliha burst out one day. "Fuck language! Let's just talk!"

And suddenly the ball was rolling again.

At the Department I felt somewhat of a stowaway. I made several attempts at setting up an appointment with Cees Draaisma, the chair and my "host," and he always said, "Yes, definitely. It's just that I'm terribly busy at the moment. If there are any practical matters that need seeing to, Dunja will help you, I'm sure."

Dunja, the secretary of the Department, was Dutch. She was married to a Russian. Her real name was Anneke. Anneke looked like a large, listless seal. Surrounded by dusty plants, she basked in her aquarium of an office, occasionally gracing visitors with a blank gaze. Nothing could get a rise out of her: she would answer any question I might have with a reluctant "yes" or "no" or play deaf.

"We were going to have a talk about my course," I said to Draaisma several times by way of reminder.

"Slavs are natural-born teachers," he would say in the voice of a football coach.

I couldn't tell whether the remark was meant in jest or in praise.

"Ines sends her regards. As soon as she tidies up the back-to-school mess, we'll have you to dinner, okay?"

Draaisma was only confirming what I'd heard from Ines each time I phoned her. ("You've got to come and see us. But not till the dust settles. You've no idea what a bother children are. I can't even get to the hairdresser. Now you, you've got it made. I tell you what. You run round to all the museums and then we'll have you over.")

The fifth floor, where the Department was, consisted of a long dark corridor and fifteen closed doors. From time to time I saw a colleague slipping into his room and paying me no heed. Anneke kept the door to the departmental office closed, and it often sported a Back Soon sign. I finally stopped trying to see Draaisma. The only living being I saw with any regularity was the plump Russian lecturer. She would be sitting at her desk behind a half-open door, moving her lips as if eating an invisible sandwich or reading something to herself.

"*Zdravstvuite,*" she would say shyly if our eyes met.

Only once did a colleague knock on my door.

"May I come in?" he asked.

"Please do," I said.

"So you're our new colleague."

"You might say so."

The man held out his hand.

"Glad to meet you. My name is Wim. Wim Hoeks. I teach Czech. Czech language and literature. Last door on the left."

I liked him immediately.

"I wonder why Cees hasn't introduced you to anybody."

"Oh, it's probably because I'm here for only two semesters."

"So what? It would only have been right."

"I suppose it's academic etiquette here."

"Well, we Dutch do take our time. It's a few years before we invite anyone home. Privacy is a great excuse for all kinds of things, including this inexcusable rudeness. 'It's not that we're unwilling; we just don't want to impose.' "

"Really?"

"Welcome to the most hypocritical country on earth!" he said. "Now tell me, how are things going?"

"Fine."

"And what are you teaching?"

"For the time being I'm just getting to know the students."

"Miroslav Krleža is a great writer," he said.

"Your Czechs are no sluggards, either."

"What about the weather? Foreigners always beef about our weather."

"Well, it's not the Caribbean, but . . ."

"Aren't you bored?"

"Why do you ask?"

"Because this is the most boring country on earth!"

"Isn't that a bit contradictory?"

"What do you mean?"

"How can a country be both hypocritical and boring?"

"Only Holland has that distinction."

"And I thought East Europeans were the masters of self-deprecation."

"No, that's another of our distinctions. Only don't let us fool you. We don't mean it. We actually have the highest opinion of ourselves. It's colonial arrogance. We've let the colonies go, but held on to the arrogance. You'll see . . ."

He glanced at his watch, stood up, and said, "Look, come and see me whenever you feel like it. We can go somewhere for coffee. Last door on the left, the smallest office on our floor. Yours is a lot bigger. You're from the former Yugoslavia. You're higher on the scale than us Czechs."

"In what sense?"

"You've got nationalism, war, post-Communism. And we're up to our necks in it all at the Hague."

"Unfortunately."

"And what a wonderful country it was! Dubrovnik is the most beautiful city I've ever seen! I'll never understand how it happened."

"You don't think I do."

"Of course not. . . . But when *you* stick a knife in somebody's stomach, you raise such a racket that the whole world knows. We do it on the q.t. We don't want people to know, and even our victims are grateful. . . . But we'll talk again. Glad to have met you."

He started off, then turned back at the door.

"That island off the Dalmatian coast foreigners can never pronounce. . . ."

"Krk."

"Right. Does the name mean 'neck'?"

"Neck? No. 'Neck' is *vrat*. Why do you ask?"

"Because that's what it means in Czech. And Czechs like to torture foreigners with the sentence *Strč prst skrz krk*."

"And what does *that* mean?"

" 'Stick your finger through your neck,' " he laughed, giving a demonstration on himself. Then, with a wave, he turned again and strode down the corridor.

The fifth floor was always so deserted that I gave up feeling like a stowaway. I also gave up asking the secretary questions and knocking at Draaisma's door. I did, however, pop in on Wim three times. His office was in fact smaller than mine. Each time he told me he happened to be very busy, and each time he pressed a signed offprint of an article he had written into my hand—by way of consolation, I presume. The first was about Karel Čapek's *Letters from Holland*, the second about misogyny in Kundera's novels, the third about "linguistic hedonism" in the prose of Bohumil Hrabal.

We never did go out for coffee. My only "live" contact at the Department remained the plump Russian lecturer, the one with the invisible sandwich in her hand. Whenever I walked past her office, she would swallow the invisible morsel and utter her timid *"Zdravstvuite."*

All things considered, the Department made a depressing impression on me, which impression was only heightened by the suspicion that the local Slavists were typical of West European Slavists. West European Slavists were wont to enter the field for emotional reasons: they had fallen in love with one of those exotic East bloc types. Or they would cement their choice of field after the fact with a politically, culturally, professionally, sentimentally correct marriage. There was another factor involved: the field made them absolute lords over minor, out-of-the-way, language-and-literature fiefdoms into which no one had ventured theretofore, which made the probability of their competence being adequately evaluated statistically insignificant. Though I should have been the last to condemn them, given that I owed my position to the fact that I happened to know Ines, who happened to have married Draaisma, who happened to be chair of the Department.

CHAPTER 8

ANA: THE PLASTIC BAG WITH THE RED, WHITE, AND BLUE STRIPES

It was just a plastic carry-all. What made it special was that it had red, white, and blue stripes. It was the cheapest piece of hand luggage on earth, a proletarian swipe at Vuitton. It zipped open and shut, but the zip always broke after a few days. When I was a child, I used to wrack my brains over how they managed to get the cherries or other fillings into chocolates without a hole or a seam. Now I wrack my brains over another childish question: who designed the plastic bag with the red, white, and blue stripes and sent it out into the world in a million copies?

The plastic bag with the red, white, and blue stripes looked like a parody of the Yugoslav flag *(Red, white, and blue! We shall e'er be true!)* minus the red star. The first time I ever saw one, I think, was at a flea market. The Poles would bring their cheap Nivea cream, linen dish towels, camping tents, inflatable mattresses, that kind of thing. If I had asked the Poles, I am sure they would have said they got them from the Czechs. The Czechs would have said, No, we don't make them; we got them from the Hungarians. No, the Hungarians would have said; we got them from the Romanians. No, they're not ours, the Romanians would have said; they're Gypsy-made.

In any case, the plastic bag with the red, white, and blue stripes made its way across East-Central Europe all the way to Russia and perhaps even farther—to India, China, America, all over the world. It is the poor man's luggage, the luggage of petty thieves and black marketeers, of weekend wheeler-dealers, of the flea-market-and-launderette crowd, of refugees and the homeless. Oh, the jeans, the T-shirts, the coffee that traveled in those bags from Trieste to Croatia, Bosnia, Serbia, Romania, Bulgaria. . . . The leather jackets and handbags and gloves leaving Istanbul and oddments leaving the Budapest Chinese market for Macedonia, Albania, Bosnia, Serbia, you name it. The plastic bags with the red, white, and blue stripes were nomads, they were refugees, they were homeless, but they were survivors, too: they rode trains with no ticket and crossed borders with no passport.

When I ran across one in a Turkish shop here in Amsterdam, I snapped it up for two guilders. Then I folded it in two and set it aside for safe keeping the way my mother set aside ordinary white plastic bags "because you never know when they might come in handy." I was aware that by purchasing one of the bags I had performed a rite of self-initiation: I had joined the largest clan on earth, a clan for which the plastic bag with the red, white, and blue stripes was colors, seal, and coat of arms rolled into one. The only thing I couldn't work out was who had unstuck the red star?

Our game derived from Ana's symbolic bag.

"The first thing to do is what 'our people' used to do," said

Meliha. "Tie it up with string so nothing falls out." You'd have thought she was describing a hedonistic ritual.

"I must say I was ashamed of 'our people' whenever I saw them picking up those wrecks from the luggage carousel at the airport," said Darko.

"It bugged me, too," said Igor. "It made me think, 'Look at the hicks I've got to travel with.' But now I think it's cool."

"How come?" I asked.

"You know who has the most expensive luggage in the world?"

"Madonna?"

"Nope. The Russians. The top whores and top mafiosi. That's what turned me on to the Gypsy look: the plastic bag tied up like a tramp's boot, the gold tooth. . . . And how right you were about the missing star, Ana. We're proletarians all! The only thing is, Papa Marx is dead and buried."

"Right on!" cried Meliha. "And turning over in his grave at this very moment."

It was with a certain diffidence that I'd proposed it as a class project—or game, really: a catalog of everyday life in Yugoslavia. Ana was the first to contribute. She brought her composition about the "Gypsy bag" to the very next class. I then suggested that we use her virtual Gypsy bag to store all the items for our "Yugonostalgic" museum.

"What museum?" they asked.

"Oh, it will be virtual, too. Everything you remember and consider important. The country is no more. Why not salvage what you don't want to forget?"

"I remember the rally they held on Tito's birthday," said Boban. "We watched it every year on TV."

"But we all remember that, man," said Meliha. "Give us something personal."

"My first bike. One of those squat ones we called 'ponies,'" said Mario. "Does that count?"

"You bet!"

"Just like a man: a phallic symbol," said Meliha in jest. "What about food? Bureks and baklava."

"Bureks, baklava, and poppy-seed noodles."

They all perked up at the reference to Balaševićs song.

"If noodles count, anything counts," said Nevena.

"Anything that makes you happy," I said.

"Or sad?" asked Selim, his eyes lowering.

"Or sad," I said. "Why not."

"What about Omarska?"

The room was suddenly still. I flinched.

"Do you want to talk about it, Selim?"

"What's there to say? It's the only virtual exhibit I've got. The Serbs slit my dad's throat there."

Selim had tossed in another of his mines. I can't say I didn't expect it: I'd been picking my way through a minefield from the start. We all had our war memories, and losses like Selim's were immeasurable. Selim and Meliha had experienced the war firsthand and in all its intensity. Uroš and Nevena refused to talk about it though they, too, were from Bosnia. Mario, Boban, and Igor had left the country to avoid mobilization and seemed thus to have avoided the virus of nationalist insanity—Boban Serbian nationalism, Mario and Igor the Croatian variant. Johanneke had followed the events from Holland. Ana, who arrived in Amsterdam with her Dutch husband before the war, had kept up with it in the Croatian, Serbian, and Dutch media, but made periodic trips not only to Belgrade but to Zagreb, where she had close relatives. Compared with theirs, my experience of the war was infinitesimal.

I realized I would have to find some common ground, because they differed in more than their war experiences; they differed in their interests. While Meliha had a degree in Yugoslav literature from Sarajevo, Uroš had only a provincial Bosnian secondary education and was just now entering the university. Mario had been studying sociology at Zagreb University. Ana had enrolled in the English Department at Belgrade University, but dropped out almost immediately. Nevena had done two years of economics. Ante had graduated from the teachers' training college at Osijek. Boban had made it through the second year of law school. Darko had graduated in hotel administration at Opatija. Selim had just enrolled in the Sarajevo Mathematics Department when the war broke out. As for Igor, he was something of a drifter: he once mentioned having done some psychology, but also told me he'd spent two years at the Zagreb Academy of Theater and Film in the program for theater directors. I never pushed him about his past; it didn't seem that important anymore.

As for the common ground, I could sense their inner fragmentation, their rage, their stifled protest. We had all of us been violated in one way or another. The list of things we had been deprived of was long and gruesome: we had been deprived of the country we had been born in and the right to a normal life; we had been deprived of our language; we had experienced humiliation, fear, and helplessness; we had learned what it means to be reduced to a number, a blood group, a pack. Some—Selim, for instance—had lost close friends and relatives. Their lot was the hardest to bear. And now we were all in one way or another convalescents.

Amidst such lunacy I had to find a territory that belonged equally to us all and would hurt us all as little as possible. And the only thing that could be, I thought, was our common past. Because another thing we all had been deprived of was our right to remember. With the disappearance of the country came the feeling that the life lived in it must be erased. The politicians who came to power were not satisfied with power alone; they wanted their new countries to be populated by zombies, people with no memory. They pilloried their Yugoslav past and encouraged people to renounce their former lives and forget them. Literature, movies, pop music, jokes, television, newspapers, consumer goods, languages, people—we were supposed to forget them all. A lot of it ended up at the dump in the form of film stock and photographs, books and manuals, documents and monuments—"Yugonostalgia," the remembrance of life in that ex-country, became another name for political subversion.

The breakup of the country, the war, the repression of memory, the "phantom limb syndrome," the general schizophrenia, and then exile—these, I was certain, were the reasons for my students' emotional and linguistic problems. We were all in chaos. None of us was sure who or what we were, to say nothing of who or what we wanted to be. At home my students resented being typecast as Yugonostalgiacs, that is, dinosaurs, but they felt little affinity with the prepacked retrofuture of the newly minted states. And here in Holland they were stigmatized as "the beneficiaries of political asylum," "refugees," or "foreigners," as "children of post-Communism," "the fallout of Balkanization," or "savages." The country we came from was our common trauma.

I realized I was walking a tightrope: stimulating the memory was as much a manipulation of the past as banning it. The authorities in our former country had pressed the delete button, I the restore button; they were erasing the Yugoslav past, blaming Yugoslavia for every misfortune, including the war, I reviving that past in the form of the everyday minutiae that had made up our lives, operating a volunteer lost-and-found service, if you will. And even though they were manipulating millions of people and I only these few, we were both obfuscating reality. I wondered whether by evoking endearing images of a common past I wouldn't obscure the bloody images of the recent war, whether by reminding them of how Kiki sweets tasted I wouldn't obliterate the case of the Belgrade boy stabbed to death by his coevals just because he was an Albanian, whether by urging them to "reflect on" Mirko and Slavko, the Yugopartisans of the popular comic strip, I wouldn't be postponing their confrontation with the countless episodes of sadism perpetrated by Yugowarriors, drunk and crazed with momentary power, against their compatriots; or whether by calling up the popular refrain *That's what happens, my fair maiden, once you've known a Bosnian's kiss* I wouldn't be dulling the impact of the countless deaths in Bosnia, that of Selim's father, for instance. The lists of atrocities knew no end, and here I was, pushing them into the background with cheery catalogs of everyday trifles that no longer even existed.

On the other hand, it was all intertwined; you couldn't have one without the other. Death chewed on Kikis. People killed and were killed, looted and were looted, raped and were raped to the sound of cheap, popular refrains. Soldiers were hit by bullets as they dragged color TVs, the new booty, to the trenches. Death went hand in hand with day-to-day detritus. A detail like Kikis could recur in an infinite number of variations—the image, say, of a girl hit by a sniper, the blood trickling from her lips sweetened by the Kiki she had been chewing. The evil was as banal as the everyday artifact and had no special status.

I did not see how we could come to grips with our past if we did not first make our peace with it. So as our common ground I chose something we all felt close to—the homely terrain of the day-to-day life we had shared in Yugoslavia.

Gradually our red-white-and-blue-striped bag filled up. There was a little of everything: the now dead world of Yugoslav primary and secondary schools, the idols of Yugoslav pop culture, all manner of Yugogoods—food, drink, apparel, and the like—and Yugodesign, ideological slogans, celebrities, athletes, events, Yugoslav socialist myths and legends, television series, comic strips, newspapers, films . . .

Boban had unearthed a cache of Yugoslav films on video, so we had lots to watch. They proved a most viable testimony to the existence of a Yugoslav life. Reading that life from our posthumous perspective, we discovered detail after detail that presaged the future, prognostications that came true.

I soon set aside the worries that had beset me: our "archeology" our "spiritualism," the reanimation of our "better past" made us so close that we found it harder and harder to disband. So we adopted another habit from the past: after class we would adjourn to a café and jabber on, dispersing only to run for the last tram, bus, or train. To an outsider we must have looked like a tribe uttering the magic words that call forth its gods; we must have seemed in a trance. Well, we were in a way.

The student I had the hardest time getting a handle on was Igor. His memory amazed me: he would have the most vivid "recollection" of things he couldn't possible have experienced.

"You weren't even born then!"

"But I've got Yugogenes, Comrade, and they remember."

He got a kick out of pronouncing the ostensibly nonsensical nonce word, Yugogenes, in the Dutch way, substituting harsh, guttural *h*'s for the *g*'s. We laughed. My students clearly liked the idea that our past was remembered not so much by us as by phantom "Yuhohenes" for which we bore no responsibility.

I frequently bumped into one or another of them in town. We were as happy to see each other as if we hadn't met for ages. We would cover each other with sweet verbal saliva and pat each other on the back, then retire to a café for an endless *kopje koffie* and aural fondling.

The student I most often ran across in my peregrinations was Igor. Suddenly the tall frame, the backpack, the inevitable earphones draped around the neck would pop out of nowhere.

"What brings you here?" I would ask.

"And you?" he would counter.

"What do you propose?"

"How 'bout a lope?"

That was how they spoke. It was their slang. For them a "lope" was a "walk," from the Dutch *lopen*. He might also have suggested a "wandel," from the Dutch *wandelen* ("go for a walk"). They'd also say things like "Let's go for a *kopje koffie*." Selim's Dutch-Bosnian combinations were hysterical.

Even though my students made it clear that they enjoyed our common project, I could never quite rid myself of the minefield image. One day when Igor and I were wandering through the streets, I tried to bring him out on the subject.

"Tell me, Igor, how do you feel about the class?"

"You know what Tito said to his future wife the first time they met?"

"No, tell me."

> Hear my thoughts, O Jovanka.
> Your hands are less guilty than mine.
> My forehead burns tonight.
> My eyelids quiver.
> I'll dream a beauteous dream tonight:
> Thy beauty shall me unto death deliver!

Thus did a line from a Croatian poetess and a stanza from a Croatian poet merge in Igor's imagination.

"Is nothing sacred?" I said, laughing.

Instead of answering, he asked, "Tell me, Comrade, have you noticed that angels never laugh?"

"I can't say I've given it much thought."

"You've never looked an angel in the eyes?"

"No, I don't think so. . . . Not that I remember . . ."

"Well, then, we have an urgent call to make."

We spent the rest of the afternoon in the Rijksmuseum looking at angel faces of the old masters.

"See? I was right," he said. "Angels don't smile, do they?"

"Like hangmen."

We both burst out laughing, though it wasn't at all funny. The laughter was a way of dealing with an invisible angst.

Convalescents, I suddenly thought—people recovering from an illness or a trauma of some kind, an accident, a flood, a shipwreck—they don't laugh, either. We were convalescents. I didn't say anything, though.

Surrounded by the indifferent walls of our imaginary laboratory, we breathed life into a life that no longer was. We took turns massaging the heart and giving artificial respiration. Clumsy and amateurish as we were, we eventually succeeded in bringing back the beat of that bygone era.

Most of them returned to their childhoods: it was the safest, least threatening territory. Whether the details were their own or what they had gathered from their parents or whether they had made them up, as Igor often did, was not important. Every detail contained its morsel of truth.

As for the whole, it was untranslatable: we were speaking an extinct language comprehensible only to ourselves. How could we have explained them to anyone, those words, concepts, and images and—what was more to the point—the feelings the words, concepts, and images called forth in us? It was alchemy: I had assured them there would be gold at the end of the line, knowing full well that a detail which shone brilliantly one moment could fade and vanish the next. As could the heart we had jointly resuscitated.

At times I wondered whether what I was doing wasn't diametrically opposed to what I thought I was doing. After all, the stigma the ideologues of the successor states had placed on memories of the collective past had backfired: it had made that collective past more attractive. Perhaps by stimulating memories of the past I would destroy its halo. Or perhaps my attempt to reconstruct the past would end in no more than a pale imitation, thus exposing the poverty of the "baggage" we deemed so powerful. Yet whenever I turned over these and related issues in my mind, the pleasure we derived from our memory game would push them aside, as I had pushed aside a discovery that hit me like a ton of bricks one day, namely, that I had forgotten a lot more than they had and was therefore not the best qualified memory tutor. But it was too late: I had set the gears in motion and could no longer stop them.

NEVENA: THE FIRST OF EVERY MONTH

My papa worked in a factory; my mama was a housewife. Our most important family holiday was "first of the month." Papa would bring home his pay in the "pay pocket" (that's what it was called) and present it to Mama. Mama took care of the money: such and such an amount for gas, such and such for electricity, such and such for rent, and such and such to pay off the things we had bought on credit. Then we would dress up, as if going out for dinner, and go out shopping.

Papa used the Turkish word for shopping—*bakaluk*—Mama the Croatianized German *fasung*. Mama led the *fasung* expedition, because only she knew what we needed (how much sugar, how much flour, how much oil, how much salt, how much coffee, and how much macaroni and noodles to last till the first of the following month), and we all pranced along behind her. Mama always bought unroasted coffee, which we then roasted ourselves in a cylindrical tin pot with little doors and a handle on one side. We'd pour the gray beans in through the doors, shut the doors, and put the pot on the gas burner. Then we'd rotate the handle and the pot would rotate and the coffee would rotate in the pot ever so slowly and roast on the fire. The whole apartment would smell of freshly roasted coffee. How I loved that smell. We needed a lot of coffee, because neighbors came to see Mama and drink coffee every day. We didn't buy many other things. Mama made jam and preserves, she pickled cucumbers, she turned red peppers into paprika and *ajvar*—that kind of thing. She was also good at making liqueur out of cherries, nuts, and chocolate, so we didn't buy that either. We kept everything in the pantry. Mama would paste labels on the jars with the name of the produce and the date. The most exciting time for us kids was dessert. Mama would buy a few boxes of biscuits and "cooking chocolate" (that's what it was called), because that was the cheapest kind. There was a kind of biscuit in the shape of a slipper with strips of chocolate on top and a kind called "housewife biscuits," which were the best for dipping in milk. And Mama always bought each of us a round, crisp chocolate wafer called a *napolitanka*. Us kids always thought "store bought" tasted much better than "homemade."

Mama would also buy ten packets of bread sticks and ten packets of pretzel sticks, but that was for company. Whenever we had company, Mama put the bread sticks in one cup and the pretzel sticks in another. The guests would sit on the couch. "Have some pretzel sticks," she would say as she put the cups on the long, low coffee table, and the guests would take a pretzel stick or a bread stick and start munching on it. They looked like rabbits. Then Mama would take out her "*ikebanas*," as Papa called them, two or three flat plates she had filled with rings of sliced pickles and sausage and peppers and cheese. Each slice had a toothpick coming out of it and in the middle she put a mound of *ajvar*. Guests always complimented Mama on her *ikebanas*, but they got on Papa's nerves.

"Someday somebody's going to choke on one of your toothpicks," he would say angrily.

"You have no sense for what's in," she would answer.

I think that "in" was the most popular word of the day. Mama always knew what the "in" furniture was, the in lamp, the in hairdo, the in curtains, the in shoes, in eyeglass frames. It was the time when everything just had to be plastic. Plastic was the innest of in.

After dessert Papa would turn the television on. Our television had a plastic filter like a rainbow across the screen to make it look like color when it was really only black and white. We would die of laughter whenever *Citizen Mollycoddle* was on.

Now that I write all this down, I'm not so sure it's the way it was. It's all so hazy and dreamlike; it's like I was telling somebody else's story rather than mine.

BOBAN: MY FAVORITE COMIC STRIP

There weren't many books in our house, but there was one that caught my fancy even when I was little. It was more portfolio than book. It had black leather covers and gilt-edged pages. In the middle of the front cover there was a round metal insignia that looked like a large metal coin. It had the profile of a bearded man engraved on it. When I was a kid, I would scratch at it and try to get it off, but I never did. Inside there were some sheets of typewriter-size paper, yellow with age: documents, paintings, maps, and photographs. There were many more illustrations than text. It looked like a badly organized comic strip.

"It's a book about revolution," Granddad would tell me.

"Levolution," I repeated after him.

"It's the book of the Great October Revolution."

After learning to read, I would mouth the title over and over: *The Life and Work of V. I. Lenin, 1870–1924.* What I liked best about the book were the portraits of the revolutionaries. The portraits always showed them with dark, brooding looks, and they were often sitting round a table arguing. Even though the book was about Lenin, Stalin was always in the foreground. Lenin usually stood behind Stalin, who was seated at the table. I liked the fact that everything in the pictures was in semidarkness. The light always came from a lamp or a window. But most of all I liked the books. There were always bookcases filled with books in the background. One painting showed Stalin visiting Lenin in his room. Lenin is standing to greet him, and there is an open book in the armchair. Another painting showed Lenin and Stalin having a chat with "delegates from the Central Asian Republics." I remember it as if it was yesterday: "delegates from the Central Asian Republics." The delegates were all wearing those Asian skullcaps, and in the background there was a big bookcase. You could see how impressed the delegates were by the number of books in the bookcase. I also remember a picture entitled *V. I. Lenin and His Wife N. K. Krupskaya in Siberian Exile.* It showed Lenin standing next to a chest of drawers engrossed in a book while N. K. Krupskaya stands next to a bookshelf.

Later I read the inscription. It was written in a fine, round hand. It said: "My very best wishes to my very best friend, Nebojša Krstić. Major Veljko Vukašinović."

My grandfather's name was Nebojša Krstić.

My grandfather was a partisan. He was what they called a *prvoborac,* which means someone who joined the resistance early. My old man called him an *udbaš,* which means a member of the Secret Police, though he didn't start calling him that until the Commies started losing ground. My old man was a shit. Then again, most people are shits. They blow hot and cold. By the way, what makes you think the Commies are so different from Sai Baba? The Commies tried to perform miracles, too. Until the lid came off, that is. And I don't believe they read all those books.

If anybody asked me to paint a representative portrait of my family, you know what I'd put next to the old man? A Zastava 101, because he paid a lot more attention to that old jalopy than to me. And next to the old lady I'd put the plastic bag she used to carry groceries back from the market. And next to me a soccer ball. And next to Grandpa the old revolver he kept in his bedside table and never let me near. The old man and the old lady were a couple of hicks. The Commies were cool!

ANTE: INVITATION TO A BALL

I remember the tea dances we had in school when we were twelve or thirteen. They disappeared after discos came in. They never served tea at tea dances, or anything else for that matter, and I'm still not clear about why they called them tea dances. The room had chairs along two walls. Boys sat on one side, girls on the other. Every tea dance had its "matron." The matron's job was to make sure we didn't drink too much of the tea they didn't serve. Somebody else took care of the music. Those were the days when they still had record players and tape recorders. They're gone now, too. Each of us would go up to a girl and stand in front of her. Like a beau or something. Without a word. That meant we were asking her to dance. Every once in a while the matron would call out, "Ladies' choice!" and the girls would stand and come over to us. That was how you could tell which girl liked you.

Those being our "hormonal years," we all looked forward to the close dances or what we called "squeezers." They were slow—"Only You"–slow—and you'd press the girl real close, so close that both of you could hardly breathe. You were almost numb with excitement, but you made believe it was nothing. Just the thought of it still takes my breath away. It was like I was diving and I'd come up with my cheek against hers. We'd be so close my eyes would lose their focus and cross. I could feel her transparent, milky white skin; I could make out the blue veins in her eyelids. Her breath smelled of green peppermint drops. Just the thought of it makes me dizzy still. The girl's name was Sanja Petrinić.

MELIHA: BOSNIAN HOTPOT

Memory aids survival.

Marcel/a Proust/ić

Ingredients: 1/2 kilo boneless pork and 1/2 kilo boneless beef, cubed; 1/2 kilo small potatoes, unsliced; 2 onions, sliced in half; 10 cloves of garlic, unsliced; 40 decagrams of fresh tomatoes; 4 green or red peppers; 30 decagrams of kale; 20 decagrams of cabbage; 2 carrots; 2 bunches of parsley; 1 bunch of celery; 1 kohlrabi; 10 string beans; 2 heaping teaspoons of sweet paprika; 15 to 20 peppercorns; several bay leaves; approximately 30 decagrams of water, broth, or white wine. Chop the vegetables coarsely. Place the meat, onions, and vegetables in a pot, preferably earthenware. Add the liquid. Place a border of dough along the pot lid's inner rim (to prevent steam from escaping) and cover. Bring to a boil, then simmer for 4 to 5 hours.

JOHANNEKE: VANILLA CONES

I come from a big family. My parents loved Yugoslavia. So did us kids. Now I see that another reason we took our summer holidays in Yugoslavia was that it was so cheap. We would make the rounds of the camping sites along the Adriatic with one of those big house tents. We were among the first foreign tourists. I had seven brothers and sisters. My father had a job, but my mother stayed at home with us, so we had to watch every guilder and couldn't throw money away on holidays. Even the Dutch were poor back then. After the war the Dutch went off to foreign countries (New Zealand, Canada, Brazil) and worked by the sweat of their brow just like the Yugos. So for us the Adriatic was heaven. Every day we'd line up, all eight of us—little, bigger, biggest—with Mama and Papa bringing up the rear, and go out for ice cream, and every day Nazif would greet us with the words, "You Dutch, you're as white as vanilla." Well, word got round, and soon everyone in town was calling us "the Vanillas." "Hey look! Here come the Vanillas!" (Our real name was Ter Bruggen Hugenholtz, which nobody could pronounce.) We each got first names, too. Summer names we called them. I was Joka, my brother Gerard Grga, Frans was Frane, Wouter Walter. After Walter in that movie everybody saw, the one about the defense of Sarajevo. "Das ist Walter!" they'd call after him in their pidgin German. "Das ist Walter!" To this day I call him Das ist Walter.

That ice cream was my earliest memory of Yugoslavia. Our parents never took us out for ice cream at home. It cost too much. The locals called Nazif the ice cream vendor a Shiptar. I didn't know about your different national groups at the time, so

I didn't know it meant Albanian. You all looked the same to us. We looked like vanilla to you, you looked like hazelnuts to us.

SELIM: HOMESICK FOR THE SOUTH

We were all required to study the history of Macedonian, Slovenian, Croatian, Serbian, Bosnian, and Montenegrin literature, as you are well aware. I never got more than a D. There was this one Macedonian poem called "Homesick for the South." I only knew the title, because I'd never read it, but the title always sounded funny to me. More like an ad than a poem. Then one day I found a fax of it in the departmental reading room here. It was written by Konstantin Miladinov more than a hundred and fifty years ago, as you are well aware. Anyway, you know how our Dutch friends are always rambling on about their summer plans, their summer holidays, getting ready for them or just back from them or wondering where you're going this year—well, this poem is like that. You'd think it was written by a Dutch rather than a Macedonian. I just had to translate it for my Mieke. So I start reciting it in Macedonian, and—Tito be my witness—my brain scans it without a glitch! I don't want to bore you, but let me remind you how it starts in case you haven't got the book handy.

> Darkness is everywhere, darkness enfolds me.
> The blackest of mists encircle the earth. . . .

Well, this weather report goes on for a while, but then he makes his point, which really hit home.

> I cannot stand to live in this place;
> I cannot live amidst snow, hail and ice.
> Lord, give me wings, that I may die,

That I may back to my homeland fly,
That I may feast my eyes once more
On sun-drenched Struga and Ohrid's fair shore.

And when I got to the end, when I got to the lines that go:

There shall I pipe my heart's last good-bye,
And when the sun sets, there shall I die.

I burst into tears, for Christ's sake. There I am, spouting
Macedonian like a son of the soil—and bawling to beat the
band. I thought I'd gone off the deep end. So anyway, I
translate it for my Mieke, the tears still streaming down my
cheeks, and you know what she says? *Mooi!* Well, when I
heard that Dutch *mooi,* I smacked her one hard, and then *she*
fucking burst into tears. I could have kicked myself, of course.
I don't know what got into me. Something in that *mooi* made
me crack. I don't get it. The word does mean "beautiful," after
all. Maybe it was the grass. Maybe the grass had something
tear-jerking about it.

DARKO: MY MOTHER HOLDS HANDS WITH TITO

This isn't a memory of my own; it comes from my mother. Like
all the kids in her school she belonged to the Pioneers, and
once, because she was at the top of her class, she was chosen to
attend Tito's birthday celebration. It was the custom to send
the best Pioneers to the celebration, Mother told us, and when
the photographer came in to take the traditional "Tito and the
Pioneers" picture, she rushed over to Tito and grabbed his
hand. I've seen the picture. She is leaning against him,
pressing her hand in his, and he has a Cuban cigar in his free

hand. When the photography session was over, Tito tried to take his hand away, but Mother wouldn't let him. She stuck to him like glue. He gave another tug, but her fingers had turned into live tongs. People started getting uneasy. One of the security guards had to come and unfasten her. She let out an unearthly howl.

"I don't know what got into me," she told me "or where I got the strength."

I once saw Tito in the flesh. It was at the Zagreb Trade Fair. Mother and I happened to be in the crowd lining the street as he passed by with his entourage. He looked smaller than in the photographs and film clips. He looked old and feeble, like a mummy. And when a sunbeam suddenly lit up the top of his head, it jumped out at me, all speckled with liver spots and covered over with strands of dyed hair turned orange.

"Come on," my mother said, tugging me by the hand, and took me for ice cream. She ordered so many scoops I couldn't eat a quarter of them. I don't know what got into her.

MARIO: TRAINS WITH NO TIMETABLES

Looking back, I have the impression that everything in the former Yugoslavia had some connection to trains. String together all the significant and insignificant trains in our lives and you get a history of the country that is parallel to—and no less valid than—the official one.

1. What united Yugoslavia more than the slogan "brotherhood and unity" were its Austro-Hungarian tracks and stations. I get a lump in my throat each time I see the stations' yellow facades, the geraniums in their flower boxes. The very sight of them means home.

2. The first train in my life appeared in the children's book *Train in the Snow* by Mate Lovrak. The first event in the history of Yugomythology—and in the history of the Yugoslav cinema—was Veljko Bulajić's *Train with No Timetable*. It is about the exodus of a group of people, by train, from the rocky Dinaric Alps to Yugoslavia's "breadbasket," the rich, fertile Baranja (or was it Bačka) region in the north. In the course of the journey they fall in love, they fight, they have ideological debates, a child is born, a man dies. *Train with No Timetable* begat a spate of train episodes in the Yugoslav cinema, all the way to the cruel love scene in the filthy WC in Emir Kusturica's *When Father Was Away on Business*. Incidentally, it was with Kusturica that the Yugoslav cinema breathed its last.

3. Railway tracks were an icon of the fifties, the time of the youth shock-worker movement, international and domestic. The younger generation was assigned construction of two important stretches: Brčko-Banovići *(Brčko-Banovići is our aim/By summer's end we'll make good our claim)* and Šamac-Sarajevo. For a time youth brigades were a hot item in movies made for domestic consumption. *The Extra Girl* starring Milena Dravić is one of many.

4. Once the tracks were built, we couldn't get enough of the trains: we took trains on school outings; we took trains to the seaside; we took trains to the army. All trains had "JDŽ" painted on them in Latin and Cyrillic letters. Many people came into contact with foreign languages for the first time on trains: "Do not lean out of the window" was engraved on small brass plates under the windows with a translation into French, German, and Russian. It became a catchword in books and movies and had its moment in

the sun in the refrain of the popular song "The White Button" *(Take the train, Selma, but don't lean out of the window. . . .)* There was a framed photograph of some Yugoslav town or tourist attraction over every seat. My favorite was Makarska-by-Biokovo because of the "by." The tastiest sandwiches we ever ate we ate on the train. The juiciest roast chicken we ever ate we ate on the train. The most important invention of the day was the thermos bottle, the most memorable sight, engraved in the memory of millions of Yugoslavs, was the sight of the Adriatic as it emerged on the horizon after a long absence. Everyone taking the train to the Adriatic played the same game: the first one to sight the sea would cry "Waaater!" and get five dinars. Or whatever the going rate was. . . .

5. The sixties and seventies were characterized by "*Gastarbeiter* trains," the preferred means of transport for the Yugoslav, Greek, and Turkish workforce making its way to and from the West until it began acquiring cars. The hunger in an anonymous Yugo on the train trip home comes out clearly in the *Gastarbeiter* ditty:

> Pull your pants down, love, it's no holds barred.
> All the way from Frankfurt I've been hard.

6. The icon of Yugoslav consumerism of the eighties was the train to Trieste. It was a train loaded with black market goods: jeans, coffee, rice, olive oil, T-shirts, briefs, panties—you name it. The peak of the Trieste shopping spree coincided with Tito's death. Tito died at the age of eighty-eight, and one of the ways the event was marked was by a flurry of agricultural activity: one community

planted "eighty-eight roses for Comrade Tito," another "eighty-eight birches for Comrade Tito," and so on. Hence the Gypsy joke: A customs official on the train from Trieste asks a Gypsy, "What have you got in those sacks?" The Gypsy responds without missing a beat, "Eighty-eight Levi's for Comrade Tito."

7. The last Yugoslav train was "the blue train" that carried Tito's body along the Ljubljana-Zagreb-Belgrade line to be buried in Belgrade's House of Flowers. Hundreds of thousands of Yugoslavs flanking the tracks paid homage to "the greatest son of the Yugoslav peoples and nationalities." And the years of Yugoslav "brotherhood and unity" were immortalized in powerful lines like:

> In the railway tunnel, in the dark,
> Our five-pointed red star makes its mark.

8. The breakup of Yugoslavia and the war it engendered trace their origins to the historic day when the Krajina Serbs in Croatia blocked the Zagreb–Split line with boulders and put an end to train service for several years.

9. The Zagreb–Split line was reopened several years ago. It took the train, baptized "the Freedom Train," an entire day to make the trip, which was broadcast live on Croatian TV. The reason the Freedom Train took so long was that the Croatian prime minister got off at every whistle-stop to make a speech. Meanwhile the Serbs we chased out of the Krajina made their way to Serbia on foot, by bus or car, by tractor or horse-drawn cart, by anything but the train.

10. Last but not least, one of the best arguments that Serbian and Croatian are different languages and that the war was accordingly a historical necessity is likewise train-related,

namely, that the very word for *train* differs in the two, the Croats calling it *vlak*, the Serbs *voz*.

IGOR: HORROR AND HORTICULTURE

(Comments on Yugoslav poetry by my friend Mikac after looking through the *New Anthology of Yugoslav Poetry* [Zagreb, 1966] I lent him)

They're all there: Serbs, Croats, Macedonians, Slovenes. There aren't any Bosniosi or Montenegrins or, rather, there are, but they don't have their own sections. The biggest eye-opener for me was reading the Slovenes in Slovenian and the Macedonians in Macedonian. Sans translation.

Okay, I said to myself, let's see what the old folks at home were reading before you were a twinkle in their eye. So out comes the calculator—you know, like in the marketplace, Dolac, say: What are your eggs going for today, love?—and do the arithmetic. Out of the 173 poets in the anthology, 56 are Serb, 62 Croat, 40 Slovene, and 16 Macedonian. Okay. Cool. So then I count up the females. The Serbs have 1, the Croats 3, the Slovenes 2. That makes 167 guys and 6 gals. And of those 6, 1 was so browbeaten she wrote under a male pseudonym. Another thing I picked up along the way is that our poets are so name-conscious they prefer three to two, like those partisan heroes they name schools after, so you see a name like Jure Franičević-Pločar or Milenko Brković Crni and you can't tell who is the man of the pen and who the man of the sword. The same holds for the current crop of wannabe Nazis: they're heavy into triple names, too. They really get off on them, the longer the better. Which makes me wonder if they're not trying to make up for an anatomical defect, you know, down where a centimeter or two can make a world of difference. Oh, and something else. Our poets have a thing about dedicating poems to one another. Know what I mean? Like one guy chatting up another. Need I say more?

Anyway, on we go. And surprise, surprise! Circa fifty percent of their output is about mama or the mamaland. Which kind of turns mamaland into mama. And vice versa. Whereupon they boo-hoo-hoo over both. Fucking unreadable, let me tell you. Oh, and then circa ten percent is made up of these horror stories, I mean literally, graves and tombs and that shit. Man, it really traumatized me. I mean, our poets are a bunch of fucking ghouls, always digging up some enemy or other. One of them marks out his territory ("This is the ground where my dead are sown") and then picks up his shovel ("I summon you, my shades"). You fucking body snatcher, I think. You'd put the fear of God into Stephen King, you would. And just as I'm getting over it, what do I see but

O mirrors of horror! Show scenes without gallows or noose!
"Blood! Blood!" screams my blood in this land of Croatians
ill used.

Shit!

But onward. To the ten percent belonging to what I would call the megalomaniac or me-me-me poems, poems where the guys talk one-on-one with the stars, the universe, like "If man you be, walk tall beneath the sky"—that shit. Poems where every man's a fucking superman.

Okay. Fine. Next category: the twenty percent that sing the beauties of nature, you know, the seasons, rainfall, crap like that. You'd think they were a bunch of—what was the name of that Serbian weatherman?—right, a bunch of Kamenko Katićes. Our freaks are into flora a lot more than fauna. True, I did find one poem about a calf, but I didn't get it till the end.

At first I thought it was about this hot little number—the language was nice and sexy—and then in the middle of it all comes this line about dung. . . . But to get back to the flora. There were all kinds of poems about fucking trees—aspens, willows, poplars, oaks. After all the horror stuff I was surprised our guys had a thing for flowers—lilies of the valley, pansies, roses, cyclamen. I didn't think horror and horticulture went together. Though one guy had something about bloody cyclamen.

How much does that make altogether? Ninety percent? Okay. So then I went through them with a fine-tooth comb on the lookout for sex. Well, you could've knocked me over with a feather: our guys don't care shit about sex. It jumps right out at you. No calculator necessary. Believe me, the only time they can write about a woman is when she's dead and buried. It's like they can hardly wait for the gal to bite the dust so they can write a poem about her. The sadder the better. Like the Dalmatians, for Christ's sake. You know the poem:

> I saw you last night. In my dreams. Sad. Dead.
> In the fated hall midst an idyll of flowers
> On a lofty bier midst the throes of the candles.

Of course you do. We had to learn it in school. Well, the same necrophiliac wrote:

> I know not what thou art: art thou woman or hyena?

Shit! Did that guy get my goat! I mean, what's the point if you can't even tell a woman when you see one. And then there was the guy who couldn't find a place to bury his broad ("Where can I bury you, O my love, now that you're gone?") and the guy—the more I read, the more they pissed me off—who was

away for so long that by the time he got back his girl had
kicked the bucket:

> But when I arrived,
> I found you no more.

What did he come back for, the shithead? And then there was
another one we had in school, remember?

> Love may yet come, befall us yet, I say,
> But do I wish it or wish it away?

That always made my blood boil. Your problem ain't whether
you want to, pal; it's whether you can! So pack up your wares
and get a move on. I'm not buying.

They're a bunch of sickos, our poets. And not only the ones
in the anthology. There hasn't been a sound mind among them
in the past two hundred years or however long they've been at
it. Serbs, Croats, Slovenes, Macedonians—it makes no
difference. Old farts all. You don't need a calculator to tell
you that.

UROŠ: I WISH I WERE A NIGHTINGALE

During our second year in elementary school the teacher
assigned us a composition about Tito. Tito had had a leg cut
off, she told us, and was recovering from the operation. It
would make him happy if we wrote something nice. I wrote I
wished I were a nightingale so I could fly to Comrade Tito's
hospital bed every morning and wake him with my song. The
teacher praised me to the skies and read my composition to the
class. My classmates made fun of me. They called me the
nightingale. "Hey, here comes the nightingale," they would

shout with a guffaw. When my family heard about the composition, they made fun of me, too, especially my old man. Then, not long afterward, Tito died, and my old man cried and the whole family sat in front of the TV for the three days of the funeral and cried. The thing that impressed them most was all the foreign dignitaries attending the funeral. "All those famous people," my old lady said. They had a good time pointing out the announcers' mispronunciations of the statesmen's and celebrities' names. But when I said that Margaret Thatcher's name is Thatcher, not Tratcher, my old man said, "That's enough out of you, Nightingale. Go and get me a bottle of beer from the fridge. And, mind you, don't drop it from your beak!" Which got a big laugh out of everybody.

Yugoslavia was a terrible place. Everybody lied. They still lie of course, but now each lie is divided in five, one per country.

I think it best to state straightaway that the northern Netherlands have always made me feel a certain Angst, which I write with the capital letter the German requires, as if in the early doctrine of the Naturphilosophen it were one of the basic elements, like Fire and Water, of which life on earth is constituted. The capital letter gives one the feeling one has been placed in a black box from which there is no easy escape.

Cees Nooteboom

Amsterdam is one of the most beautiful cities in the world. Overused a platitude as it is, I would have no hesitation putting my name to it, and with nary a blush at its banality, were it not for what it leaves out: a sensation, an almost physical sensation of absence about the city, a sensation that occasionally pursued me and whose source I was unable to pinpoint.

Roaming through the city, I would pass through a number of olfactory zones, urine ceding to the mould that grazed my nostrils as I ran down a flight of stairs, the mould ceding to the rancid oil that wafted from the cheap seaside food concessions and lodged in my hair, the oil ceding to the human sweat that clung to me as I made my way through the crowds, the sweat ceding to the heavy, sticky aroma of hashish. The ever present physicality all around me had no power to arouse; it produced the same impression as the eccentric old man who did circus tricks on a tightrope in the middle of the Leidseplein stark naked. That naked superannuated human body twisting and turning on a rope was a grotesque example of the city's incongruities.

Detail after detail threw me off guard. I was constantly confronted with a certain dualism: everything seemed to go hand in hand; each plus had its minus. The absence of beauty took the classic forms of ugly civic sculptures, the iron fly lying on the Haarlemplein asphalt, the metal caterpillars crawling through the Leidseplein's lawns, the miniature, rubber-ball-sized busts sticking up out of the wet grass in park after park. But beauty, too, was present, and it, too, took classic forms: museums, patrician houses, canals, reflections. . . .

Besides the first platitude I often heard another, namely that "Amsterdam is a city of human proportions." For me it had the proportions of a child. Shop windows in the red-light district displaying live dolls for grown-ups, porno shops decked out to resemble toy shops, kindergarten-like coffee shops with plastic mushrooms "growing" at the entrance and Dam's theme-park attractions. It's not that this urban infantilism is subversive or derisive—it would appear to have no ulterior motive whatsoever; it's just that it has turned Amsterdam into a kind of melancholy Disneyland. I often experienced a vague sense of shame as I walked through the city, playing its pornographic game and wondering whether I wasn't the only one who perceived it as such.

If Amsterdam's famous curtainless windows expose the interiors behind them, the interiors behind them expose the absence of privacy. Thus the sacred right to privacy is paradoxically confirmed by its absence. The front verandas—scarcely big enough for a chair or two—represent another exhibition space of absence: when the weather is hot, residents sit out on the verandas like live exhibits watching other live exhibits, the street traffic, amble past. Amsterdam is a permanent stage, but if that is a characteristic it shares with all other cities on earth, it differs from them in the almost mechanical effort the inhabitants invest in performing on that stage, in making over their windows into display cases, in promenading their bodies on walks or bicycles. Like any tourist I was charmed at first by this Disneyland for grown-ups, but before long I found it repellent. Perhaps I projected my own nightmares onto the city and read meanings into it that were not there. The fact remains, however, that it was Amsterdam and no other city I had chosen for my screen.

If Amsterdam was a stage, I had a double role: I was both audience and performer, watcher and watched. The water and sky and windowpanes layered and reflected one another, and stopping in front of a window that fairly forced me into voyeurism I would catch my own image melting into the interior, the picture on the TV screen, the owner staring at the screen from his armchair, the reflections of other passersby. If I passed a window in the red-light district, my reflection would cross the prostitute's face like a shadow. Everything reflected everything, everything merged, the reflections of the houses swimming in the canals together with the windows mirroring the sky. The very thought of it made my head spin.

Some of the front doors had mirrors sticking out on metal stalks, the purpose of which was to enable the inhabitants to see who was ringing without themselves being seen at the window. I often caught my reflection in those mirrors. I had the feeling I might slip through them into a parallel world, and I was frightened at the thought of seeing myself from inside, hidden behind the curtain, ringing the front doorbell.

———

One day, passing a group of American tourists that had gathered round an old Kalverstraat organ grinder and hearing them gush over him with the word "cute," I was reminded of its equivalent, *leuk,* in Dutch and realized that *leuk*ness was the key to the problem. *Leuk*ness was an antiseptic, a disinfectant that removed all spots, all bumps, put everything on an equal footing, made everything acceptable. Near my house there was a gay bar called the Quinn's Head with a display of ten male dolls, ten Kens, in the window. It was a *leuk* display. Whenever I passed it, I thought of the live Barbies—young women from Moldavia, Bulgaria, Ukraine, Belarus—the traffickers, traders in human flesh, bought up for export. I thought of the fresh East European flesh setting off on the long journey west. If it didn't get bogged down in some Serbian or Bosnian backwoods, it would end up here. I thought of them and of the Eastern European Kens who had come to this Disneyland to entertain the grown-up male children here, to give them alien flesh in which to insert their male members. How *leuk* it all was. And what is *leuk* is beyond good and evil; it is amoral not immoral; it is simply take it or leave it.

Early one morning I witnessed a scene that pierced me like a knife. The streets were still empty when the porcelain quiet of dawn was rent by a scream. I saw a woman coming toward me, her arms flailing, her fists clenched in a threat, her mouth emitting a mixture of words and moans. I glimpsed a mask that seemed to have merged with her face, a mask of pain. Her eyes were tearless, locked in a dull stare, her mouth twisted downward. She walked past without noticing me, though I was the only living being in sight. On she went, her fists in the air. She seemed to be rehearsing a list of insults gathered over a lifetime. Even though I could not understand them, they penetrated me to the quick. It was the combination of the vital shrieks and the dead, papier-mâché face that did me in.

And when on one of my nervous train trips I got off at The Hague and went to visit Madurodam, I found myself in the very heart of the metaphor I had been seeking. Madurodam is a perfect mock-up of the Netherlands, a Dutch Disneyland. It had every-thing—the cities, the houses, the canals, the bridges, the wind-mills—and everything was "true to life": the water ran, the bonsai were budding and the grass sprouting, the boats plied the waterways and the bridges raised to let them pass, the air was abuzz with helicopters. It had people, too: the drivers of minia-ture buses and trams, switchmen, conductors, pilots, pedestri-ans, doctors, shopkeepers, shop assistants, tourists, children, grown-ups, senior citizens, farmers, firemen. It had Schiphol with all its runways, planes, control towers, terminals, and pas-sengers. It had the parliament in The Hague and the cathedral in Utrecht. It had the famous Alkmaar cheese market, Amsterdam's Rijksmuseum, Rotterdam's Erasmus Bridge, the Groningen rail-way station, the Ameland lighthouse. . . . And suddenly I had an epiphany: I saw myself sitting on a bench in Vondel Park like a butterfly in an album or admiring a painting the size of a child's fingernail in the Rijksmuseum. Amsterdam-Madurodam. Madurodam-Amsterdam. I suddenly realized that I lived in the largest doll's house in the world. I refused to look out of the win-dow. What would I see? Only the giant pupil in the giant eye of a child.

Then I would alter my perspective and Amsterdam would again become "one of the most beautiful cities in the world," a "desert rose." I thought of desert winds ingesting indifferent desert sand, grinding it with their teeth, burnishing it with their burning tongue and spitting out a stone flower. On rainy days, when the sky came down so low it seemed to rest on the roofs, the stone rose had a dirty, ghastly cast to it. But the moment the sky lifted, the "rose" would fill with light and shine with a glow that left me breathless.

For the most part I adjusted my pulse to the pulse of the city and went on with my life. I went to the market, bought fish, fruit, and vegetables and sampled the myriad varieties of Dutch cheese; I kept up with the latest films; I people-watched in cafés; I went to galleries and museums. And life seemed its normal, laid-back self again. I lived in the heart of Amsterdam, which, or so it sometimes seemed to me, pumped more cotton candy than blood. Though maybe my own heart was broken and my view distorted. Maybe the instinct of self-preservation was the glue that held my heart together and made me believe that everything was "normal."

CHAPTER | 11

We are Pioneers,
Soldiers brave and true.
Every day we sprout
Like the grass anew.

I kept thinking we had time to burn, but the first semester was over before I knew it. And since the end of the semester coincided with my birthday, I proposed that we all go out and celebrate the two together. I had a plane ticket to Zagreb, where I would spend a week before coming back to prepare for the second semester.

The kids chose an old Dutch pub near the main railway station. One of them knew the owner. It was nearly empty: there were no more than three or four regulars at the bar, the local drunks.

"Look," said Darko, "we've got it to ourselves."

Meliha had brought a box of genuine Bosnian *urmašice* her mother had baked. Igor, Nevena, and Selim, all of whom worked at the "Ministry," brought me artifacts they had gathered at work: Igor a pair of handcuffs concealed in a bouquet of yellow roses, Selim a leather collar with metal spikes, and Nevena a black whip wrapped in purple paper and a red ribbon.

"Many happy returns of the day, Comrade Makarenko!" said Igor, kissing my hand. "Now you've got everything you need."

I asked him where in the world he'd dug up Makarenko, whose account of his work with Soviet juvenile delinquents, *The Road to Life, or A Pedagogical Poem,* had been long forgotten even in its country of origin.

Johanneke had gone to the Bosnian delicatessen in Rotterdam to buy spicy Macedonian *ajvar,* chocolate *napolitanka*-filling, and a package of Minas coffee, all of which she then packed in a box labeled "FIRST-AID KIT FOR YUGONOSTALGITIS." Ante gave me a rosemary plant, Ana a photocopy of the first postwar Yugoslav primer. I wondered what lengths she had gone to get that photocopy to Amsterdam.

Mario, Boban, Darko, and Uroš came, too. Even Amra—the young mother, who almost never came to class—put in a brief appearance. Zole, the guy who had claimed he was living with a gay partner to keep from being thrown out of the country, looked in for a while, as did Laki, whom I had completely forgotten about.

Ante had brought his accordion, and while the first mugs of beer were emptied and refilled with alarming alacrity, he started in on his prodigious repertory of partisan songs, urban folk songs, Bosnian love songs, Serbian and Macedonian *kolo* dances, Medjimurian ditties, Dalmatian glees, Slovenian polkas, with some Hungarian and Gypsy tunes thrown in for good measure. He knew all the old favorites: "Emina," "Biljana Bleaches the Linen," "What Jet Black Hair You Have, My Sweet," "I Was a Rose," "My Father Has Two Little Horses," "The Girl from Bileća," "From Vardar All the Way to Triglav" . . . Once the music had set their memories in motion, line led to line, chorus to chorus, and soon they were competing to see who could remember the most. It was like a crash course in the history of the Yugoslav popular song.

We went through the Opatija Festivals year by year: Zdenka Vučković, Ivo Robić, Lola Novaković, Lado Leskovar, Zvonko Špišić, Djordje Marjanović, Ljupka Dimitrovska . . . We took great pleasure in merely pronouncing the names as a group.

"Remember when Lola Novaković sang 'You Never Came to Offer Me Your Hand,' and all Yugoslavia cried along with her, because of course everybody knew who hadn't come."

"I didn't know. Who was it?"

"Why, Cune Gojković , you idiot!"

"But how do *you* know?" I asked, breaking in on them. "Most of you weren't even born yet."

"We've got Yugogenes, Comrade, remember?" they replied in a raucous chorus. "They take care of it."

Ante kept feeding them songs, and they kept begging for more: "Good for you, Ante! Hey, Ante, how about . . ."

They eventually got to Djordje Balašević, whose bittersweet songs were calculated to reduce all former Yugos to hopeless melancholy, and moved on to the classics of Yugoslav rock: the Indexes, White Button, Azra. During one of Ante's breaks we pieced together the wording of the Pioneer vow ("I solemnly promise to uphold the achievements of our homeland . . .") and the Yugoslav national anthem ("Hark, fellow Slavs! The word of our forefathers lives as long as their sons' hearts beat strong . . ."), which we recited in an updated rap rhythm. We made a list of all the composers of the commercialized pseudo–folk music so popular in the seventies and of the turbo-folk that succeeded it. We roared with laughter over the silliest of doggerel:

> Buy me a car, Papa. Oranges too.
> Or buy me a teddy bear straight from the zoo.
> Buy me a bunny, some sweets, or a ball.
> No, buy me everything. I want them all.

And by the time we got to "The Bunny and the Brook," we were in our second childhood, Nevena shedding a tear at the line "And now poor bunny weeps and weeps . . ." On we went to Yugoslav television, chronicling first the children's programs *Letter by Letter, Mendo and Slavica, Neven, The Smog Dwellers,* then the first American series—*Peyton Place, Dynasty, Dallas*—the Polish Captain Klos and the Soviet Captain Shtirlits, the Czech series *Hospital on the Outskirts.* From there we moved back in time to Radmila Karaklajić , who could have been our mother or grandmother, and her "Zumba, Zumba, Salted Codfish." We went through all the ethnic jokes: the Bosnian ones (about Meho and Mujo, Fata and Suljo) and the Vojvodina ones (about Lala) and the Slovenian ones (about Janez) and the Montenegrin and Dalmatian and Macedonian ones. We imitated the way Kosovo Albanians speak "our language" ("When I love I kiss, and when I don't I kill") and all kinds of regional accents. No one could finish a sentence without someone else jumping in. It was one long rat-tat-tat of quotations from life in Yugoslavia. I kept worrying that our plastic bag—the one with the red, white, and blue stripes—would burst and with it the newly established foundation for our imaginary museum of Yugoslav daily life.

Nor did they steer clear of the war.

"There's something fundamentally fucking wrong with a language that instead of saying 'The child is sleeping soundly' or 'sleeping deeply' says 'sleeping the sleep of the butchered.' "

"That's what brought the war on."

"What do you mean?"

"If you think your kid's about to be butchered, you pack a gun and fire at the drop of a hat."

My kids didn't know that I'd heard the same thing from any number of Yugoslav émigrés. They even cited it as their main reason for having left the country. ("Why did I go? Because in other languages children sleep the sleep of the just and in mine they sleep the sleep of the butchered.")

At that moment I felt a wave of compassion come over me; at that moment I felt sorry for them and loved everything about them—the way they looked, the things they said, the way they said them. . . . They were *my* kids. As my eyes traveled over them, I snapped Polaroid shots of their salient features: Selim's unusually long, fine fingers and the nervous way he had of flapping his arms like wings; Meliha's face when a smile spread across it like oil; the deep incisions between Ana's eyebrows, a brand almost; Uroš's restless, half-shut eyelids and whitish eyelashes; the ticlike twist Nevena gave to her head before she raised her eyes. I was the only one without a Polaroid: the place at the table set aside for me was empty, a void.

The group temperature rose like beer froth. We must have been temporarily insane, the lot of us. We had no idea where we were. A Pioneer meeting? A Party rally? A school field trip? All of a sudden—from too much to drink or overexcitement or fatigue or some kind of group dynamics—Meliha burst into tears. Others followed suit or felt a lump in their throats. Something told me that we'd drunk the cup to the dregs and that from one second to the next the positive group dynamics could turn into something else.

Which is what happened.

Uroš, who had clearly had more to drink than the others, stood and called out, "Quiet, everybody. Quiet down. I've got something to say."

His face was pale, and trying to take a deep breath, he swayed slightly.

> In a land of peasants
> In the mountainous Balkans

In a single day
A martyr's death came
To a band of children.
All had been born
In the selfsame year.
All had gone to the same school,
All attended
The same celebrations;
All received
The same vaccinations.
And they died on the selfsame day.

We listened without a word. Ante was playing the partisan song "Mount Konjuh."

And fifty-five minutes
Before that fatal one
The band of children
Were at their desks
Hard at work on a hard-to-solve problem:
How far can a traveler go
If he walks at a speed of . . .
And so forth.

It was a painful scene. Desanka Maksimović's "A Bloody Tale" was known by heart to generations of schoolchildren in the former Yugoslavia. It figured in all textbooks and anthologies and was recited at "official events," celebrations and school assemblies. The incident it treats actually occurred: the Germans did in fact execute an entire class in Kragujevac in 1941. But overexposure had cost the poem its potency, and in time it turned into a parody of itself. People had simply grown sick and tired of it. While Uroš droned on, I recalled some TV footage of the ninety-year-old poetess in a hat with a brim three times larger than her head. She was sitting in a first-row seat listening to a warmongering speech by Slobodan Milošević, beaming and nodding like a grotesque mascot or mechanical dog.

> A handful of the selfsame dreams
> And selfsame secrets—
> Secrets of love and love of country—
> Rested deep in their pockets,
> And all of them thought they had
> All the time in the world
> To run beneath the firmament
> And solve the world's problems . . .

The path taken by the innocent poem had begun with a historical event: the death of a group of children during a war. Once the event was embedded in the poem, the poem was embedded in the school program. By the time fifty years had passed, what was meant to be an antiwar poem had turned into its opposite: the smile the poetess gave the nation's leader represented symbolic support of the war he was waging and everything it implied. Here in the Amsterdam pub the lines trickled from the mouth of the young refugee like a repulsive drool. It couldn't have been more painful, more wrong. Uroš had missed the mark. Fatally. If we listened without a peep, it was not because we were shocked by the poem or Uroš's performance; it was because we were shocked by Uroš himself. Uroš had pricked the balloon that was holding us together, and our collective nostalgia whooshed out and disappeared. The magic of the moment had turned to alarm.

> Row after row of children
> Joined hands and left the classroom,
> Going from their last lesson

> To the firing squad meekly,
> As if death had no meaning.

Having recited the final line, he collapsed into his chair. No one said a word. The only sound in the room was Ante's soft accompaniment. Uroš pulled a twenty-five-guilder banknote out of his pocket, spat on it, and slapped it onto Ante's forehead. The accordion fell silent. Uroš brought his hand down hard on the cup in front of him, breaking it to pieces. Then he slammed his head against the table.

As he raised it, I saw thin jets of blood trickling down his face. I heard a shriek coming from Nevena or Ana or Meliha. I saw Mario and Igor lifting him from the table and dragging him to the men's room. I was numb. I felt completely cut off. I could hear what people were saying, but their voices sounded infinitely distant.

"That was like in the Petrović movie *I Even Met Happy Gypsies*."

"With Uroš in the role of Bekim Fehmiu."

"Fehmi."

"Since when are you an expert on Shiptar names?"

"Since when do you call Albanians Shiptars?"

"Why do 'our people' always end up like this? Why do we make a bloody mess out of everything?"

After a while the guys came back. Uroš looked fairly together. Igor and Mario had done a good job: they had washed the blood from his face, bandaged it up with some help from the owner, and wound somebody's scarf round his hand.

"Sorry if I . . . ," Uroš mumbled on the way out.

By now the voices sounded normal again, but I didn't respond. I didn't know what to say.

"Hey there, Comrade. You okay? You're as pale as a ghost." It was Igor.

I nodded and asked for a glass of water. The waiter appeared. We paid. I put the presents into my bag. We left the pub in silence.

We came out into a thick fog. You could barely see your hand before your face.

"Christ! A pea-souper!"

My only response was a few deep breaths.

The students looked at me, bouncing up and down to keep warm, then began to disperse.

"I have the feeling I'm in one of those Carpenter movies," Mario cried out through the fog.

"Look, don't get all upset over Uroš," said Meliha by way of consolation. "Balkan bashes have Balkan endings."

"I'm okay," I muttered. "See you in two weeks."

"Going to Zagreb for the holidays?" Nevena asked.

"Yes."

"When?"

"Tomorrow."

"Have a good trip!" she said, kissing me on the cheek. "Bring back some of that good Zagreb chocolate."

One by one they disappeared into the fog. Before long only Igor and I were left. I was grateful when Igor offered to see me home. He took the bag with the gifts, and I took his arm and leaned against him. I still felt weak.

The fog was as thick as cotton candy. The pain I had felt during the Uroš incident was giving way to the pleasure of Amsterdam and its childlike charm.

"Fog becomes Amsterdam, don't you think?" Igor whispered.

"How come you're whispering?"

"It's the fog," he said, flustered.

I looked at him. I found it touching he was flustered. The fog was exciting. Like a child's fantasy about vanishing into thin air.

Now you see me, now you don't. It was tempting and scary at the same time. Like the invisibility hat in the Russian fairy tale.

"What is it?" he said. "Why are you looking at me like that?"

"What a child you are!"

"You're the child! I bet you have no idea where you are."

"Remind me."

"In Macondo."

"Why Macondo?"

"Remember how everyone suddenly stopped sleeping and totally lost their memories? So they had to paste labels on things to know what to call them and directions to know how to use them. And remember how Arcadio Buendía invented a memory machine?"

Everything around us seemed to stand still. There were no more sharp edges. Everything was soft—sounds, voices, lights. Everything was quiet, lying low, holding its breath. We practically had to feel our way through the fog. Everything was unreal.

"No, I don't remember."

"Remember who saved them?"

"No, I don't."

"Melquíades the Gypsy, who came back from the dead and brought them sugar water in little bottles."

"Coca-Cola?"

I saw a man with dark, glittering, slightly slanting eyes staring out of the fog at me. His large lips were moist and swollen, his body taut as a string. He seemed to be trembling.

A picture seeming to emerge from a forgotten past flashed through my mind. I saw myself unbuttoning Igor's coat warm with moisture and letting my head fall on his chest, then standing on tiptoe and chewing his upper lip until it bled, lifting it with my tongue, gliding the top of my tongue along the smooth enamel of his teeth . . .

"Good night," I panted, and slipped into the entrance.

PART 2

"I'll pick you up at the airport," she said. "Don't bother," I said. "I'll take a cab." But when I stepped off the plane, I felt a twinge of disappointment: her face wasn't there. A foreign country is a country where nobody meets you at the airport, I thought. I was surprised at my own sensitivity: it was so childish. I hadn't had time to don my armor.

I had vowed to suppress all "émigré emotions." I knew the standard list of complaints: *Nobody asks how we are; they just go on about their own problems* (Mario), "we" being the ones who had left the country, "they" being the ones who had stayed behind. "They" lived "there"; we, "here." *They know best. They jump in the minute we open our mouths. They've got an opinion about everything. Why must they have an opinion about everything?* (Darko). *To hear them, they know Amsterdam better than we do, not that they've ever been here!* (Ante). *They're always whining about how bad things are for them and trying to make me feel guilty for having left* (Ana). *Whenever I go back, I feel I'm attending my own funeral* (Nevena). *And I feel like a punching bag. I ache all over!* (Boban). *I used to play Santa Claus. I'd go loaded down with*

presents. It made me feel good. Things are different now (Johanneke).
*I don't know what it's like. I haven't gone back and have no desire
to* (Selim). *I haven't been, either. I'm afraid of the face-to-face
thing* (Meliha).

The door to Mother's flat was ajar. I was moved by her
thoughtfulness: she was on pins and needles, afraid of missing
the doorbell or of having misplaced the key, needing to look for
it and then run to the door, which she might have trouble opening: you never knew when it would get stuck. . . .

She flung herself into my arms like a child. ("Heavens! You're
a wraith! Where do you live? Bangladesh? No, you live in a country that supplies the world with tomatoes. Which taste awful, by
the way.") She sat me down at the kitchen table and started chat-
tering about the dishes she had to offer ("No, no, I'll put it on a
plate for you, no need to get up"), whether I wanted salt or a little more of this or that. . . .

She looked shorter and more frail than the last time I saw her.
She had more wrinkles and was losing hair on top. Just seeing
the top of her head through the now sparse gray hair aroused a
painful tenderness in me. Heavens, how she'd aged!

Mother had an inborn gift of turning people into her "bat-
men." She'd done it to everyone around her—me, her menfolk,
her friends—and no one uttered a word of protest. I was forever a small, quiet page in her court, or at least that is how I perceived myself. She would shower me with a cooey confetti of
pet names—I was her "bumblebee," her "apple dumpling," her
"froggy-woggy," her "missy fishy"—but she had never allotted
me much time. She had kept an eye on me, that was all: she didn't
care about me; she took care of me. Though she had often left me
in the care of others—students, housewife neighbors, day-care
"aunties." I was always enrolled in "after-school activities" and
would wait patiently for her to fetch me. Once she "forgot" to
fetch me from a hospital where I had undergone a minor opera-

tion. I remember sitting on my bed the whole night, fully clothed, outwardly stalwart, yet inwardly terrified: I might never see her again. She showed up the next morning. She refused to let me "dramatize" such "twaddle," and I eventually grew accustomed to it and to making do without her. I was "Mama's independent little froggy-woggy." She had worked hard. She was an economist and ended up heading a bank. She had also run back and forth between several steady lovers and two husbands. And through it all I was "Mama's little gold-star pupil" and "Mama's only treasure."

Now she was carrying on with forced gaiety about the neighbors, to whom she'd never given a second thought, about relatives, of whom she'd never spoken before, and about people I'd never heard of. This long, detailed report was her way of filling the void and hiding the fact that she had fewer and fewer friends; it was her way of warding off the fear of death, of avoiding a genuine confrontation with me, of alleviating the pain of my arrival, which was after all the beginning of an imminent departure, of erasing the time that had elapsed since my last visit, in sum, a way of "setting things right."

"Remember Mr. Šarić on the second floor? He died recently."

"What of?"

"A stroke."

"Sorry to hear it."

"And the Boževićes on the eighth floor—they lost their son."

"What happened?"

"Car accident. You won't recognize Mrs. Božević. She's aged twenty years. Turned gray overnight. But listen to me. I'm only telling you the sad things. I've got some good news, too."

She was testing me, measuring my compassion level. Would it be satisfactory or would she have to scold me? ("You take no interest in our neighbors," as if she thought of them all the time.)

This concern for feelings had come with old age: she used to make fun of people who paraded their emotions.

She stood, left the room for a moment, and returned with a notebook in her hand. With the eagerness of a child who has a new toy to show the world, she handed me her "diary." It seemed to be mostly numbers.

"What is it?"

"My diary."

"Your what?"

"My sugar diary. I've got diabetes. I have to monitor my sugar level daily."

"Is it bad?"

"So-so. But I give myself insulin injections."

"Why?"

"The doctor says it's better to start early with small doses than to wait until you need large ones."

She talked about the malady so intimately and with such understanding and concern that she made it sound like a pet dog or cat. She pointed a pudgy finger at various dates, explaining why the sugar level had jumped there and was normal at other times.

"I'll show you how I measure it," she said, and added quickly. "How long are you staying?"

"A week."

"You're going to be very busy," she said, pursing her lips.

"What do you mean?"

"You've got to get a new ID, for one thing. There's a new system. The lines are horrendous. People wait a whole day. I almost fainted. And then you have to see a lawyer about your flat. And get a new health card. There's a new system for that, too. They keep changing things."

Yes, the nonstop chatter was a sign that she had learned to mask her fear, vague as it was, with words.

When she opened the drawer in the dresser to let me see what the new IDs looked like, I noticed a Berlin picture of Goran and me in the place where she kept the family photographs.

"You should pay a visit to Goran's parents," she said, following my glance. "Marko's not doing well."

We cleared the table and did the dishes. Then I unpacked and gave her the present I'd brought, a warm housecoat and slippers. Putting the housecoat away in the wardrobe, she showed me the clothes she had bought since I'd last seen her.

"I've acquired quite a few new things, not that I have anywhere to show them off." She sighed. "This one I've worn only once, on my birthday."

Then we watched a Brazilian soap opera, Mother trying in vain to clue me in on the plot. Sitting glued to the screen hour after hour, obsessed with the fates of Marisol and Cassandra or whatever their names were—that, like the chatter, was a strategy of self-defense. Mother had three television sets—one in the bedroom, one in the living room, and one in the room she styled as "the guest room." This total submersion into the world of cheap soaps, this TV hysteria, TV stupor, this categorical refusal to confront reality had come with the war, when reality sneaked into households in the form of skimpy subtitles, skimpier even than Marisol or Cassandra's actual lines. That was all the space it was allowed. Soaps were the foam you sprayed on fear to put it out, a foam you applied twice daily, preferably in the company of friends. Mother watched with two neighbors, Vanda and Mrs. Buden. For them the Brazilian anesthetic had become an addiction.

Mother, who had once cringed at the thought of intimacy with her neighbors, could not now stop talking about them, and the ways she referred to them enabled me to establish where they stood on her emotional ladder. If she called them "Mr." or "Mrs." ("Mrs. Francetić on the fifth floor says Croatian Oil has been sold to the Americans"), she had a good relationship with them. If she called them "my neighbor" ("My neighbor Vanda can't wait to see you"), they were close. If she used their surname alone ("Marković on the third floor is drunk all the time"), she was less than fond of them. She had gradually made a family of the people she had on hand. ("No great shakes, perhaps, but beggars can't be choosers. Not at my age. And should anything happen to me, they'll be here, whereas you . . .") It was the gravest accusation she could have leveled at me: her parents were long gone; her brother had died ten years before, her husband at the war's outset; then I left to get away from her.

She made believe she no longer had opinions, she who had once had an opinion about everything, and whereas she had never paid much attention to other people's opinions she now seemed to dote on them ("Mrs. Ferić says that Amsterdam is smaller than Zagreb"). It was all an act, of course. It was as if she were sitting in an invisible wheelchair demanding respect for her invalid status and granting her favor to all who complied.

"Vanda will be coming at five," she said. "You might want to shower and change."

I dutifully trotted off to the bathroom to shower and change.

While the three of us drank our coffee, Mother gave Vanda a vivid report of my life in Amsterdam.

"Tanjica says Amsterdam is one of the most beautiful cities in the world. Well, I recently saw a TV documentary and you know it's more beautiful even than Venice."

Tanjica says this, Tanjica says that. It was as much a way of getting through to me as it was of making small talk with Vanda.

After Vanda left I took a tour of the flat. I praised the new bathroom cabinet and pointed out she should do something about the yellow stain on the bathroom ceiling. She perked up. It came from a leak in the Ivićes' bathroom, but they were in no hurry to get it fixed. That's the way people were, wasn't it now. Causing damage and then denying they had anything to do with it.

"I'll take care of it," I said.

She nearly blushed with excitement. You'd have thought my offer was an offer of marriage. I was going to take things in hand, do what needed to be done, care for her. ("Tanjica's come and taken over, thank God. Thanks anyway, but Tanjica will take care of it.")

We watched the news, and she filled me in on everything television-related: the new anchorwoman, the master of cere-monies on the new quiz show, the new series.

"You're totally out of it!" she said. "You might as well have been gone a hundred years." This was no accusation, however; it was an excuse for a long conversation. And she was right. I was totally out of it. At least life on the TV screen looked totally different.

"I don't know what to do," she suddenly sighed. "Every-thing's so expensive. I've got a pretty good pension, and even I have to worry about making ends meet. I may eventually have to sell the cottage."

"Go ahead."

"You mean you wouldn't mind?" she asked.

She was testing me again.

"I can't say I wouldn't mind," I said, "but go ahead if you think it's called for."

"But it's yours!"

"No, it's yours," I said.

"It just sat there all summer. I thought you and Goran would be coming back eventually and would want a place at the seaside, a place where we could spend our summers together. But it makes no sense now. I hate to think of it just sitting there."

She was embroidering the story a bit. Goran and I had used the Cres cottage only rarely. It was her projection of the family idyll. She had spent the summers there with her husband until he had had a heart attack—at the cottage, as it happened—and from then on she had pretty much stayed away. So it did in fact just sit there.

After a bit more chatter—television again and high prices—she said she was tired, and off she went to bed. She was asleep in no time, like a child. I turned off the TV, turned out the light, and went to my room, the "guest room."

Draping one of her woolen scarves over my shoulders, I went out onto the balcony and stared into the darkness. I thought of how little there was left of me in the place. A few pictures, some clothes—that was it. Not that I felt pained at the thought. Why should I have expected there to be more? There had been little enough while we were living together: she took up all the space; I was always in a corner somewhere.

Now I was present in frozen, carefully selected fragments. She held absolute sway over her realm, arranging and rearranging its contents as if life were an installation with photographs. The reason she'd held on to the picture of Goran and me was that it kept our relationship going, and as director of the family soap she refused to recognize our separation.

Yes, I'd come "home." I chewed on the concept like an old piece of gum, trying to extract the last bit of flavor from it. "Home" was no longer "home." Mother was all that was left. Not only was Goran gone, our friends were gone, too. Many had moved to far-flung parts of the world, and the ones who had stayed behind were friends no more. It was none of their doing or mine. It had just happened.

Looking over at buildings that seemed to be looking back at their reflection in a mirror, I tried to make my mind a blank. I enjoyed sinking into the darkness. Then I went to bed, dragging Mother's scarf behind me. I fell asleep cradling it in my arms like a teddy bear.

CHAPTER 2

"Once I'd left, I could never quite get it together," said Meliha. "I'm never sure what time it is, know what I mean?"

Time for them was divided into *before* and *after,* and while they could reconstruct the *before-the-war* period with no difficulty, the *after-the-war* period, which included the war itself, was pure chaos. The simplest question was enough to trip them up.

"You mean when did I leave *the country?*"

That's the way they put it, reducing it to the lowest common denominator.

"Right."

"Well, I didn't come straight here."

This is what happened first. Or that. First they did that and went there, and then they came here, to the Netherlands. Exile narratives were dateless. Dates came more easily in Dutch because Dutch officials were forever asking, "When did you first arrive in the Netherlands?" Yet much as they learned to shoot back the answer, the content behind it evaded them. *After the war* was a mythic time in which it made no difference whether a hundred or two hundred or three hundred years had passed. Too many things had happened in the brief *after-the-war* period, and their mental clocks went haywire under the strain. Everything had gone haywire; everything had cracked, broken asunder. Place as well as time had divided into *before* and *after,* their lives into *here* and *there.* They were suddenly without witnesses, parents, family, friends, without even the daily acquaintances with whom we constantly reconstitute our lives, and lacking these tried-and-true mediators, they were thrown back on themselves.

The feeling I got upon entering the room was that by sheer force of will they had held back the hands of the clock. They had lured me into their capsule to delay the thought of death. But death was all around them, their invisible subtenant. The very air reeked of it.

Papa was wearing pajamas and a wrinkled, unbelted bathrobe. A tube stuck out of the open fly—a catheter. I was startled by the lack of self-control it signaled. I could scarcely recognize him: he was thin and unshaven, his complexion was sallow, he had dark circles under his eyes. Mama was in better shape: she was wearing an attractive blouse and had some lipstick on. I was touched by her effort to show me that she at least still had things under control.

I called them Mama and Papa. Olga and Marko had been teachers. They had had Goran late in life. Papa graduated from a teachers' training college just before the war broke out and had joined the partisans. After the war he had been given a high post in the Croatian Ministry of Education. In forty-eight he made a political slip of the tongue and, like so many others, was sent to Goli otok, Naked Island, where he spent three years at hard labor. After his release he was assigned to an elementary school in a small provincial town. It wasn't until Goran entered the university that they were able to move to Zagreb.

Papa had always been laconic and reserved: he had learned to keep his mouth shut on Goli otok. Mention of the labor camp and its atrocities was banned until the seventies, and even then not much was said. So basically Papa had kept his mouth shut all his life. He was a good listener, though, and asked the right questions. He was less than demonstrative in his love for Goran; he seemed to have left that side of things to Mama. I think he loved me, too, after a fashion.

And suddenly you couldn't get a word in edgewise. He talked nonstop, not only asking questions but answering them, too.

"I hear you're teaching. Have you got many students? I've been trying to calculate the number of pupils I had during my thirty years as a teacher. The number Olga had, too. I can't tell you how much time we've put in on it, and believe it or not we never get anywhere. So I said to Olga, Olga, I said, we've got a mathematician in the family, haven't we? Write and ask *him* to do the calculations."

"Put it out of your mind now," Mama said. Then she turned to me and gave me a tug. "Come and give me a hand in the kitchen, will you, Tanja?"

"Now you see what it's like," she whispered.

I made no response.

"Talk, talk, talk. Never any letup. I've stopped listening."

"What's the catheter for?"

"Don't ask. It just has to be. . . . Fetch the biscuits from the pantry, will you?"

I was touched by her willingness to share her secrets with me. I opened the doors of the cupboard she dignified with the name of pantry. I was surprised to find the title page of a magazine ineptly taped to the door. It was a picture of Tito in his marshal's uniform. I always thought Mama and Papa hated Tito, even if they'd put nothing of the sort into words. Papa had spent four years with Tito's partisans only to land a year later, and for no reason whatever, in the worst of the country's labor camps. And now Papa's "hangman" was lolling in domestic bliss amid their modest reserves of rice, flour, onions, and potatoes. They'd decided to rehabilitate him. In Mama's pantry. Clearly they preferred the Tito years to the current situation, though they didn't dare say so out loud, just as there had been many things they didn't dare say during the Tito years.

"When did the logorrhea start?" I asked, taking down the tin box with pictures of shortbread on it.

"I can't say, really. It came on gradually. But in the end I couldn't help noticing. He talks to the walls when I'm not in the room. He just keeps talking. I can't take it anymore. I really can't. I've heard it all a thousand times. I even think I hear him muttering in his sleep." She bit her lip and added, "I can't wait for it to end."

"What about Goran? Does he know what's going on? How is he anyway?"

"You can read his letters if you like."

"No. What's the point?"

She left the room for a moment and reappeared with a snapshot in her hand.

"I shouldn't show you this, but maybe you're better off knowing."

She handed me the picture. It was of Goran and a Japanese woman.

"Pretty," I said.

"Her name is Hito," she said with relief. "Papa and I call her Tito. It's our little joke. Looks nice, doesn't she?"

Glancing down at the picture again, I felt a twinge of jealousy.

Mama sighed.

"Life goes on, Tanja. Oh, not for us. We've had our day. But you children, you deserve a better deal. . . . Your mother tells me you're doing well in Amsterdam."

"Pretty well."

"You were always at the top of your class."

I had the feeling she meant to say something else—that she was "on my side"—but couldn't find the words for it.

"Goran took it hard when you refused to go with him."

"I know."

"Time heals all wounds, fortunately."

Papa appeared at the door.

"What secrets are you two telling in here? I don't like to be left alone. And what's that 'Time heals all wounds' stuff? You women, you pick something up and parrot it all over the place. Time doesn't heal wounds; it makes them."

"You've been reading too many novels," Mama said, as if speaking to a child.

We went back into the living room and had some coffee. Mama opened the box of shortbread. The shortbread had been made in the former Yugoslavia and was so old it had lost all semblance of flavor.

Papa kept up his patter. From time to time Mama waved an arm in the air, as if chasing away flies. Then she got up and turned on the TV. Papa started grumbling that she hadn't been listening to him, she never listened to him, all she cared about was that idiotic box. Mama turned down the sound. She was watching a soap opera with subtitles. She didn't need the sound.

Glancing round the room, I had the feeling things had shrunk. Even Mama and Papa seemed smaller. Everything looked older, too; everything looked as gray and shabby as the dusty rubber plant in the corner.

Papa's words inundated the room, settling accounts, justifying actions, raging, grousing. The words had an almost physical reality. They came with old age, the lack of bladder control. He was unaware they were spurting out of him.

I don't know how much time went by, but at one point I stood as if waking from a dream.

"Time to go," I said. "Mother's making dinner for me."

They didn't try to stop me.

"Well, now you know what our life is like," Mama said by way of apology.

"What's so wrong with it!" Papa barked. "We live better than people in a lot of places. And if things hadn't happened the way they did, we'd be living better than the Americans."

Breathing heavily, he went and pulled out three notebooks from under the table the TV set was standing on. They were large—stationery format—and hand-bound.

"Here," he said, "have a look at these. My scribblings."

I gave them each a kiss at the door. Papa was clearly uncomfortable. For all his attempts at a smile the corners of his mouth turned down. The expression made him look like an abandoned child doing his best to overcome the slight. It must have been the expression I was wearing when I arrived at the airport.

I watched her pricking her finger with the needle and sucking out a drop of blood through a miniature dropper, then sticking the dropper with her trembling hand into the opening of a tiny instrument, following the numbers on the display and entering them carefully into her sugar diary: such and such a date, such and such a time, such and such a sugar content. I watched her cast a worried glance at the clock and open the fridge, take out the makings for breakfast, and lay everything out neatly on the table: two plates, two cups, two spoons, two napkins.

"You make the coffee. I've had to cut it out. On account of the sugar."

I poured some Nescafé into cold milk.

"Warm up the milk. Aren't you going to eat anything?"

"I can't."

"Well, I've got to. Regular meals at regular times. That's the way it is with diabetes." She sighed.

I watched her crumble the bread with her fingers, the way children do. Another of her new habits.

"You're observing me," she blurted out suddenly. "I feel like a guinea pig."

"What do you mean?"

"You've been observing us since the day you arrived," she said, switching to the plural.

"That's not true," I said.

She picked up a moist scrap of bread and began kneading it into a ball. I felt a lump in my throat. I was going to cry. And then she would, too.

"It makes me feel you're blaming me for something. You think I'm the reason Goran left you."

I must not let myself be caught in this trap, I kept repeating to myself. I must not let myself be caught in this trap.

"After breakfast we'll pack and call a cab," I said as calmly as I could. I noticed that I, too, had switched to the plural.

"Amsterdam is in the same time zone as Zagreb, isn't it?" she asked, moving into attack mode.

"Of course it is. You know that."

"So it's half past eight there, too?"

"Right, only in Dutch you don't say 'half past,' you say . . ."

"I don't know why, but I thought it was one hour earlier there."

"No. It's the same time."

"Well, you should know." She sighed and added, "I can't say I like thinking of you there."

"Why?"

"Those canals, I bet they stink."

"Not at all."

"But the water is stagnant. It's got to stink."

"Oddly enough it doesn't."

"Well, I wouldn't live there if you paid me."

"Why not?"

"Because it never stops raining and the canals have rats swimming in them."

"What gives you that idea?"

"I saw it on television," she lied.

"I haven't seen a single rat."

"You never see anything. Your head's always in the clouds."

It was heartbreaking, I thought. The need to give offense as I was about to leave. I was abandoning her, and she had to find a way to punish me. At one time this kind of thing would have driven me to tears, but I'd learned to protect myself. Now it was like water off a duck's back.

"I'm going to pack," I said, getting up and heading for my room. She followed.

"Want to take anything as a keepsake?"

"What, for instance?"

"I don't know. I've got some homemade plum preserves."

"You made plum preserves?"

"No, Mrs. Buden. And I can't eat them. On account of the sugar."

"Then I'll take them," I said to make her happy.

She brought out a glass jar in a plastic bag.

"Heavens, will you ever learn how to pack?" she said, smoothing out the clothes in my bag. "Wrap it up in a blouse or something so it doesn't break. Is there anything else? Any of your things?"

"I don't need anything, Mother," I said, zipping up the bag. I glanced at my watch and saw there was plenty of time. "Why don't you give my things away. Maybe Vanda can use them."

Whenever I go back, I feel I'm attending my own funeral (Nevena).

She intentionally ignored what I had said.

I mixed another coffee for myself.

"How can you drink that Nescafé cold?" she asked. "Let me warm it up for you."

"I like it cold."

"You always did have a mind of your own. . . . Why haven't you phoned for the taxi?"

"There's plenty of time."

"It takes them ages to get here."

"There's plenty of time."

She looked over at me, then lowered her eyes. We were both searching desperately for neutral ground.

"Let me take your blood pressure," she offered. "I bet you never have it taken."

"Good idea," I said, though the blow was so stunning I could scarcely breathe.

Whenever I go back, I feel like a punching bag. I ache all over (Boban).

She brought out a plastic pouch and carefully removed the blood pressure monitor. She wound the cuff round her left arm and pressed the button with her free hand. She watched the numbers flash past to the buzzing of the machine. It was over in a minute. "Your blood pressure is normal," she said, slightly distracted but serene.

She raised her eyes, starting as they met mine.

"I was just testing it," she hastened to say, like a child caught lying. "I wanted to see if it was working. Now give me your arm."

I gave her my arm. Her fingers, thick with age, took hold of it and wrapped the cuff around my upper arm. The monitor was in her lap. She gripped it in both hands. Then she pressed the button and three eights appeared on the display. When they disappeared, she carefully pressed "start." We said not a word. I felt a swelling in my arm. We listened to the humming of the machine and followed the rise and fall of the numbers on the display. As the numbers came to rest, I had a sudden desire to remain in that position, just as I was, forever.

"You're normal," she said, removing the cuff. "You've got nothing to worry about."

That was our farewell hug and kiss. The blood pressure monitor was a visible substitute for something invisible, a bloody umbilical chord, all fresh and shiny like a metal string. Our blood pressure was normal, our heartbeat even. At that moment we had told each other everything we had to say.

I called the cab. It came immediately. She saw me to the elevator. I kissed her on the cheek. I took a deep breath, inhaled the fragrance of her skin, and entered the elevator without releasing it.

"*Love you!*" suddenly wafted in to me. In English. She must have picked up the phrase and intonation from the American movies she watched on television. I was touched: she had never before used those words to me, never told me *I love you*. And now that melodious American "*love you*" in a cracked voice, perhaps, but brimming with everything she wanted to say and didn't know how. It went straight to the solar plexus. I imploded.

Through the narrow, diver's-mask window in the elevator door I could see her touching her cheek with her hand. She could only have been brushing away a tear. As I pressed the button, I could hear her shuffling off in her slippers.

"*Love you . . .*" I thought I was singing back to her, but what came out of my lips was rather more like a whimper.

I bought a few boxes of the requisite chocolates at the airport duty-free shop. The well-known Kraš brand came in a box embossed with the Croatian coat of arms and designed to resemble the new Croatian passport.

After takeoff I felt a vague sense of relief. Leafing through the in-flight magazine, I stared blankly at the list of destinations, then dipped into articles on Istrian truffles, the beauties of Korčula, the meteoric career of pianist Ivo Pogorelić, and the latest successes of tennis champ Goran Ivanišević.

I'd accomplished nothing during my seven days in Zagreb. I hadn't obtained a new ID; I hadn't contacted a lawyer. Of course, the flat was a lost cause: there were thousands of similar cases. Besides, I was not particularly fond of the things we'd left behind. True, I missed the books, Goran's and mine, but even if the current tenant had agreed to give them back I wouldn't have had room for them.

I had, however, persuaded the tenants living in the flat above Mother's to find a handyman to take care of the ugly yellow stain on her bathroom ceiling. I had also left Mother some money for similar emergencies and bought a new tap for the sink.

During my seven days in Zagreb I had watched seven episodes of the Brazilian soap opera. I learned who was who in the extended family of characters. At least one of Mother's three television sets was on from the moment she got out of bed.

"It gives me the feeling I'm not alone," she said by way of self-justification.

"Why not try reading?"

"I can't. It makes my eyes hurt."

"Get new glasses."

"I did, but it didn't help. It's like I had sand in my eyes."

I'd made no phone calls: I had no one to call. I'd skimmed through the numbers in my old address book, and once I even picked up the receiver and dialed the number of a former friend, but before anyone could answer I put the receiver down. I was relieved.

I'd thought about Mother. About how she defended her turf. What mattered most to her was that the stain be taken care of, the tap stop dripping, the curtains be clean, and life take its normal course. But she was a fighter, too, and she had found an enemy: sugar. She refused to recognize any other: she was too weak now; she would have lost the battle. So she had staked out her territory, and there she reigned supreme.

The picture of Goran and me was in the china cabinet in Mother's living room. Seeing it there had made me realize how close her "exhibit" was to the ones I saw in the living rooms of émigrés. Émigré souvenir exhibits did not express nostalgia for a former life or the native country; on the contrary, it expressed lack of same. All the gingerbread hearts, peasant-shoe ashtrays, miniature Dalmatian or Montenegrin caps, handmade embroideries and lace, leather drinking gourds, and Adriatic shells were so many minuscule shrines, Lilliputian graves marking the end of a way of life, an unequivocal choice and a willingness to accept the losses that choice entailed.

Whether I had accepted them I couldn't say. What I can say is that throughout the week I spent there I was constantly ill at ease. Not so much when I was with Mother as when I was outside, in the street. I wandered the streets of Zagreb with an invisible slap on my face, viewing things slightly askance, like a rabbit, and hugging the facades of the buildings for safety's sake. Everything looked run-down and gray, now *mine,* now *alien,* now *former.*

I never told Mother I'd tried to get a new ID. The thing was, I couldn't find the office. Even though I'd been to the building several times before, even though I knew the area intimately, even though I have a good sense of direction, I couldn't find the place. When I asked for directions, people pointed to the left and to the right, but I still couldn't find it. I kept circling the narrowly circumscribed space—two or three streets at most—until panic suddenly overflowed my inner spaces and I burst into tears. The refugee trauma, the equivalent of the sudden disappearance of the mother from a child's field of vision, had surfaced where I'd least expected: "at home." The fact that I'd managed to get lost in an area I knew like the back of my hand filled me with horror.

I recounted the incident to the passenger sitting next to me on the plane. He was from Zagreb and maybe a few years my senior, an architect by trade. He had left Zagreb in 1991. He was on his way back to America, where he had found work with a firm and settled down.

"I thought I was out of my mind."

"How come? You had every reason to get lost," he said. "So many street names have changed."

"But the streets are the same."

"Not if they have new names," he said.

"Still, I can't believe it happened."

"A minor blackout. Too many changes in too short a time."

"But how could I get lost in my own city?"

"What if Zagreb is no longer your city."

"Zagreb will always be my city," I said stubbornly, hearing how ridiculous it sounded.

"Next time take the trouble to learn the new street names and everything will be just fine. The sooner you forget the old ones, the better."

"You think that's easy?"

"Not in the least. I can see how upset you are about it. I used to be, too. But I got over it. Or rather it took care of itself. Because they've written us off. Me, you, all of us who've left. All right, we're dysfunctional, but we don't count. We're a negligible minority. Look, you've been home now. Did you get the impression that people are particularly disturbed by the events of the past ten years?"

"I don't know."

"People were relieved in 'ninety-one. Life in the old Yuga had been tough on a lot of people, dog eat dog. There was always some damn goal you had to work toward: the radiant future or this or that reform. And those cursed neighbors poking around to see whether your hens were laying more eggs than theirs. So a lot of people breathed a sigh of relief when the old Yuga broke up: they could pick their noses, scratch their asses, put their legs up on the table, turn their music on full blast, or just sit and stare at the box. The Croats kicked out the Serbs, the Serbs kicked out the Croats and beat up the Albanians. And the poor Bosnians— well, they've been written off like us émigrés. By both Croats and Serbs. True, the place is riddled with criminals now, and the criminals are making fools out of the lot of them, but they still think they're better off than before: the criminals are their own at least, and nobody's setting impossible standards. They should be grateful to Milošević: he pulled the plug on Yugoslavia, after all. Nobody else had the nerve. And everybody was dying for it."

"But what about the aftermath? The responsibility for it all."

"What concern is it of yours?" And what good are questions like that? Look, in a year or two nobody will remember Vukovar. Or Sarajevo for that matter. Not even the people who live there. So don't get all hot and bothered. It's not worth it, believe me."

"But I do."

"Tell me, have you ever met any of the émigrés who left after World War Two? Or even the ones who left after the crackdown on the nationalists in '71? Well, I have. I've got an uncle in America, and he introduced me to them. It was like meeting ghosts. They'd go on and on about things that hadn't the slightest relevance to our lives. It was their perception of time that did it. You change more than your space when you leave; you change your time, your inner time. Time in Zagreb is moving much faster now than your inner time. You're stuck back in your own time frame. I bet you think the war took place yesterday."

"But it did!" I said heatedly. "And it isn't over yet."

"Well, it is for the people who stayed behind! Your 'yesterday' is their ancient history. Remember the émigrés who rushed back from Canada, Australia, Western Europe, and South America after Croatia declared its independence? Croats tried and true. The crooks and legionnaires and hitmen and losers who responded to Tudjman's clarion call."

"Exhibits from a provincial museum."

"Precisely. Well, in a few years we may look like them to the people who stayed behind. So the thing to do is forget, forget everything."

"Then who will remember?"

"Why do you think people invent symbolic surrogates? To get others to suffer and remember for them."

"I don't know if I . . ."

"Well, let me tell you. Our story is not an easy one to tell. Even numbers tell different stories to different people. What we experience as a deluge, others experience as a shower: a few hundred thousand killed, a million or two displaced, a fire here, a bomb there, a bit of plundering. . . . Mere bagatelles! More people lost their lives in the floods in India this year."

"You must be mad!"

"People have no bent for misfortune, believe me. They can't identify with mass disaster. Not for long, at least, and not even if the disaster is their own. That's why they've come up with the surrogate solution."

"I don't understand."

"More people know that Elvis Presley is no longer with us than that the Sarajevo Library is no longer with us. Or the Muslim victims of Srebrenica. Disaster puts people off."

"It's horrible what you're saying."

"You ain't heard nothing yet. Once I get going, you'll be itching to ditch me . . ."

He was interrupted by a stewardess announcing the descent into Amsterdam.

"Saved by the bell," he said with a cordial smile.

I feel more comfortable in Dutch, said Nevena, as if Dutch were a sleeping bag.

"I feel more comfortable in the air," I said.

My fellow passenger overlooked the remark, as if finding it slightly off-color.

Visibility was perfect—the air clear, the sky blue, the sun shining brightly. The land beneath us was like a matzoh, divided into thin, regular segments. The Netherlands. Malevich's *White Square* in tens of thousands of cheap reproductions. All at once I realized I had not one single picture of Zagreb in my head. I tried hard to conjure something up, but all I could muster was a series of fuzzy and, oddly enough, black-and-white images. My subconscious had for some reason whisked my Zagreb files back to the precolor era.

"Tell me," I said, turning abruptly to my neighbor, "is that Vartcks shop still in Republic Square?"

"You mean Governor Jelačić Square."

"Whatever."

"Hmm. I don't know."

"Nor do I. I was there yesterday and I can't remember whether I saw it."

"I've never bought anything there," he said. "How come it bothers you so much?"

"It just does," I said.

PART 3

CHAPTER 1

A hand grenade fell smack in between
The little boy and his pa. What a scene!
Of the poor little lad precious little was left,
And Papa was of both arms bereft.
They tried to stuff the lad in a bag,
But were soon cursing God in despair.
Because no more of him could they snag
Than a shoe and a tuft of hair.

Neno Mujčinović

The day after I got back to Amsterdam I paid a visit to the Department. Classes didn't begin for a week, but I thought it best to check in.

"I hear one of your students has killed himself," the secretary said in a voice she might have used to inform me of a change in the teaching schedule.

"What are you talking about?" I managed to come out with.

"That's what I hear."

"Which student?"

"How should I know?"

I could have strangled her.

"Who told you?"

"Another student of yours. Just now."

I rushed downstairs and over to the café, where I found Nevena and Igor. From the expressions on their faces I could tell there was something wrong.

Yes, they'd heard that Uroš had killed himself. No, they didn't know how it had happened. They'd heard that Uroš's brother had come to Amsterdam to take care of things. Oh, and that Uroš's father was suspected of war crimes and was currently under interrogation at the Hague Tribunal. No, they'd had no idea, no idea about his father. Uroš was so reserved.

I had noticed that, too. And like me they had never seen him outside class.

"It was the shame of it, Comrade," Igor said simply.

The war had brought a rash of suicides in its wake.

Mama told me the story of a soldier back from the front—a boy, less than twenty—who had paid a visit to his former school. He apparently spent the whole day in the schoolyard, plying the kids with sweets and showing them what a hand grenade looks like. The next morning his remains were scattered all over the place. Parts of the body had landed in a tree and were still stuck to the branches. He had blown himself up a few hours before classes began. The staff didn't know—how could they?—so the kids came trooping in on the bloody remains.

Yes, a whole rash of suicides. Quiet, peaceful, unobtrusive suicides, because there was too much misfortune and death in the air for people to have much compassion for them. Suicide is a luxury in wartime, compassion in short supply.

They had various ways of doing the deed: they would drink themselves to death—that was the cheapest way—or take an overdose (as a result of the war the borders were wide open, and drugs fairly flowed in), or simply "die of a broken heart," the euphemism for the untreated heart attacks and strokes that spread like wild-fire during the war. Other diseases left untreated could likewise come under the rubric of suicide. Then there was the case of the student daughter of a Serbian general war-criminal who took her own life out of shame. Or of the elderly Belgrade woman who slipped and fell just as a bus pulled up before a waiting crowd. The crowd stampeded onto the bus, trampling the body beneath their feet. No one thought to help. The doctors managed to patch the woman up, but soon after they sent her home she threw herself out of a fourth-floor window. Shame again.

There were suicides among people who had escaped the war, too. We heard all kinds of stories in Berlin. About a Bosnian woman who had hanged herself in a psychiatric hospital the day before she was to be released. About a Bosnian refugee who had hanged himself in a refugee asylum after smothering his wife and two-year-old with a pillow. Here in Amsterdam a Croatian woman at one of the asylum centers had turned on the gas and then burned herself to death. They did it out of humiliation, de-spair, fear, loneliness, and shame. Quiet, anonymous deaths, the lot of them, war victims, though absent from the statistics of the war dead.

We learned the details from Darko, who showed up at the café before long. Darko was the only one who had maintained a more or less personal relationship with Uroš. He told us that Uroš had shot himself in the temple with a revolver. He'd had no trouble getting hold of the weapon: all he had to do was make contact with Yugoslav mafia circles. Amsterdam was awash with Yugo weapons: the police were constantly running across discarded grenades in the parks. Two children had recently perished after stepping on one.

Uroš had given his flat a thorough cleaning before pulling the trigger. He threw away everything he owned—books, clothes, everything, including what he had been wearing just before the fatal shot. He left behind only a black plastic bag. On the bag he had stuck a Post-it with his brother's name and address in neat block letters. He had killed himself on Saturday or Sunday, when his landlady was out of town. She had found him on Monday evening and immediately notified the police. He was lying in the middle of the room stark naked. His body had risen to the occasion: except for a few drops of blood and urine, it was pristine. It was flanked by seven cardboard children's suitcases, the kind sold at Blokker's. Each one had the same contents: an unused toothbrush, a pad, a well-sharpened pencil, and a yarmulke.

"Was Uroš Jewish?" Nevena asked.

"Not that I know of," said Darko. "His father was a Bosnian Serb. That you all know."

The setting of Uroš's death as described by Darko seemed infantile, yet at the same time cold as a knife. The children's cardboard suitcases were the baggage Uroš felt necessary for his journey: yarmulke, toothbrush, and pad and pencil seven times over. They were likewise Uroš's will in hieroglyphs for anyone who wished to decipher it.

"Oh, and one more thing," said Darko. "He had a bullet in his mouth."

"What for, I wonder," Nevena said.

"I don't know."

"Right," said Igor distractedly. "What for?"

"Like I say, I don't know. But what if—once he'd cleaned up the place and stripped and put the gun to his head—he realized it was going to hurt. He might cry out. Somebody might hear him. Maybe he thought of a scene in a war film where they put something hard between the teeth of a wounded man they had to operate on with no anesthetic. To keep the man from screaming.

And for a second he panicked because there was nothing left: he'd set everything in order. But then he took a bullet out of the revolver, put it between his teeth, and shot another one into his head."

Darko could scarcely get the words out. He seemed on the point of tears the whole time he was trying to reconstruct the scene. It was as if he were simultaneously thinking how senseless Uroš's death was, protesting against it—there was such a thing as a noble and meaningful death, after all; why was Uroš's death meaningless?—and in the end sympathizing with Uroš, precisely because his death was so meaningless. But I was only guessing at what had gone on in Darko's mind. The protest was in fact my own.

Igor showed us a short article in the *NRC Handelsblad* dealing with the trial of three war criminals, one of whom was Uroš's father. They were among the first to come before the Tribunal, mere small fry. The big guns wouldn't make their appearance for a few years.

"Shall we go and have a look at him?" he asked, meaning Uroš's father.

"You mean the trials are open to the public?"

"I got two passes today at the Department."

"Like for a movie."

"They think of it as language practice," he said ironically. "Free of charge."

"When?"

"Tomorrow, if you like."

Nobody said a word. I had forgotten about the war during the course of the semester. So had the students. Uroš's death had sent me back into the fray, the nightmare. I was beside myself. How could I have failed to know? Because I had never asked. And I'd never asked because I'd been afraid to. Now that it was too late, I was tormented by the questions I could have asked.

"Uroš's brother has taken care of everything. He's got friends who've lived here forever, and they helped. There isn't a thing that you or any of us could have done. We can't even go to the funeral."

"We can drink to his soul, can't we?" said Nevena, moving in the direction of the bar. "My treat."

We sipped our Dutch *rakija* in silence. I was no longer thinking of Uroš; I was thinking of a sequence I had seen on television early in the war. It showed a young man Uroš's age, a Slovene in the uniform of the Yugoslav National Army, who had been taken prisoner by the new Slovenian Territorial Defense force. There he stood—his hands up, the tears running down his cheeks—shouting, "Don't shoot, guys! I'm one of you!" A few seconds later the Slovenian "guys" shot their own "guy."

Our drinks duly downed, Nevena, Darko, Igor, and I went our separate ways. That day Amsterdam looked like the set for Fellini's *Amarcord*. The snowflakes had an unbelievably Extra Large look to them.

CHAPTER 2

Now and then someone
Will dig up rusty arguments
From under the Bushes
And take them to the dump.

Wisława Szymborska

I didn't know what to do. I paced the cramped space of my flat, shivering with a mild fever. I couldn't concentrate on anything, the thought of Uroš's death having taken over like a migraine. And then my eye lit on a notebook, one of the three Papa had just given me in Zagreb. I'd left the other two with Mother, knowing I'd have neither the time nor the inclination to read them. If I took even one, it was to assuage my conscience. I plucked it off the shelf and started leafing through it.

The text had been typed single-spaced with virtually no margins. The print was fuzzy. He must have given me the third or fourth copy. He had stapled the sheets together, covered them with light green cardboard and written "Memoirs of a Small Town Schoolmaster" on it in his own hand. He called the notebooks "books." I don't know the title he gave to "Book One," which presumably dealt with his early childhood. "Book Two" may have been called "School Days, School Days, Good Old Golden Rule Days." I had "Book Five," which bore the dedication "To my future progeny." Papa had little hope of "future progeny," the progeny being merely a romantic excuse, but since he had made several copies of this, his life's confession, he apparently did hope that somebody else would eventually read it.

> I went to the town of N to do what I had been trained to do: teach. I was a teacher like so many others except for one thing: I had gone to the school and the town of N from—Goli otok.

Papa's confession was infused with his experience as a political prisoner on Goli otok for his Cominform sympathies. It had completely derailed him: even after his release he did not feel absolved. While he was "inside," "absent from life," while he spent "all day, every day carrying a ten-kilogram rock up a fifty-meter incline and, if the guard happened to be in a good mood, dropping it to the ground for a moment's respite before proceeding back down the incline with the rock in tow," the people on the outside had learned, ever more shamelessly, to "pick the state's pockets." He called his postprison life posthumous and himself "the corpse," forced to hide his Goli otok past like a case of syphilis. He felt exiled from life on other accounts as well: he had lost his partisan status (at one point he describes how he was stripped of all military honors) and was no longer a Communist (he had been expelled from the Party). All he was now was a "schoolmaster."

Tone and mood varied: self-pity would yield to a schoolmasterly sermonizing or the indignation of the true believer or the activism of the provincial social worker–cum–political functionary. At first I thought he was addressing a set of invisible prison walls, but before long I realized that his true audience was neither his future progeny nor Tito nor the Party nor the secret police nor the Yugoslav state nor the brutal Goli otok guards; it was the small town where he had taught.

What gradually emerged was a picture of everyday life in the Yugoslav provinces during the fifties and sixties. Papa gave a minute description of how after several years as a teacher in N he started renovating the dilapidated school—cementing over the muddy courtyard, then gathering some discarded boards and putting up a workshop; how much later, when he had become head of the local university-extension branch, he undertook the construction of a House of Culture and the creation of a Workers Society for the Arts; how he set up an amateur theater group for which he managed to acquire real floodlights; how the first cinema came to be built and how they procured films for it; how they founded the first genuine public library and reading room and how they financed books for it; how they put new life into the much neglected municipal park; how they built a secondary school complex and the first swimming pool; how they organized a basketball club; how they instituted the first music school. . . .

The pages devoted to his pupils were particularly warm. At one point he recounted having misspoken and said "Go up on the board" instead of "Go up to the board," and while his back was turned the pupil thus bidden had taken him at his word. "The boy had removed the blackboard from its wooden stand and, to the great merriment of the class, stepped onto it. That boy eventually earned two university degrees."

Upon retirement—he had moved to Zagreb by then—he received the standard symbolic gold watch for having done his duty, but he was deeply wounded that no sign of gratitude came from the town where he had spent the best years of his life.

At the very end of the "book" Papa devoted inordinate space to descriptions of the various cupboards, wardrobes, and shelves in his life, from childhood to old age (coffins belonging for him to the same category). He was especially expansive on the bookshelves in the Zagreb flat, out of which all kinds of documents, posters, and medals were wont to fall. One such document praised him for his "selfless educational endeavors on behalf of the younger generation during the War of National Liberation," another for his "selfless endeavors to develop and strengthen the social and cultural life of our country." Yet another was called "The Partisan Teacher Certificate." ("It reminded me of the days when the three Rs were taught to the roar of German bombers in one direction and Allied Flying Fortresses in the other, of cannon fire in the distance and machine-gun fire close at hand. Our pupils would sit beneath a tree with slates in their laps and chalk in their hands, learning words, reading, and doing sums under the watchful eye of the partisan teacher. . . .")

One day I started riffling through those yellowed documents and what did I find but a single sheet of paper with the state seal at the top. And what did I see but my name and the fact that I was being awarded a medal for service to the nation. I sat there thinking to myself, "What kind of a nation can this be if I've done it enough of a service to deserve an award and have all but forgotten I received it?" Yet as I sat there holding that sheet of paper, suddenly, in a flash, the fear of having wasted a life went up in smoke. My eyes ran down the text and sure enough there it was. It might as well have happened yesterday. . . .

I arrive in Zagreb with no idea what I'm doing there, but dressed up to the nines, tie and all (not even my worst enemy could have devised a greater torture). The auditorium I'm ushered into has a ceremonial feel to it—people are whispering, looking expectant, there's not a smile in the place—and then the director of the University Extension

Association of Croatia walks onto the stage, a sheaf of important-looking papers under his arm. "The first certificate for major contributions to the consolidation, growth, and further development of education and culture in the Socialist Republic of Croatia goes to . . ." and he reads out my name.

Papa belonged to the generation that truly believed it was building a brighter future. He had joined the partisan movement as a convinced anti-Fascist and felt he had won the war. If he had ended up in a camp for the politically unreliable, it must have been because he had stated somewhere in public that he refused to accept the existence of Stalinist camps. Upon his release, "unshaken in his convictions," he went back to "building a better tomorrow," but by the time he retired he had lost his illusions—hence the "books." There he lined up the shades of the people who would eventually bring down everything he had believed in, many of whom, too weak to withstand the herd instinct, were members of his own generation. And once he had put down everything he knew, he threw open the window to take a deep breath and examine the ruins. Time had regressed. He was back where he had started from. It was wartime again. There were camps and barbed wire.

I wondered whether anyone would ever read what he had to say. The grandchildren he hoped for, should he have any, would speak Japanese. Olga, who had heard it all a thousand times over, was more concerned about when she would be able to paint the walls white. Over the years Papa had turned from victim to torturer and turned Mama into a mother confessor whom he constantly battered with words.

I could just picture Papa plastering the walls with his plaints, sending out signals no one wished to receive, justifying his existence, whining, rehearsing the slights to which he had been subjected, tracing list after list of them in the air, galled by disillusion and petty, filthy, human betrayal. I pictured him standing in the middle of the room in his striped pajamas—the tops unbuttoned, the catheter sticking out of the bottoms—emitting swarms of kamikaze-fly words splatting the walls and leaving blood specks behind.

I thought of Goran, too. Goran like his father nurtured his share of slights. He had doubtless dragged them to Japan with him, smuggling them across the border like a cache of jewels. Like his father he had been tainted ("tainted" is a word his father uses somewhere) by the experience of exclusion. *Expunge—eliminate—delete—expel—excommunicate—ban—interdict—keep out—shut out from—prohibit from—banish—erase—exclude . . .* And out goes Y-O-U!

Goran no longer loved me. That was why I refused to go to Japan with him. It had happened quietly, imperceptibly, for no one specific reason. Goran tried his best: he did everything he could to stimulate his heart and quicken his pulse; he didn't believe that love could simply slip away like that. But little by little the feeling he'd had for me yielded to a feeling of having been slighted. Maybe I have the same feeling; maybe it was hibernating in me. It's hard to find our own fault lines and sense the taint as it enters our veins.

Goran was of the same stuff as Papa. The moment he scored a victory, he would submit it mentally to his own, personal "town of N." And the greater his achievements, the deafer the town was to them. The only thing the town cared about was his failures. Those it was willing to hear about because they confirmed it had been right about him. So for both Goran and Papa the country was divided into two opposing, equally passionate camps: the victims and the victimizers. And then for the first time I realized they might be on to something: perhaps that now defunct country had in fact been inhabited exclusively by victims and victimizers. Victims and victimizers who periodically changed places.

How do you find release from the past? I kept wondering. . . . I had asked my students to make their peace with it as the necessary first step. I had offered them the painless territory of the past, trying to protect them as parents protect their children and children their friends, as my mother had protected me and Goran's father Goran. But no, there was no release; there was only forgetting. And that came from those miraculous little erasers we all have in our brains. Every one of us drags a closet behind him, and every closet has its skeletons. Sooner or later out they tumble, though in disguise, in a form we feel comfortable with, like the documents that came tumbling down from Papa's shelf. The past is our "installation," amateur stuff but with artistic pretensions. With a touch-up here and a touch-up there, here a touch, there a touch, everywhere a touch-touch. (Retouching is our favorite artistic device.) Each of us is curator in his own museum. And we can't make our peace with the past unless we have access to it, unless we can stick a finger in its dike like Hans Brinker, the boy who saved Holland from inundation. Stick your finger in the dike. Fill your screen with pictures. Keep your life dust free. Make occasional changes. Get rid of a thing or two. Uncover A; cover up B. Remove all spots. Keep your mouth shut. Think of your tongue as a weapon. Think one thing and say another. Use orotund expressions to obfuscate your intentions. Hide what you believe. Believe what you hide.

I grew sick at the prospect of all those repetitions, recapitulations, renewed complaints and justifications, of virus-transmitted misfortune and the umbilical cords that encircle and entwine us, tying us all together into the awful, painful, bloody mess we're forever flailing in—parents, children, grandchildren, hanged man and hangman, victim and victimizer, guard and prisoner, judge and defendant. . . .

I needed air. I tossed Papa's notebook onto the floor, pulled on my coat, and went out. I walked along the Zeedijk for a while, then went into De Verdwenen Minnaar, a pub where I had an occasional coffee. I took a seat at the bar and ordered. The hum of human voices and the heat given off by the bodies served to calm my nerves. I needed warm human flesh to put out the pain pounding in my temples as one puts out a cigarette. There was a man sitting next to me. We exchanged a few words, drank a few drinks, looked a few looks, and let our bodies graze against each other: we were working toward a minor transaction of mutual aid involving the commixture of bodily fluids. The transaction was successful: I got what I needed—the consolation of self-humiliation. The pain disappeared.

In the wan morning light coming through the barred window my sleepy eyes picked out a banknote on the bedside table: the man, whose face I had not had time to fix in my mind, had left me a hundred-guilder note. My mouth drew into a smile. *Snip voor een wip!* as the Dutch say. A hundred guilders for a lay. It had completely slipped my mind I was living in the red-light district!

The complex housing the ICTFY, the International Criminal Tribunal for the Former Yugoslavia, reminded me of nothing so much as Yugoslav socialist architecture of the sixties and seventies, in which functionality took a backseat to the ideals of the radiant future, internationalism and justice for all. It was architecture UN style adapted to the more modest proportions of the Netherlands. The building of the International Tribunal was meant to make everybody feel "at home," Yugo criminals included. Though I wouldn't be surprised if the latter were disappointed in the modesty of the interiors.

After showing our passes, submitting to a thorough search, and stuffing our backpacks into the lockers, Igor and I went through one last checkpoint and finally made our way down a flight of metal steps—the kind they have on ships—to the courtroom. The spectator area was divided into two sections, one on the left for journalists, the other on the right for the general public. We picked up earphones on our way in. A small sign informed us of the languages available on the various channels. Channel six was reserved for the language called "Croatian/

Bosnian/Serbian" Our seats faced a glass wall covered by a series of screenlike rolling shutters. There were television monitors hanging in the right and left corners. At nine on the dot the shutters went up and we stood as the judges entered the courtroom. The three judges, dressed in red-and-black robes, took their places on a platform in the very center of the room. Their three assistants, in black robes with white collars, sat just below them. The counsels for the prosecution and defense sat even lower and off to the side. We thus had an unobstructed view of them all. Each had his own computer. The defendant sat next to his lawyer. He was a middle-aged man in a gray suit with lackluster eyes, a potatoey complexion and a kind of lackluster, potato-sack posture to go with it all. I was disappointed, as was, I imagine, Igor. We had expected a criminal and what we got was a man, a man with an eminently forgettable face. Except for one detail: his lips turned downward and his jaw was clamped shut. It was a replica of Milošević's face, but of Tudjman's, too—the same clenched teeth and thin, crooked slit of a mouth in the form of an upside-down U. The kind of flat face one sees in children's drawings. An evil face.

The prosecutor had called a witness to the stand. The shutters went down for a time, then back up, all but the one blocking the witness. The witness's TV image was indistinct, but we could hear his voice. He was reading from a computer screen. There were long pauses between his responses, because he had to wait for the translation of each question to appear on the screen. Every once in a while the cameras would turn toward the spectators and we would see our own faces on the monitors. We could also see the reflections of our faces in the glass wall superimposed on the faces of the people beyond it.

At first we followed the trial through the glass, throwing only an occasional glance at the TV monitors, but more and more I caught my eyes lingering on the screen, as if I found its image more reliable than the live proceedings. The words we heard, switching channels from time to time to hear how things sounded in English, French, or Dutch, were in any case unreal. The reality the glass wall separated us from inspired no more confidence than "real" reality: both of them—the one that churned out lies, lies, and more lies and the one that promised the truth, the whole truth, and nothing but the truth—were equally fantastic, if that is the word for it.

The questioning centered on a carp hatchery. Uroš's father had been the head of a carp hatchery in a small town in Bosnia. He was being asked about repairs that had been made on the leaky roof of the main building, about the sheet metal that had been used to cover the roof and how much it cost and who was supposed to pay for it, and then about some truck or other and the driver and so on and so forth. The endless, tedious stringing together of details that made no sense whatever to us was intended to show whether Uroš's father and two accomplices had had enough free time to slip off to a nearby shack where the town's Muslims were being held, force them to play humiliating sexual games—their favorite allegedly being "father and son"—and then beat them to death with their fetid-carp hands and toss their corpses into the ponds.

All the defendants in the production sounded like amateur actors: all they were doing was reading out prepared statements from the computer screens in front of them. By speaking Robot rather than Human, they turned evil into a mechanical plot line, as mechanical as any other. None of the accused felt the slightest guilt. Of all the people who had destroyed the country—leaders, politicians, generals, soldiers, crooks, murderers, mafiosi, liars, thieves, villains, and volunteers—not a one was willing to come out and state, I am guilty. I had not heard the word "guilty" from them before, I did not hear it while sitting in the courtroom with

Igor, nor do I ever expect to hear it. They were all just doing their duty. Do you feel guilty when you hammer a nail into a wall? No. Do you feel guilty when you hang a picture on that nail? No. Do you feel guilty when you beat a hundred people to death? No. Of course not.

I wondered how things stood with the hundreds of thousands of nameless people without whose fervid support there could have been no war. Did they feel guilty? And what about that herd of foreign politicians, diplomats, envoys, and military personnel who had stampeded through the country? Not only had they been liberally paid; they had earned the epithet of savior, to say nothing of promotions in the UN or whatever institutional hierarchy they chanced to represent. (And Croatia and Bosnia weren't exactly hardship posts: the hotels were quite serviceable, the food decent, the Adriatic close at hand.) Did they feel guilty? They too were only doing their duty. Just like the sniper on the hill who gunned down the woman in the streets of Sarajevo. Just like the foreign photographer who took the woman's picture (though it never occurred to him to call an ambulance) and won a prize for the best war photo of the year. Even the poor woman writhing on the pavement, the blood gushing out of her, even she, little as she was aware of it, was doing her duty by her authentic representation of war. Who is guilty of the death of Selim's father? Who of the death of our Uroš? Who is guilty of riveting Igor and me to our seats, hungering for absolution?

There we were, Igor and I, watching television! It was the image of the perverted reality in which all of us, perverted as we were, were accomplices. In a way there was no difference between me, who sat there glued to the TV screen, and Uroš's father, who sat glued to his screen reading out canned responses in a metallic voice. In a world thus mediated—and mediated so many times over—everyone was guilty. Crime was unreal. Everything was unreal. I felt it would take no more than a single click of the mouse to do away with the judges, the defendants, and us, the spectators. One blissful, conciliatory *delete*. Only one thing was real: pain. Pain was the speechless, useless, and only true witness. The pain that would surge through Selim's veins and surface at his temples. The pain that pounded dully in me. And Igor. The deaf, dumb, and blind pain that could suddenly bowl us over, that signaled something was radically wrong.

So there I sat facing the glass wall and musing. . . . What would happen, I wondered, if all that pain came together in the feeble mind of an Oskar Mazerath and he stood and opened his mouth and let out a scream? I pictured the glass wall shattering into thousands of tiny slivers, the computer screens, the lights, the eyeglasses, the porcelain caps on people's teeth—all smashed to smithereens. I pictured that piercing, earsplitting voice shooting the gray potato head of Uroš's father into the air, sending all the heads of all the blood-drenched murderers flying through the air, bursting their hardened eardrums and callous hearts. . . .

I glanced over at Igor. Feeling my glance on his face, he turned and gave me a questioning look. I took the earphones off his ears.

"Let's get out of here," I said.

Leaving the courtroom was like leaving a funeral at which one wasn't quite sure who was being buried.

"Where to?"

"Home," I said. "Amsterdam."

We got onto a tram. The visit to the Tribunal had been a bust: we had come to see instant punishment meted out to Uroš's father and were leaving empty-handed.

"The Hague is no Nuremberg," said Igor, guessing my thoughts.

"That's for sure."

"And the trial is nothing like Eichmann's in Jerusalem."

"You've made your point," I said with a snort.

"Hey, what's got into you? Why are you being so crotchety?"

"Because you shouldn't make light of institutions of justice."

"La-di-da! Will you listen to her! Institutions of justice. I didn't know you were a romantic, Comrade."

"Well, I didn't know you were a cynic. And where it least becomes you."

"Okay, okay. Pipe down."

"Look, those people are trying to clean up the shit we left behind. Because we don't feel obliged to do it ourselves. Because it doesn't even smell so bad to us. But they're not into American movies, so we didn't see Uroš's father strung up the way we'd have liked."

"They may even set him free," he said.

"It's worth it if they sentence anybody."

"All that exorbitant rigmarole for one crook?"

"What do you care? It's not coming out of your pocket, is it?"

"Okay. Pipe down, pipe down," he grumbled. "I'm not Karadžić, am I? Or Mladić."

"Those people are trying to help us, and we look on from the sidelines, grinning like morons! You and me—we didn't even have the patience to sit it out a few hours."

"But it's a tribunal, not a church."

"It wouldn't do us any harm to think of it as a church. And sit through the service for humility's sake."

"Well, I wasn't the one who wanted to leave."

I blushed. He was right. I felt like belting him one. He gave me a piercing glance. I could feel him reading my mind. People in the tram were looking in our direction.

Just then the tram stopped and Igor pulled me out of my seat.

"Come on. Let's go."

"Why did you want to get off?" I protested when we were in the street.

"First of all, because you embarrassed me by talking so loud, but also because I want to introduce you to my girl."

"You've got a girl in The Hague?" I said like a student in a course of Croatian for foreigners.

"What's so strange about that?" he replied. "It's no different from saying, 'I've got a girl in Bjelovar.'"

A sudden onslaught of fury lodged like a ball in my throat, and I made several attempts at a deep breath.

"Don't hyperventilate on me now," he said playfully.

I spat the invisible ball out of my mouth and was finally able to breathe.

Igor stopped in front of the Mauritshuis.

"Taking me to another museum?"

"This is where my girl works," he said.

We climbed a flight of wooden stairs covered with a thick, red carpet. At the top of the stairs Igor turned to the left. On the wall of the first room, next to the door, hung Vermeer's famous *Girl with a Pearl Earring*.

"So that's your girl!"

"Yup," he said in English. *"That's my chick."*

I knew the picture—I'd been to the Mauritshuis—but I didn't let on. It took my breath away. The original looks like a pale imitation of its numerous reproductions. The first time I saw the painting, I was surprised at how light the blue of the girl's turban and the gold of her raiment were, much lighter than in the reproductions.

"You look a bit like her," he said cautiously.

"I'm not angry anymore. And you've got your A. You don't need to flatter me."

"You might be her elder sister. No, really. There's something in the facial expression. It reminds me of the 'human fish.' "

"How can you say such a thing! Did you ever see the human fish?"

"Only in a picture," he confessed.

"Well, I did. When I was a kid, all Yugoslav elementary schools took a day trip to the caves at Postojna."

"Well? What does it look like?"

"Like something that lives in a cave. And it's one of a kind."

"Now that's what I call an exhaustive description."

"All right, then. *Proteus anquinus*. The human fish. Length: between ten and twenty-five centimeters. A kind of amphibian reject. A unique case of unsuccessful metamorphosis. It breathes through its gills mainly, but can use its skin, too. It is blind, and while it does have arms and legs of sorts they seemed to have been abandoned along the way: the legs are mere stumps and the arms end in hands with three fingers. It can apparently survive several years without food, and its life expectancy is unusually long—a hundred years or more. It has no pigment, and its skin is a pale, milky white, all but transparent. You can see the slightly bloody gills, the thinnest of veins running through the body and a minuscule heart. In short, it is a failed mutant, something between lizard, fish, and human embryo. The human fish was our Yugoslav miracle. We should have put it on our flag instead of the red star. It's our E.T."

"Pretty impressive, Comrade," he said in English.

"Oh, there's something else. I believe it reproduced in the larval stage, though I can't be certain."

"Where did you pick all this up?"

"I haven't the slightest idea. And one more thing . . ."

"What?"

"The human fish is a cannibal. For some reason there are times when it eats its young."

"Well, well," said Igor, though his mind seemed elsewhere. "So I was right after all."

"What do you mean?"

"My girl emerges from the cave a unique, endemic specimen."

"Tell me more about it."

"The thing I like most about her is the color of her skin. It's the color of a stalactite."

"You mean stalagmite, don't you?"

"Get off my back!"

"But I like the way you describe her. Go on."

"I have the feeling her skin is desiccated, yet moist to the touch. I like her expression of gentle, pliant helplessness. And the half-open mouth, the shiny, dry film over the lips and the drop of saliva at one side of them. The dewy quality of the gaze, the barely perceptible tear about to be shed. The fascinating duality of absence and constant presence in the eyes. Look at them: they seem to be following you. And the white collar cradling her slender neck. The sweet little face that can't wait to fall into someone's warm, protective hands—or under the guillotine. . . . There's something unfinished about her. She's like the human fish in that way, too. See? She has no eyebrows. My girl's a beautiful larva waiting for metamorphosis."

Igor, who had been standing behind me, took me by the shoulders and moved me slowly up to the painting.

"Now take a closer look at the earring in her ear," he said.

"Okay. . . ."

"And what do you see?"

"Nothing. The pearl."

I could see our reflection in the glass protecting the picture. Igor's hand remained on my shoulder.

"Look closer."

"I don't see anything."

"That's what I thought. Wait a second. I've got a magnifying glass."

"You've got a magnifying glass?"

"Yes, I happen to have a magnifying glass in my pocket."

"What else do you happen to have in your pocket?"

"*None of your business,*" he said. "Just have a look at the painting through it."

"I see the pearl . . ."

"And in it?"

"A reflection."

"Boy, you really are blind! Look again."

"I don't know. Given the genre, you might expect to see a representation of death."

"Haven't got a clue, have you? The pearl contains Vermeer's face!"

He was jubilant.

"What makes you think that?"

"You mean you still don't see it?"

"No. Come on, admit it. You're making the whole thing up."

"Isn't it fantastic?"

"Even supposing it's there, couldn't it be a convention of the time?"

"The painter, her creator, in the pearl in her ear!"

"There are those who say that the girl in the picture is Vermeer's daughter, Maria, in which case it could be seen as the first symbolic representation of DNA."

"Which would make it even more fantastic! The old man becoming one with her. The first symbolic representation of piercing!"

"But there are also those who say it's the portrait of someone completely different or a character study. Rembrandt did turban portraits too. Right here in this museum you can see . . ."

"The ones who say she's his daughter are right."

"If so, your *chick* is wearing her *old man* in her ear."

"Tell me," he said abruptly, "who do you wear in yours?"

"I don't know. Just as she doesn't know she's wearing the image of her creator and hypothetical father. But then neither do we. It isn't everyone who goes through life with a magnifying glass at the ready."

"There's Sherlock Holmes. . . ."

I could feel the weight of his hand on my shoulder and the warm, gentle flow of his breath on the nape of my neck. Suddenly I bristled. I carefully removed the hand and turned to face him.

"And you?" I asked. "Where's your tattoo?"

"Haven't got one," he answered.

"Uroš had one."

"Uroš?"

"Well, a brand, the stigma of his father."

"That man's a murderer, not a father."

"Remember the questionnaire I handed out on the first day of class?"

"Yes, I remember that stupid questionnaire," he said, stressing the word "stupid."

"Well, the answer Uroš gave to my question about what he expected to get out of the course was 'To come to.' "

"Sounds a little *corny* to me. Though Uroš wasn't, how shall I put it, *the sharpest tool in the shed*."

"What's that supposed to mean?"

"He wasn't particularly bright."

"That's not a nice thing to say."

"Sorry."

"Uroš sent out plenty of SOS signals. We just didn't notice. Or didn't care to. It's all my fault."

"And now your conscience is bothering you, right?"

"Those children's suitcases. . . . There's a message in them, a message we haven't deciphered. It's right in front of us, there are all kinds of signals in the air, and we're blind. It's like your putative Vermeer image. Maybe the world would look different if we all walked around with magnifying glasses in our pockets. Or if we had the gift that fairy-tale characters are given, the gift of understanding plant and animal language, or even just human language, really understanding how people talk."

"Forget it, Comrade," said Igor. "People don't talk; people bullshit. But that's enough for now. They're closing. We've got to go. Can I offer you a hot chocolate?"

Igor and I were the last to leave, but I managed to buy a souvenir in the museum bookshop: an oval glass paperweight. Under the glass was a reproduction of Igor's girl.

A light, wispy snow was falling as we came out of the museum. We crossed the small square and went into a cafeteria. We found a seat at the window and ordered our hot chocolates. Now that I had started in on Uroš's death, I couldn't stop.

"Maybe I'm the one who pulled the trigger," I said.

"What trigger?" he shot back at me.

"I mean, maybe I'm the one to blame for Uroš's death. He sent me a signal, and I failed to decode it."

"That's a load of crap!" said Igor. "You've got to stop romanticizing Uroš's death. What's the point? Does it make you feel any better? Heaven only knows why he killed himself. Maybe he went off his rocker. Maybe he got tired of the journey and jumped the train. Maybe it was just his way of saying good-bye, ta-ta, *tot ziens,* adieu, and *fuck you one and all.* . . . Tell me, why am I the one you picked to bug with all this?"

"Because there's no one else for me to bug."

"Pull yourself together, will you? Those tears are going to ruin your hot chocolate."

"I'll stop. I promise I will."

"I wish I knew what movie I've fallen into. *The movie of the week?* Or maybe it's a Danielle Steele novel."

I wiped away my tears.

"There's a good girl! I was afraid you were turning into a—squid."

I laughed, and the laughter gave momentary relief.

"Tell me a little about yourself," I said cautiously.

"What do you want to hear?"

"About your life. Are your parents still alive? Where do you live? Who with? Have you got a girl? Who are your friends?"

"You and your stupid questionnaires! Well, I know what you're after, and you don't need to worry. For one thing, I'd never kill myself for a crook like the one we saw in the courtroom. But even more important, I'm not the suicide type. *I'm a player. I'm sharp as a tack.*"

We didn't talk much in the train on our way back to Amsterdam. We were each very much self-absorbed: Igor was reading a Dutch newspaper; I had unwrapped the paperweight and was running a hand over the oval glass, thinking of the pictures Mother had put in the china cabinet. They did not include a picture of my father. I didn't remember my father. I couldn't. I was three when he killed himself. Mother refused to talk about him. She had burned her bridges and was not about to reconstruct them for me. Not only did I know nothing about him; I didn't have his name: she had further erased his traces by giving me hers. No wonder there was no trace of him in her china cabinet rogues' gallery. She was absolutely certain she had "saved" me by excluding my father from my biography. Saved me from what— only she could say. She had done everything she could to fill in all cracks I might pass through, remove all threads I might grab hold of. She managed a goodly part of my past, occupying my father's place as well as her own.

The invisible pearl in my ear was empty. I peered at its turbid surface in search of a magic picture. I could not tell whether the scene in the picture, which would emerge from a deep, dense darkness into my memory, had actually taken place or whether the man in the picture was my father, but he could have been. I am three. A man is giving me a piggyback ride, and I am holding on to his hair. The man is holding on to my shoes as if they were the ends of a scarf around his neck. We are walking through deep snow. It is twilight. There is a magic glitter to everything. Suddenly the man shifts his hand to my shoulders and collapses into the snow in slow motion. I am deliriously happy. . . .

"You're scratching your ear," Igor said, looking up from his newspaper.

"I am?"

"A penny for your thoughts."

"Oh, I don't know . . . I'm not thinking anything, really."

At the station we went our separate ways. I turned to see his tall frame, slightly stooped under the backpack, hands in pockets. In the dark, from the back, speckled with tiny snowflakes, he looked more robust, more of an adult.

"See you in class on Monday," I called out.

He did not turn or reply; he simply raised one arm slowly to show he had heard.

CHAPTER 5

Eventually Ines and Cees did invite me over. Truth to tell, Ines and I had never been particularly close. The whole Amsterdam thing had come about pretty much by chance. A mutual Berlin friend happened to be in Amsterdam and happened to run across Ines, and while they were chatting about who was where and doing what he gave Ines my address. She and I had studied awhile together and double-dated awhile together. She had her Vladek; I had my Goran. She and Vladek had known each other since their school days and got married as undergraduates. They disappeared from Zagreb the moment they graduated. Rumor had it they'd gone to Amsterdam. Vladek had earned his way through the university dealing in Croatian naive artists, in Italy mostly. He had now opened a gallery in Amsterdam.

I had hoped Ines would have me over as soon as I arrived in Amsterdam. I had phoned her several times with proposals that we meet, but she always had a polite excuse: she was so busy, she had to be with the children, but "we'll get together, just the two of us, and have one of our good old gab fests, okay?" I tried to recall whether we'd ever spent any time together without Goran and Vladek.

Ines was a typical Zagreb product. She was attractive and took inordinate care of herself: she had *her* cosmetician ("You really ought to go to her. You won't recognize yourself!"), *her* hairdresser, *her* dentist, *her* dressmaker. She bought all her clothes in London ("Trieste is for peasants!"). Everyone she knew was *hers*, from the woman in the visa office ("Vikica got us our visas in five minutes!"), the bevy of doctors and the pedicure to the butchers and cleaning women ("Milkica is top-notch. She's great at windows and nobody can beat her at the ironing board. Whenever you need her, just say the word"). Her intimacy with the world around her, her ability to subject it completely to her will, her absolute at-homeness with her crowd—it the butter, she the knife—her utter lack of concern for anyone who did not think as she did, the authority and efficiency with which, as if engaged in a high-salaried position, she lived the "adult life" while still an undergraduate—all this put me off, yet beguiled me as well. She had that "Zagreb girl" quality about her: a femininity one inherits from one's mother or acquires with entry into the privileged class and a coy way of talking—a slightly nasal voice combined with high-pitched *sh*s and *ch*s, a tendency to stress the final syllable, and an ingratiating intonation designed to show she was on the side of whomever she happened to be talking to. But much as the voice oozed compassion and understanding, it made no commitments.

I wasn't all that eager to see her, but it rankled a bit that during what was now the months I'd spent in Amsterdam she hadn't once phoned. I put on makeup for the first time in ages, donned earrings and high heels. Walking down Bloemstraat looking for her house, I felt somewhat abashed at my desire to go all out for her. I wanted her to see me at my best and was using the costume to disguise the true state of affairs.

Ines hadn't changed a bit. She offered me her cheek at the door, took me by the arm, and led me into the house, babbling all the while ("Tanjicaaaa! Spin round so I can have a good look at you! Why, you look simply marvelous! Like a girl of fifteen! And that dress! Did you get it here? I still pop over to London whenever I need something. You should see Cees fume! 'What makes you think you can't find one here!' he says. Well, you can't. Oh, they do their best for a pitifully short stretch along the P.C. Hooftstraat, but as department stores go, Bijenkorf is barely a cut above our NaMa. . . . God! Remember NaMa? Why, any girl from Virovitica dresses better than your average Dutchwoman. You've noticed it, too. I'm sure you have.")

Anyone would have thought that Ines and I were old friends coming together after a long separation, and her nonstop jabber had me believing it, too. I felt I'd fallen down on the job, neglected the friendship.

Ines gave me a tour of the house before we sat down to eat. First she showed me the children's rooms. ("The children are with Cees's mother. Piet has just turned seven, and Marijke is three. Here's a picture of them. Piet and Marica, as I call her.") The house was spacious and furnished simply, though the walls were covered with paintings by Croatian naive artists ("I wanted something to remind me of home," she said, noticing my look. "And something to show the Dutch that we weren't beggars; know what I mean?"). My eyes lit upon the masters of Croatian modernism on the bookshelves: the collected works of Krleža, Ujević, Matoš ("I do so like to read an Ujević poem before I go to sleep. Don't you? Though you read oodles more than me, I'm sure. You can't imagine how those children wear me out!"). The curtains on the kitchen windows were made of Slovenian lace, and on the windowsill there was a small wooden shelf housing a

gingerbread heart. It was there she put the box of Kraš chocolates in the shape of a Croatian passport, my house gift to her.

"And did he just disappear?" she asked me coyly in the
kitchen.

"Who?"

"Why, Goran, of course."

"He didn't disappear. He's in Japan."

"Are you in touch?"

"No."

"Who would have guessed it! The model couple! To think it
happened to you!"

"Well, it did."

"Serves you right for getting mixed up with a 'Milošević,' "
she said jokingly.

I didn't respond. I was surprised she had remembered Goran
was officially classified as a Serb.

"Hey, don't get your back up! I was only joking. I can see
right through you, old girl. You locked him in your heart. He said
you'd never part. But he's now fancy-free. And you have lost
the key."

I couldn't help smiling at the lines of the old scrapbook ditty,
and suddenly the tension was gone.

"If you'd married a Croat the way I did, you'd have had an easier time getting over him," she said. "You'd be on your second
marriage by now."

"Missed my chance."

"Vladek went off the deep end the moment we got to
Amsterdam. He got into grass and stuff. I mean really into it."
She pronounced the word "grass" as if it were a euphemism and
whispered it as if our parents might be listening in.

"Where's Vladek now?"

"Not even the police know. But I don't care. He's not my problem anymore. . . . Well, let's have something to eat."

Cees spoke a pretty decent Croatian. ("See what I've made of him? Done a pretty good job, haven't I? Though it was really his mother-in-law, wasn't it, Cees? Oh, and by the way, how's your family doing? I don't even know who you've still got back home. . . .") Ines kept the chatter up the whole time I was there. The perfect hostess, she put out her best silver ("I put it out for you, to remind you of the way we used to live: it comes from my grandmother"), "our" wine and "our" olive oil ("We go home every summer. We've got a sweet little place on Korčula. You'll have to come and see it some time. And we come back laden down like Gypsies with wine and olive oil and prosciutto, everything you can imagine. Cees just loves it there. The kids, too. It means a lot to me for the kids to speak Croatian. And to Mama, too, of course. Mama spends a full two months every year with the kids"). On and on she went about the seashore, the kids, her mother, Cees's mother, the Dutch. I hardly got a word in edgewise.

In other circumstances I might have been bored, but that evening I found the conversation relaxing. The coy nasal babble was like a balm. For the first time in ages life seemed "normal" to me. Time itself seemed to come together, its stitches healed. I was on firm ground at last, basking in the pleasant warmth of Ines's words. For a second I thought we were all in Zagreb. True, we were a bit older and we had Cees with us rather than Vladek, but Goran would be right back. He'd just run out for another bottle of wine. . . .

"You must try my poppy-seed cake. I made it just for you. Thank God for the Austro-Hungarian monarchy. Otherwise we wouldn't know what real pastry is, if you know what I mean. I had to bring the poppy seed from Zagreb, too. You can't find it here anymore, not even from the—what shall I call them?—the

Turks." She clearly expected me to get her mildly racist reference and to approve it with a wink.

" 'Bureks, baklava, and poppy-seed noodles,' " I sang.

"You and your Yugonostalgia," she grumbled. I was taken aback by the remark. She made it sound as though I were the one who hadn't stopped going on about the country.

Over coffee Ines switched to the plural.

"We're glad we were able to help you. It's so rare people can help one another. And you were up there with the best of them, so I said to Cees, I said, Tanja's the one to invite. We've heard a lot about your students. About that boy, too. Dreadful!"

Again I was taken aback. I sensed the prattle was leading somewhere.

"That boy's name was Uroš," I said.

"Every generation has its suicide," she said.

"What do you mean?"

"We had one when we were at the university, remember? What was his name?"

"Nenad."

"Right. Went off to India, came back and did himself in. His father was a general. It was drug related, I think. God! Remember all the people who made the pilgrimage to India? But you and me, we never fell for all that chakra and mantra stuff, right?"

"Have you found out anything about that student?" Cees asked, cutting off Ines, for which I was grateful.

I told him everything I knew.

"I'm sorry to have to tell you this," he said, "but I've had some complaints from the students about you."

His words were a punch in the solar plexus.

"What kind of complaints?"

"Students have a right to complain if they feel an instructor isn't doing his job, and we are obliged to take their complaints seriously. The upshot of it is the students aren't happy with the way you've been teaching your class."

"That can't be true," I managed to say.

"I'm afraid it is."

"What have they complained about?"

"They say they don't do anything connected with the field. They say it's a waste of time."

"They say that?"

"They say you have no clear-cut program and your classes are chaotic. Not only do they sit around with you in cafés; you *require* them to."

"Who says that?"

"I'm not at liberty to tell you," Cees said evenly.

"You can't tell me they've all complained!"

Cees made no response.

Ines tried to console me. She said I was blind; I refused to see that things had changed. People here in the Netherlands didn't side with either camp, but they could see that "one and one make two," couldn't they? She said I was too bighearted and had got too close to the students. And "you know the old saying: sleep with a baby, wake up wet." That "wake up wet" and the way she said it made me feel all but a physical revulsion for her. She told me that a proposal had been made to the Dutch Ministry of Education, a proposal Cees himself had drafted, to separate Croatian and Serbian at all Dutch universities, a move, after all, "long overdue, dictated as it was by a political reality of long standing." If Cees's proposal was accepted, then starting next autumn Amsterdam would teach Croatian language and literature and Groningen would teach Serbian, which made sense, since Groningen already had Bulgarian. Which meant there was a good chance I'd get a full-time job come September. No, they had no other candidate in mind, absolutely no one. She couldn't do it because of the children and anyway there was a rule that man and wife could not work in the same department, especially if one was head of the department. Besides, she'd never quite put the finishing touches on her dissertation. She said I should think about myself; I wasn't getting any younger, and I certainly wasn't thinking of going back to Zagreb, was I? I'd never get a job there. I knew what "our people" were like. Once you leave, you're gone forever. And they're right in their way. "You fall between two stools, no matter how big a rump you've got." Yes, rump. That was the word she used, and again I felt that revulsion for her. Cees was all for me, but Cees was not alone. The students were much, much more sensitive to "national lines" than I had realized. She was amazed I could be so naive, so blind to the way things were, to "political reality." And then there was the matter of that poor Serb, the one who'd done himself in, yes, right, Uroš. Look at the dreadful things that dogged those kids even after they thought they'd escaped it all. . . .

"We didn't invite you here to give group therapy sessions," Cees said.

"I don't give group therapy sessions! You know how different their educational levels are. I had to base the class on something they could all relate to. They've had everything taken from them, don't you see? How can I force Renaissance comedy on people who've escaped a living hell?"

"Haven't you had everything taken from you?" she cackled. "Of course you have. And thank God Yugoslavia is no more!"

"You haven't got the training for it, and you're not being paid for it. We have experts for that kind of thing in this country. They're called psychotherapists. Your job is to do what we asked you here to do. And what we're paying you to do."

"Listen to Cees, dear. He's got your best interests at heart."

"You gave them all inappropriately high grades. Everyone in the Department noticed it. You can't tell me they were all so outstanding."

"They were," I mumbled.

"That's just like you. Tanja of the big heart! She always was bighearted, Cees. I remember her once ripping off a brooch and giving it to me when I complimented her on it."

I didn't remember anything of the sort. I wondered whether she had made it up or I had forgotten it.

"Well, now—you see that bribing them with high grades doesn't work. Your students insist on a curriculum. I think you've underestimated them. They're serious about their studies, and I'm glad of it."

"Listen to Cees, dear. He knows what he's talking about." She was being coy again. She might have been talking to a child.

"I wasn't bribing them! How you can fail to see that they're convalescents! We're all convalescents! And I have no doubt that what I did with them is more important than any academic curriculum." But even as I spoke, I knew I was speaking into a void.

Cees shrugged his shoulders.

"If they thought it was more important, why did they complain about the lack of a curriculum?"

As far as Cees was concerned, my position was nothing but a weak excuse for having failed to do my academic duty. Something welled up in my throat, and I burst into convulsive sobs. I felt betrayed on all sides: I had been betrayed by my students, and I had betrayed myself by bawling in the presence of Cees and Ines. I could not believe, I simply could not believe that one of my students had gone and tattled to Cees about what we had done in class. Or had there been more than one? Cees had used the plural. Could the whole class have gone to see him? I felt ashamed, abandoned, bitter, and furious. I no longer knew why I was crying, yet I couldn't stop my tears. And I was so panicked that, strange as it may seem, instead of wanting to make the quickest exit I wanted nothing more than to curl up on their couch and stay there until morning. The thought of returning to my basement flat filled me with despair.

In a genuine desire to be of assistance Ines rushed to the phone to call a taxi, which she saw as an ambulance. ("I won't have you traipsing from tram to tram in your condition!") When the taxi came, Cees held out his hand.

"I hope I've made myself clear," he said awkwardly. "See you next week at the Department."

Ines offered me her cheek.

"Everything will be just fine," she cooed. "Believe me, Tanjica. Just do as Cees says. You know we love you and want nothing but the best for you."

As I was going out of the door, she thrust a small package into my hand.

"I've sliced you a piece of poppy-seed cake. You can have it for breakfast tomorrow morning."

As the taxi pulled away, she threw me a kiss and disappeared into the house.

The next morning I noticed a long scratch on the back of my left hand. The skin was red, the scrape having gone quite deep. I was frightened at first, unaware of how it had got there. But then I vaguely remembered having sat for a while in my armchair and run my hand back and forth over the radiator ribs. I wondered how long it had taken to inflict such a wound on myself.

I paused in front of the door. A mere two weeks earlier I would have rushed in, full of enthusiasm; now I seemed to lack the strength to cross the threshold. I took a deep breath, gripped my briefcase like a shield, and went in.

"Hey there, Comrade! How was Zagreb?"

"Bring us the chocolate you promised?"

"Glad you're back. We've been looking forward to it."

The loud greeting, clearly sincere, threw me off balance. I didn't know what to say. I waited for it to die down, then distributed the syllabus I had made up over the weekend. It consisted of a list of the lectures I would be giving until the end of the semester. Each was accompanied by a date and a brief summary of the topic to be covered. Next I distributed a list of required reading, which came to approximately two hundred pages a week. I told them I would be sticking religiously to the schedule and they would be expected to have read the texts by the time I lectured on them. I announced that there would be two papers and a final oral examination. I said I would no longer tolerate poor attendance: a poor attendance record would be reflected in the final grade.

"What's going on here?" Meliha called out, laughing. "New regime in power?"

I chose to ignore the remark.

"How can we read all these books if the library's got only one copy of each?" Mario protested as his eyes ran down the reading list.

"You'll have to share them among yourselves or photocopy them," I said. I'd spent a good part of the weekend in the departmental library photocopying the first books on the list myself.

"Has the library even got all the books on the reading list?" Selim asked.

"All the books on the reading list are in the library. Otherwise I wouldn't have included them."

I gave a copy of the syllabus to Cees as well.

"Two hundred pages a week? Isn't that overdoing it a bit?"

"Not at all. American students read as many as four hundred a week. Besides, that's what you asked for, isn't it?" The fact about the American students, which I'd read somewhere, seemed to have the desired effect. Cees's only answer was a shrug of the shoulders.

The lectures were devoted to a brief comparative survey of the histories of Slovenian, Croatian, Bosnian, Serbian, and Macedonian literature, which amounted to a strenuous jog through a field full of facts, names and dates, though I'd left some time at the end of the semester for a thematic analysis of several Croatian novels.

The disbelief stuck to their faces for a while. They tried to put my behavior down to a whim and forgave me, hoping the whim was only temporary and the next time things would go back to how they had been. For my part I kept studying their faces, searching for the one who had denounced me. At times I thought it might be Meliha, then Nevena, or Igor, or Boban . . . I went through hell trying to work out if it was only one of them or if two had worked together. I pictured Meliha and Igor delivering regular reports on class activities to Cees. Or Selim rushing to Cees to tell him the crazy things going on, the resurrection of a country that its own citizens had destroyed in the name of historical necessity. Though could it have been Johanneke? Or Ana?

I would leave immediately after the lecture was over. I never went to my office. I did everything I could to discourage contact. Gradually the disbelief on their faces turned to puzzlement and finally to disappointment. Yet they would still come up after class, waiting for me to invite them for coffee. Meliha tried once, then Nevena.

"Hey, Comrade. You up for a *kopje koffie?* Our treat."

"Thanks, but I'm very busy at the moment," I said both times.

I could see them absorbed in conversation in the café opposite the Department. A joint meeting of the chiefs of staff. I knew they were talking about me. "*The bitch.* Lucić has turned into a real *bitch.*" I imagined one of them, the informant, sitting there tight-lipped and frowning. I tried to guess who would be first to stop coming to class. Igor? Ante? Nevena?

Only once did I lose a grip on myself. I had required them to memorize Ujević's "Everyday Lament." I had asked them to be able to recite it from beginning to end and from end to beginning. It was a silly trick I'd picked up from a much-hated professor of Croatian poetry who delighted in torturing us with like assignments. I remember swearing to myself at the time that I would never inflict anything like that on my future students.

Nevena refused to learn the poem in either direction. I asked her to read it aloud. She made an awful muddle of it. I then asked her to read it backward. She just stood there, at a loss. It was a painful, humiliating scene. Finally Igor came to the rescue by standing and reeling it off beautifully.

"Thank you, Igor," I said. "And, Nevena, you may come back once you've mastered the poem."

Nevena packed up her things and, hissing *"Bitch!"* through her teeth, stomped out of the classroom. I think I heard her burst into tears as she slammed the door behind her. Sorry as I felt for her, it was too late. I had no idea how to escape the role I had assigned myself.

I could sense their dissatisfaction grow. I could sense it every time I entered the classroom, sense it almost physically, like a change in the temperature. At times it seemed to fill the room, fill it so full that I was afraid it would shatter the windows. Yet they said not a word. I kept wondering when they would reach the breaking point and rebel or at least whether any of them would finally confront me and ask why I was behaving as I was. But they said not a word. Only Igor appeared unaffected by it all. He looked straight at me, as if seeing into my soul, and would occasionally put on his earphones, which he never removed from around his neck.

"Turn off your Walkman, Igor. This is a classroom, not a rock concert."

"I don't use a Walkman at rock concerts."

"How can you hear what I'm saying when you . . ."

"Don't worry. I hear you better with the Walkman on."

"We'll see about that," I said. "At the exam."

It was terribly trying. I kept mouthing things that weren't my own and hated myself for it. If I persevered, it was because I couldn't rid myself of the thought that one of them had gone to Cees and told him everything that had gone on during the first semester.

And yet the routine of the new regime gradually wore down my animosity until at one point I began taking a certain pleasure in giving "real" lectures. The students reacted accordingly. Meliha assumed the role of the diligent student, Igor never missed a class, Ana took down everything I said, and Johanneke showed such enthusiasm that for a while I suspected her of being the one who had denounced me to Cees. But by then the class had shrunk to them and only them: Nevena never returned, and one by one Mario, Selim, Boban, and Darko stopped coming.

We got through the historical survey without much trouble. Our race through the periods and schools, the authors and titles had a kind of anesthetic effect. I left the theme of "return" for the end. None of them knew whether they wanted to remain or return, but they all felt they were living here "only temporarily" and they concentrated their energy on getting their "papers." Once they had their papers, they thought, they would be able to make up their minds. The "motherland" still glittered somewhere inside them as a possible Exit sign.

So here I was, packing my students' refugee suitcases again. It was the same thing I'd done during the first semester with one difference: this time the suitcase contained no contraband. I was familiarizing them with their own literary family, their forebears. The examples I selected amounted to a kind of biography of fictional heroes. Often the narrative began in the third person and ended in the first in the form of the protagonist's diary or letters to a friend. And although the protagonists were "homegrown," they all—especially their Croatian variants—bore a distinct family resemblance to young Werther and Childe Harold, to say nothing of the Russian characters dubbed "superfluous men" by the critics, characters like Griboedov's Chatsky, Pushkin's Eugene Onegin, Lermontov's Pechorin, Turgenev's Rudin and Lavretsky and Kirsanov and Bazarov, Goncharov's Oblomov, Chekhov's Ivanov, and Olesha's Kavalerov, all of whom crawled around the other Slavic literatures like so many crabs. So much for the male line. The female line consisted principally of three types: the young and beautiful patriot, whom the hero generally abandons; the femme fatale, who taunts the hero but likewise inspires him; and the silent martyr, who faithfully accompanies the hero to the end of his days.

I was amazed at the regularity with which the protagonists' common features returned. I felt I was reading genetics rather than literature. It was like discovering something one had always been vaguely aware of but never considered important, like finding a mole at the same spot on one's skin as on the skin of one's parents or children or grandchildren. I often felt I was reading installments of a soap opera that had dragged on for more than a century (though I would never have admitted it in public).

We read two novels by K. Š. Gjalski, *Janko Borislavić* and *Radmilović*, both of whose protagonists have gone mad by the end of their lives; we read Vjenceslav Novak's *Two Worlds* and *Tito Dorčić* and M. C. Nehajev's *Escape*, all three of whose protagonists commit suicide; we read Krleža's much acclaimed *Return of Filip Latinowicz*, which like the others deals with the theme of exile. And while the protagonists in all the works feel isolated abroad, it is their inability to adjust to the return home that triggers their tragic deaths.

"But what would really grab us," said Meliha, "is a novel about the *Gastarbeiter*, about our fathers and grandfathers who trudged off to Germany and Sweden and France and Holland and slaved away for years only to come back and pour their hard-earned nest eggs into huge houses—something solid to leave behind, to make them die happy—that then stood empty like memorials to the utopia of carefree retirement, like pyramids, like tombs. Because the war came and everything went up in smoke."

"Maybe," said Ana uneasily, "but is that really our story?"

"You bet it is, sister, if your parents spent half their lives in Germany and you're living abroad without a penny to your name. Ask my friend Alda. She'll tell you. Her parents retired after thirty years. Put every penny they'd saved into a bank in Sarajevo. Thought they'd build a house and settle down. And where are they now? Back in Cologne! That's how it is with us: every generation starts with nothing and ends with nothing. My grandmother and grandfather—and my parents after them—they had to start from scratch after the Second World War, and this new war put them right back where they'd started from. And now here I am, starting from scratch, with nothing, zilch, zero."

Nobody said a word. Meliha's zero was dangling above our heads like a noose.

Anthropologists studying migration have taken over the term "sleeper" from popular spy novels. Sleepers are emigrants who make "normal" lives for themselves in their new environment: they learn its language, adapt to its ways, seem fully integrated— and suddenly they have an epiphany. The fantasy of a "return to the motherland" takes over with such a vengeance that it makes them into robots. They sell everything they have acquired and move back. And when they realize the mistake they have made (as most do) they go back to the land where they had "slept" for twenty or however many years, forced to relive (as they would on a psychiatrist's couch) the years of adjustment until—twice broken, yet twice restored—they make peace with their lot. Many live a parallel life: they project the image of their motherland on the neutral walls of the land where they are living "only temporarily" and experience the projected image as their "real" life.

My students were far from being "sleepers," nor could they ever dream of becoming them. They belonged neither here nor there. They were busy building castles in the air and peering down to decide which place suited them better. Of course I was up there with them. I too belonged neither here nor there. The only difference was that I couldn't bear to look down. I had vertigo.

I couldn't quite pinpoint what had brought it on. There were times when I found myself stopping in the middle of the street because I'd forgotten where I was going. I'd just stand there like a child afraid to be thrown out of a game if he moves a muscle. "And out goes Y-O-U!" Maybe the confusion came from the fact that it didn't really matter where I was going, that I could just as easily have been standing on a street in another city, that my very presence in the city was a matter of chance, that, when all was said and done, everything was a matter of chance. Many of us had ended up in places we'd never dreamed of seeing no less inhabiting. And it would happen from one day to the next. It was like going to sleep in one life and waking up in another.

Sometimes my sleep was interrupted by an oppressive but nondescript pain, a painless pain. I would get out of bed and make my way to the bathroom, switch on the light, let the water run for a while and take a series of small gulps, trying to quench a thirst I seemed to have had for ages. Then I'd lean my forehead against the mirror of the medicine cabinet and watch the mist of my breath spread gently over the surface.

"O my wound, O my soul. The autumn has come, O my wound. Woe is me, O my wound, my festering wound . . ." Wounds are intimates in my country; they are our sons and daughters, our sweethearts. Wounds are love; love is pain. Goran and I once heard a turbo-folk rendition of "O My Wound" blaring out over a Berlin street. The street vendor showed us a cheap cassette with *Ach, meine Wunde* on the cover. As Goran handed over the money, he said to me with a smile, "Our wounds are our hottest export."

"O Germany, O stranger. I gave you my lover, I gave you my brother," they wail, as they have wailed, keened, and howled for decades over migrant workers, refugees, émigrés, exiles, *Gastarbeiter,* adventurers, conmen, crooks, deserters . . . "O Australia, O stranger," "O America, O stranger," "O Canada, O stranger."

I could never understand the point of the cheap, patriotic video clips—half travel commercial, half political campaign—of swarthy, mustachioed men recently back from stints abroad expounding on the magnetic pull of the motherland. With crammed suitcase in each hand and gold chains and crosses on their hairy chests, they tramp the hills and vales leading to their native villages, where mustachioed crones in black await them by sooty hearths. "My Moootherland! My naaative soil!" my musical compatriots bellow, gazing into the beautiful distance, which is usually the sole beautiful thing they have to gaze into. Maybe all émigrés are character actors condemned to endless soaps; maybe the very genre of exile keeps them from transforming what they do and how they feel.

———

Whenever I found myself in the subgenre of émigré insomnia, I would wrack my brains over how things would be were they not as they are. Hoping to make a warm spot for myself, I would shuffle together everyone I know as if they were packs of cards. I would think of Goran cuddling up to his Hito. They have an orderly way of sleeping, nestled together like spoons. He groans; she awakens. *Anything wrong?* she asks. The groaning ceases; the breathing goes back to normal; Hito goes back to sleep. I would think of Goran's mother going to the kitchen for a glass of milk. She takes a cookie out of the canister with "Danish Cookies" written on it, then changes her mind and takes out another two. And one more. She dips them in the milk, then pushes them all the way down with one finger, then eats them with a spoon. The sweet mush calms her nerves. "I don't understand it. I can't stop eating," she laments. "Especially at night." I would think of myself curled up in the bed in Mother's "guest room" and hear the shuffle of slippers, the scrape of a door, and the tinkle of urine in the toilet bowl: my mother is urinating in the toilet next to my room. The room swells like a sound box with the noise. Then it stops and she shuffles back to bed. And as she falls asleep, she decorates her past like an Easter egg. Deliberately. Complacently.

Only at such times, lying awake on the bed in my Amsterdam burrow, was I able to gain a clear picture of myself. I picture myself pulling on my jeans, throwing a jacket over my pajama top, and sailing out of the basement. I attempt a deep breath, but the air is tepid and as sticky as cotton candy. A numbing subtropical wind whisks litter along the street. Two plastic bags caught on the branches of a nearby tree make a snapping noise and glow dully in the dark like messages from another world.

I see a compatriot of mine, a short, squat woman with a sprightly gait. She has a tall, gray-haired woman in tow. The older woman is walking with the aid of crutches. "Get a move on, Mama," the younger woman commands in a voice that penetrates my eardrum like a needle. All "our people" know this woman. *"She's a genius,"* they say. Sometimes she sports a veritable troop of fictive offshoots, sometimes a fictive eight-and-a-half-month stomach, sometimes today's fictive cripple of a fictive mother, but she is always accompanied by a glowering man who follows her like a shadow, his hands thrust deeply into the pockets of his short jacket. They claim she can steal anything "our people" care to buy: clothing, jewelry, VCRs. . . . *"Let's go, Mama,"* she grunts. *"Get a move on."*

A drunk young Englishwoman pulls my sleeve and asks, *"Got a match?"*

"Sorry," I say.

"Fuck you!" she says back and totters away.

I am standing in front of a tattoo studio. The studio is closed, but the TV in the display window is showing a documentary. "I began getting myself tattooed to learn what pain means," says a young Japanese man, turning to expose a richly tattooed back to the camera. "Each of these patterns is a memento of pain." Another young Japanese man covered with tattoos nods vigorously and says, "No pain, no gain!"

The thick, black water in the canal round the corner shimmers ominously. A white swan emerges abruptly out of the darkness and freezes ghostlike. Just then the TV set in the display window shuts off and the screen goes blank. I keep standing there for a while. The plastic bags in the branches are still snapping like children's kites. The subtropical wind licks my face. Sweat trickles down my back. "And out goes Y-O-U." Then I scamper back to my hole like a mouse.

CHAPTER 8

We have come to the end of our primer. We have learned all our letters.
We can read print and we can read script. Now we can read all sorts of
nice children's books. Now we can read everything. We know how to
write, too. We know how to write everything we see. Now we can read
and write by ourselves. The more we know, the better we are.

—First-Year Primer

And then came the exam. There they were—all four of them:
Johanneke, Meliha, Ana, and Igor—in the corridor outside my
door. Johanneke came in first. I asked her several questions, all
of which she answered correctly. I gave her an A. She had worked
much harder than the rest and proved a discreet observer of the
goings-on. Only now did I realize I'd never had a serious conversation with her. We had adopted her, and she was "ours." That
had apparently sufficed.

"I hope you'll stay on," she said.

"I may," I said, trying to sound cheerful.

I stood, walked to the door with her, and held out my hand.
She looked uneasy.

"Good luck," I said like a fool, realizing that I needed it more than she did.

The moment Meliha entered, I knew I couldn't go on with my role.

"Forget about the exam, Meliha," I said.

"What do you mean?"

"I can't bring myself to quiz you," I said honestly. "Exam or no exam, you deserve an A."

"Now you tell me! And here I crammed all night, just like when I was a student. It was great, by the way. Really! . . . So you'll be back next year?"

"I may be."

"Well, if you are," she said cheerfully, "I'll be back, too."

We talked a little about her parents, her plans, the status of her studies. . . .

"I don't know what to do," she suddenly blurted out. "I'm in love!"

"Who is it?"

"A *Dačer!*"

So we talked a little about her *Dačer.* A great guy. And wild about Bosnia. Works for an NGO. Violence prevention, something like that. Spends more time in Sarajevo than here. Knows the language. Maybe she'll end up going there with him. Who'd have thought it would take a *Dačer* to make her want to go home. "And then there's . . . well . . . My dad—he's going downhill. All he can say is, 'Life's one big joke.' He's like a parrot. You ask him how he wants his eggs, fried or scrambled, and he says, 'Life's one big joke.' Though it may be I should take some lessons from the guy."

She stood. I followed suit, and we shook hands. She was on the point of opening the door when she paused and a shadow drew across her face. It made her look ten years older.

"What's the matter, Meliha?"

"Nothing. Sometimes I think I'm going mad. I'll be walking along, and suddenly I have to stop and pick up the pieces, the pieces of myself. My arms, my legs, and phew! there's my crazy head. You don't know how glad I am to find them. So anyway I glue them together and they hold for a while. I think that's it for good, and then I'm in pieces again. And again I pick them up and put myself together like a jigsaw puzzle until the next time. . . ."

She opened the door and added, "Now my face is all wet, and my *Dačer*'s downstairs waiting for me." Then she forced a smile over her face and slipped out.

Ana was next.

"I want you to know I didn't come for the exam," she said, entering the room.

"What do you mean?"

"There's no point. I'm not going on."

"Why the sudden decision?"

"I'm going back to Belgrade," she said.

"Hold on. Back up a little. What's made you decide to go back?"

"Geert has always preferred Belgrade, and this place is getting on my nerves."

"You won't miss anything?"

"No."

"But you've spent several years here, haven't you?"

"They could have been anywhere."

"Are you sure you don't want me to give you a grade?"

She didn't seem to hear the question.

"I only came to say good-bye," she said, then added impulsively, "Are you on your own?"

"Why do you ask?"

"Living in a foreign country—it's much harder when you're on your own."

"That depends," I said. I was not eager to pursue the conversation.

"You know . . . ," she said, "what happened would have happened no matter what."

"What do you mean by that?"

"You didn't realize it, but you were the last reason for us to get together. Things would have fallen apart without you."

"Why is that?"

"Because that's how it goes. At first we were in an up mood: we got a kick out of life. Life was a blast, a never-ending party. And then one morning we woke up to find a clearing all around us."

"A clearing? What do you mean by 'a clearing'?"

"I don't know. I suppose what I mean is the awful feeling that there's no one behind you and no one in front of you."

"But you've got Geert."

"The Dutch are much better on foreign soil than on their own."

"What's that supposed to mean?"

"They take swimmingly to living abroad, but they're like fish out of water when they're at home."

"What do you expect to find when *you're* 'at home'?"

"One horror after another."

"And what would you have here?"

"The absence of horrors."

"For many that's enough of a reason to stay."

"Though Holland is tough, too, in its way," she said calmly.

Then she took an envelope out of her bag and put it on my desk.

"What's that?"

"The key to the flat."

"Whose flat?"

"We don't need it anymore, and you may be staying."

"I haven't made up my mind yet."

"But it may turn out that you will."

"Is it your flat?"

"No, Geert's. Government subsidized. All you have to pay is the gas and electricity, and they come to almost nothing. Oh, I should tell you: it's not in the center of things. The address and telephone number and everything else you need are in the envelope. The furniture's pretty old, but you can chuck it. You can make all the changes you like. Geert and I are leaving in a week. Let me know when you decide. Go and have a look at it. Leave the key in the box if it doesn't appeal to you."

I was surprised at Ana and for a split second jealous of her. She seemed to have a certain knowledge I lacked. I stared at the envelope for a while after she left, then stuck it into my bag. Ana's key had briefly opened the door that was holding back all my fears.

That left Igor, but I couldn't bring myself to move. I kept thinking about Ana and Meliha and the lives they'd been leading, lives I'd known nothing—but nothing—about.

Igor's paper lay in front of me, and I leafed through it absentmindedly though I'd read it before. As the basis for the paper on the theme of "return" in Croatian literature Igor had chosen a completely unexpected work, the fairy tale "How Potjeh Sought the Truth" by the classic children's writer Ivana Brlić-Mažuranić.

In a clearing in an old beech forest there lived old man Vjest and his three grandsons. One day the god Svarožić, whom Igor calls "the Slav Superman," appears to the three brothers. And when he had spoken, Svarožić gave a wave of his cloak and lifted Ljutiša, Marun, and Potjeh onto its skirt. And he gave another wave of the cloak and it took to twisting. And the brothers on its skirt took to twisting with it, to twisting and turning and turning and twisting, and all of a sudden the world started passing before them. First they saw all the treasures and the fields and the estates and the riches that were then in the world. Then, twisting and turning and turning and twisting, they saw all the armies and the spears and the javelins and the generals and the spoils that were then in the world. And then, twisting and turning and turning and twisting even more, they suddenly saw all the stars, all the stars and the moon and the Seven Sisters and the wind and all the clouds. And these visions did greatly perplex the brothers, and still the cloak fluttered and rustled and swished like a skirt of gold. But then they found themselves back in the clearing, did Ljutiša, Marun, and Potjeh, with the golden lad Svarožić facing them as before. And thus did he speak: "This is what you shall do. You shall remain here in the clearing; nor shall you leave your grandfather until he has left you; you shall not go into the world for good or for ill until you have returned him his love."

When Grandfather asks his grandchildren what they saw in the world and what advice they received from the god Svarožić, Potjeh cannot remember—Igor uses the English word *blackout*—so he leaves his home for the forest to seek his lost memory and Svarožić's advice. There he is set upon by wood demons, whom Igor calls Lex Luthor's adjutants. . . .

I beckoned to Igor. He came in and sat down. I saw my own reflection in his face. It was like looking into a mirror. He seemed to have recorded every word I'd said during the second semester and had now switched on the tape. He began spitting back at me the dry, academic list of names and dates I'd crammed into the four of them, and he made precious little pretense at concealing his scorn for me. I interrupted him.

"I was a bit perplexed by your paper," I said.

"It's on a perplexing work."

"What do you mean?"

"What's the important truth Potjeh can't seem to remember? Svarožić's message? All Svarožić told him was to stay at home. *As simple as ABC.*"

"So?"

"So Svarožić appears to Potjeh one more time and tells him the same thing: go home. But what happens now that his memory has returned? He dies. 'A quick wash and back I fly to my dear grandfather,' he says, leans over a well, falls in, and drowns."

"Well, what do you make of it?"

"Given the rules of the 'there's-no-place-like-home' genre, they should all live happily ever after. Fairy-tale heroes find wisdom, riches, and princesses on their travels; they don't fall into wells. Something must have got into Mažuranić to keep her from giving the fairy tale its conventional ending."

"But Potjeh ends up in Svarožić's court."

"Mažuranić puts Potjeh in heaven, which is death plus a happy ending, but it's a *cop-out* of an ending, because we're all guaranteed heaven or hell in one way or another. So from a technical standpoint the work is pure *crap;* from a psychoanalytic standpoint, though, it's pure genius."

"Why?"

"The message is clear: 'exile' equals defeat—Potjeh wanders through the woods in a total fog; he has amnesia—and the return home equals the return of memory. But it equals death as well: no sooner does Potjeh's memory return than he falls into a well. So the only triumph of human freedom resides in the ironic split second of our departure in this, that, or some third direction. For the sake of that inner truth Mažuranić strayed from the genre and wrote a 'bad' fairy tale."

He looked up at me, his dark, slightly crossed eyes weighing my soul.

He had defeated me: he had shown me something I would never have seen by myself. The work could support any number of interpretations, but Igor's reading struck me as both valid and terrifying. What if everything he said was true? What if return is in fact death—symbolic or real—and exile defeat, and the moment of departure the only true moment of freedom we are granted? And if it is true, what do we do with it? And who are "we" anyway? Aren't we all smashed to bits and forced to wander the earth picking up the pieces like Meliha, putting them together like a jigsaw puzzle, gluing them together with our saliva?

"What's the matter, Comrade? I mean Professor Lucić," he said with a tinge of mockery, as if reading my mind.

That jerked me back into my role. The talk we'd just had was a step toward reconciliation. I'd held my hand out first, but now I pulled it back.

"Thank you, Igor. That will be enough. I'll be handing in the grades today. Come back tomorrow or the next day and the secretary will tell you what you got."

The moment I said it, I hated myself more than I ever had in my life.

He shrugged, picked up his backpack, and made for the door. But then he turned and said, "Just a footnote, Professor. In literature it's always the men who go out into the world. Go out, come back, and shed their 'prodigal tears.' Where are the women?"

I didn't respond. I squinted in his direction, deaf and dumb. I could barely make out his features. I dug my stumps into the ground and turned the color of my surroundings. I felt the *Proteus anguinus,* the human fish that had got stuck in the process of metamorphosis, stirring somewhere inside me: gills breathing, blood flowing through the thinnest of veins, a minuscule heart beating all but inaudibly. Help me, beat the heart. Touch me and I shall turn into a beautiful maiden; leave me and I shall be prisoner of my darkness forever.

Once Igor had left, I settled down to grading the students. I decided to pass Nevena, Selim, Mario, Darko, Boban, and Amra, and gave Meliha, Johanneke, and Ana A's. But what to do with Igor?

I don't know why I did what I did. I was like Brlić-Mažuranić, who didn't know why she had tampered with a genre that had proved its worth many times over. Something had gone wrong, something inside her; something had prevented her from ending that tale in the prescribed manner, the manner in which she had effortlessly ended so many others. All I know is that I was unable to control the impulse to turn my tale in the wrong direction, and when after a long period of vacillation I finally gave him an F—together with a brief, guileful explanation for it—I felt physical revulsion combined with a feeling of shame and shame combined with a feeling of relief.

Now all I had to do was take the grades to Anneke, give her back my office key, and see Cees. I looked around the room. I was in a clearing. There was a wasteland behind me and nothing in front of me but the key in the envelope at the bottom of my bag.

But then I opened the desk drawer to make sure I hadn't forgotten anything, and saw a piece of paper folded in two. It was an anonymous note that had been placed in my box in the departmental office a few months earlier. I had dropped it into the drawer and completely forgotten about it, and I now read it as if I'd never seen it before.

Yugobitch
Fuck you. When I think of the people who died trying to brake out of the Commie shithouse, & you go spreading that brother-

hood & unity shit. No more of your Yugoslavia crap, you hear?!
Death to the people & freedom to Fashism!

Captain Leši

P.S. Up yours.

Not a single word in the note gave away its author's identity as a
Serb, Croat, or Bosnian. It would have thwarted the most assidu-
ous linguistic inspector. I realized that with all the practice I'd ac-
cumulated lately I'd willy-nilly become an expert in the field of
hate texts. And yet how hard it would be to elucidate the contents of the text to, say, a Dutchman. How could I convey the use
of assonance in the inventive coinage *Jugokuja,* "Yugobitch," or
the resonance of the stock phrase "brotherhood and unity"?
How could I explain what lay behind the slogan "Death to the
people and freedom to Fascism!" or the reference to the fictional
Yugoslav hero from the early fifties, Captain Leši?

The anonymous note was a leftover piece of shrapnel. But
even though it had landed in my drawer, I had no interest in discovering where it had come from. I picked up a red (yes, red) felt
pen and corrected the spelling mistakes with a kind of affection-
ate apathy. Then I tore the sheet of paper into tiny bits and threw
it into the air like so much confetti. The war was over.

CHAPTER  9

I walked slowly down the five flights of stairs and who should I run into on the ground floor but Laki, Laki the Linguist from Zagreb, who had attended a few classes during the first semester only to disappear. He paused for a moment, as if in doubt as to how to proceed, then screwed up his eyes, looked away from me, and said in a lazy drawl, "So how are we doing, Mrs. Lucić?"

"I'm fine, thank you. And you?"

"Fair to middling. Still hanging around the Department, as you can see."

"Right. Otherwise we wouldn't have run into each other."

"And starting September I'm going to be here every day."

"Really?"

"They're giving me an office. So I can finish up my dictionary."

"Good for you."

"Not bad, and things will be even better once the dictionary comes out."

"I'm sure they will."

"We could never have dreamed of this when the Commies were in power."

"That's for sure," I said, the irony in my voice clearly going over Laki's head.

"I've got some funding from the Ministry of Tourism in Croatia. It's in their interest, after all. It'll help the Dutch tourist trade. I've managed to squeeze something out of the Ministry of Culture, too. And the Department here is doing its bit with the office. No great shakes, of course, but they may also let me teach a few drill sections."

"Sounds great."

"Not bad. . . . By the way, you going home for the summer?" He used the word "home" as a neutral substitute for the country that, while it was still in existence, the *Gastarbeiter* had all called Yuga and pronounced with extra-long vowels.

"I may."

"Well, I can't wait. My parents have this great house on Hvar. I spend two months there every year."

"Yes, well. . . . See you."

"Best of luck, Mrs. Lucić," he said.

The screwed-up eyes that refused to hold your glance for more than an instant, the anti-Communist stance so fashionable after the changing of the guard (though Laki had had nothing to do with Communism one way or the other), the mishmash of "now" urban speech, dialect, and literary affection (it was as if grandfather and grandson were speaking out of the same mouth), the ever so forced "Mrs. Lucić"—it was all vaguely nauseating, like a premonition of something unpleasant.

Instead of going out, I went back upstairs and knocked on Cees's door. He was alone.

"Come in, Tanja. Good to see you. I've been meaning to track you down."

Neither he nor Ines had made any attempt to "track me down" since I'd been to their place that evening. In fact, I had phoned them once or twice and been treated to Ines's warm words about how busy they were and had no time for anything and I'd been constantly on their minds and they'd been hearing such good things about me from my students and we'd eventually get together and "have a good chat." She made the "good chat" sound almost physical.

Now Cees explained that despite the excellent reports he'd had about my class that semester (did he mean "reports" in the literal sense or was it just a polite phrase?), he would be unable to hire me back come September, because he'd been unable to find the necessary funding. The Dutch Ministry of Education had been cutting the budget for higher education for the past few years now, and until he could come up with funds for a position in Croatian language and literature—and he was doing everything in his power to do so—Ines would have to take over on a volunteer basis. It was a real sacrifice on her part, but it was the only way of keeping the program alive. The Department was in trouble: even Russian, its bread and butter, was losing enrollment. He couldn't ask me to work for nothing. No, he wouldn't dream of it, knowing the situation I was in; he wouldn't want to exploit me. I'd find something, he was certain. After all, I had a doctorate, I had teaching experience and "a big heart." And what was most important, *Slavs are natural-born teachers, aren't they?* Ines had sent her regards and was sorry she hadn't been able to see me. She'd just left for Korčula with the children, and he would be leaving soon as well, as soon as he handed in his grades. Would I see Anneke in the next few days about the formalities of moving out of the flat she had found me: keys, deposits, and the like.

Cees's voice radiated sincerity. There wasn't a hint of ill will.

Of course he didn't broach the question of where I would be going after Amsterdam—cautious people don't ask questions whose answers might bind them to something—but the whole time he held forth I had only one thought in mind.

"Cees," I broke in, panic-stricken, "my visa is running out."

"I don't see how I can be of any help."

"You can write a letter stating that as head of the Department you confirm that I will be teaching here next year."

"But that would be unscrupulous. I couldn't risk it."

"The authorities don't care about truth; they care about documents. There's no risk whatever."

"I don't know . . ."

"I'll come for the letter tomorrow," I said in a voice I barely recognized. "You can leave it with Anneke."

I left the office secure in the belief that the letter, departmental stamp and all, would be waiting for me the next day. Then I sailed down the stairs and into the café across the street. I reached the toilet just in time. Never in my life had I vomited with such vehemence.

Later I asked myself what I'd meant to accomplish with the letter and why I'd humiliated myself so to get it. What good was an extension when there was no job to go with it? I'd seen émigré fever symptoms in others—Goran, for example—but I thought I was immune to them. All that talk about "papers," the willingness to go to any lengths for the proper "papers." And then what? "Then we'll see." I'd watched faces change expressions in quick succession or combine cunning, condescension, and fear; I'd watched the tense, sad, half-criminal look that goes with the scramble for the last mouse hole. I'd heard lively conservations break off abruptly as an invisible shadow of despair descended, but people would snap out of it and conversations resume with the same intensity.

I am not an émigré. I have a passport in my pocket. Why did I humble myself before Cees, to say nothing of Ines, who would certainly hear of the incident immediately. ("I mean, we did everything we possibly could for her. You have to help your own, after all. It's never so clear as when you're abroad. . . .") Oh, Ines! All sweetness and light, all airs and graces, the Austro-Hungarian charm, the *soft* Croatian chauvinism, the warmth of the south, the complacency that comes of a house whose walls are resplendent with booty, the booty of the first marriage ("Something to show the Dutch that we weren't beggars, know what I mean?"). They saw themselves in a solid, bourgeois bunker, while I saw them balancing on an ice floe, smiling all the while, babbling all the while, as they take down Grandmother's silver. The silver and the naive paintings are their only weapon against fate, against evil: they are sure signs that they belong to a class which no harm can befall. As for me, I'd find something. I had a doctorate and a big Slav heart. *Slavs are natural-born teachers, aren't they?* I'd get the visa and a few crumbs from the table, and then what? Then we'd see. . . .

After calming down a bit, I realized Cees hadn't promised anything. Nor was he to blame for anything. I was without resources, inner or outer. I was vulnerable, up for grabs. Anybody could pick me up, toss me on my back, do what he wanted with me, and leave me battered and bruised. That's why I was such easy prey for Ines's babble, why I got stuck in the honey of her words. Nor was she to blame any more than Cees. I had lost my integrity. I had put on a mask as a means of defense, and it had merged with my face, made deep inroads into my person. I was no longer myself.

On my way out of the café, I passed Igor. He was in his usual pose: earphones on and book open. He didn't notice me. Sud-

THE MINISTRY OF PAIN | 191

denly I thought of the Americans whose children I'd sat for in Berlin, the ones who never failed to introduce me to their friends. *"This is Tanja, our babysitter. She comes from the former Yugoslavia. Tanja is wonderful with children. She really has a way with them."*

CHAPTER 10

"You one of us?" he asks with a shrewd look and a grin that shows a gold tooth. His pal has a moist cigarette dangling from the corner of his mouth.

"Yes, I'm one of us," I say. "Where are you two from?"

"I'm from Smederevo, and this guy here's from Kumanovo. You?"

"Me? I'm from Mars," I say.

Now both are grinning.

"There ain't nothin' like our guys," the Gypsy said to his pal. "It's the lip on them." Then he turned to me. "Want us to play somethin' for you?"

"Why not."

"Somethin' from home how's 'bout. From Mars."

"Great."

He picked up his clarinet, and his pal slung his accordion around his shoulders and threw down his cigarette.

I pulled a hundred-guilder banknote out of my bag and dropped it in the hat.

The accordion player glanced down at the banknote and

wailed, "For God's sakes, sister. You crazy or somethin' throwin' away money like that? Keep it for a 'mergency, for one of them rainy days. Sure, leave us a guilder or two, but this? Aaaii! Don't be crazy, man. Money don't grow on trees!"

I dismissed his concern with a wave of the hand and moved off into the crowd, feeling the painful Gypsy shrapnel—"*Set, O golden sun, go down. Make the sky dark for the moon . . .*"— explode in my heart and lodge there. And suddenly my heart was bathed in blood, and the ice coating its walls started to melt, and I staggered through the marketplace dripping blood.

The Albert Cuyp Market is the largest and most famous in Amsterdam. It is located in the Pijp, a former working-class district. Its scales, of which there are said to be over three hundred, come out every morning and don't come down until late in the afternoon. The idea of buying fish, fruit, or vegetables was only a rational cover for the vague magnetism that would draw me toward the market, engulfed as it was in a mist of pollen and the strong scents of spices from beyond the seas—cinnamon, cloves, nutmeg—shot through with wind and salt. The air fairly sparkled with the bolts of rich silk and thick plush, of exotic jewels, of gold and beads, of the mother-of-pearl of immodestly open shells, of the glittering silver of fresh fish. The apples in my marketplace had a golden luster all their own; each grape glowed like a tiny lantern; the milk was as rich and white as a Vermeer woman's skin.

There were times, however, when the magnetism lost its force, when a dead fish lay heavy on the scales and the apples, though still red, and the lettuce, though still green, had lost their sheen. Not far from the scales were seedy vendors of cheap clothing, the air around them electrified by the synthetic fabrics; not far from the scales were vendors of bric-a-brac one would be hard put to find names for: cloths that might be dusters, plastic brushes of various shapes and sizes, nylon chignons in all colors, wooden backscratchers with plastic fingers, packaged snack foods. Not far from the scales were vendors of soap, shampoo, face cream, shabby handbags, artificial flowers, shoulder pads, patches, needles and thread, pillows and blankets, prints and frames, hammers and nails, sausage and cheese, chickens and pheasants, moth-eaten scarves . . .

Wandering among the stands, my heart full of Gypsy shrapnel, I chanced upon something that immediately caught my eye: a plastic tote bag with red, white, and blue stripes—Ana was right; I paid only two guilders for it—and like a wound-up mechanical toy, I made for the butcher's called Zuid (South), a code word to the local Yugos, who were its principal patrons. The butcher's window proudly displayed jars of pig's knuckles, and the shelves were lined with a modest selection of Yugonostalgic delicacies: Macedonian *ajvar,* sausage from Srem, olive oil from Korčula, Plasma Biscuits (whose ridiculous name made them an instant cult item the moment they appeared on the market), Minas coffee (which of course came from Turkey), and Negro Chimney-Sweep toffee (also a cult item because of the name). I bought a jar of *ajvar* and some toffee. It was a ritual purchase, purely symbolic: I hated *ajvar* and the toffee was bitter.

Thinking of the thousands and thousands of émigrés who leave their countries for countries like this one, who buy *ajvar* they hate and toffee they know is bitter, carryalls they will never use, ludicrous plastic-fingered backscratchers, and nylon chignons, I proceeded on my mechanical-toy journey, now heading toward the side street off the Oosterpark where a Bosnian café by the name of Bella was located. There I found a group of sullen, tight-lipped men playing cards. The looks they gave me were long but completely expressionless: not even a woman entering their male space could throw them off guard. I took a place at the counter, ordered "our" coffee, and sat there, penitent, so to speak. Before long I began to feel the invisible slap on my face and noticed I had hunched over like the men.

Having finished the coffee, I picked up the relics I had gathered on my pilgrimage—the Macedonian *ajvar* and Negro Chimney-Sweep toffee in the plastic carryall with red, white, and blue stripes—and set off for home. The Gypsy shrapnel had dissolved in my heart in the interim, and I was no longer bleeding, but I was confused as to whether I had just bid farewell to something or filled in an invisible application form. "For God's sakes, sister. You crazy or somethin'?"

PART 4

I'm like a stepping razor
Don't you watch my size
I'm dangerous, I'm dangerous

Treat me good
If you wanna live
You better treat me good.

Peter Tosh

I knew it was Igor the moment I heard the doorbell ring. I knew he'd be coming for an explanation. He came in, walked around the room as if it were too small to contain him and he wasn't yet sure whether to stay or not, but then he put his backpack on the floor and said, "Hmm. So this is your pad."

"Yes, this is my 'pad.' "

"Living room—bedroom, kitchen facilities, and bath," he said ironically. " 'Tight quarters, two meters by three.' " He was quoting a Yugoslav TV commercial.

"I hope your place is better."

"So you've made your little nest in the basement."

"Let's just call it the lower level."

"Don't have many books, do you," he said, glancing around the room, "considering your profession, that is."

"Would you like something to drink?" I asked, ignoring the remark.

"Coffee will do. I don't see you stocking anything else in this place."

While making the coffee, I thought of what to tell him. Although the cups were clean, I gave them another wash. It took me forever to find the sugar bowl. I did everything I could to buy time.

She is from Zagreb, Count, a true product of Zagreb and a truly remarkable young woman. Though still in her salad days, she has a will of iron and is steadfast and intrepid. I hardly need state that she is at home with the standard school subjects, but she also knows French and Italian, can sing and draw, and is a dab hand at embroidering. She is so taken with her calling that she performs her duties with great passion, and there is an idealistic strain to her nature, which makes her regard the reform and en-noblement of the souls entrusted to her as a sacred mission.

It was an excerpt from Šenoa's *Branka*, that classic of Romantic prose in which a young teacher, imbued with the ideals of the Croatian national revival movement, leaves Zagreb for the remote village of Jalševo to teach the village children. Pouring the coffee with my back to Igor, I listened to him read from the copy I had taken out of the library. I could feel my chin trembling. I was afraid I was going to cry. It was a childish way to provoke me, but I sensed it was no more than an introduction to the extravaganza he had planned.

"So you've been spending all this time staring at people's

legs," he said, putting down the book and nodding in the direction of the barred window.

"You can cope with anything if you know it's temporary," I said in as calm a voice as I could muster. "Besides, I'm leaving in a few days."

"What makes you so sure it's temporary?" he asked, either unconcerned about where I was going or feigning lack of concern.

I took him his coffee on a tray. I knew what he'd come for and decided to take the bull by the horns.

"Look, Igor, I'm terribly sorry . . ." I began, putting the tray down on the table.

"Great. You're sorry."

"Sit down," I said, and sat down. He remained standing. He had turned his back on me again and was staring out the window.

"I know you've come because of the grade."

He turned and trained those dark, slightly crossed eyes on me.

"And if I have?"

"I don't know," I said. I heard my voice crack and felt my chin tremble again.

He turned again and crossed the room to the basket I used for various knickknacks including the presents I'd received for my birthday. Igor started going through them.

"Everything was so good at first, wasn't it?" he said, picking up the two pairs of handcuffs.

"Yes . . ." I said cautiously.

"By the way, Comrade, have you ever tried these on?"

"What for?"

"Oh, out of curiosity. Didn't you even wonder how they open?"

"No."

"And I thought scholars were supposed to be inquisitive," he said.

The sneer in his voice made me blush, and again I was on the verge of tears.

Igor came up to me and took the cup out of my hands. He put it down on the tray.

"What do you say we give it a whirl?" he said, taking my hand and placing his lips on my wrist. They were cold and dry.

Then he lifted the wrist and skillfully handcuffed it to one arm of the chair.

"There," he said sweetly. "Now you're my slave."

"What kind of joke is this?" I said, mouthing words that didn't sound like mine.

Igor drew his chair up closer and took my free hand. "That was quick, wasn't it? Bet you were impressed. I practiced for hours."

I pulled my hand away. "Come on now. Take this thing off, will you? You shouldn't have any trouble after all that practice." I was doing my best to smile.

He took back my free hand, put it up to his cheek, and gave it a few strokes.

"Ah, Professor," he said, "you've got a nineteenth-century hand."

"A what?"

"Your hand is like the descriptions of hands in nineteenth-century novels: a dainty white hand."

He put my hand in his and turned it over like a glove.

"Only you bite your nails. Like a little girl." Then out of the blue he buried his head in my lap and said, "Help a poor student, won't you?"

I tensed up, wrenched my hand free, and started stroking his hair. For a while he stayed where he was, but then raised his head, took my hand, and, giving the palm a lick, snapped the other pair of handcuffs around my wrist and the other arm of the chair.

"There," he said, satisfied. "Now you're mine, all mine."

"Let's stop this stupid game, shall we?" I said, blushing again.

"So you still hope it's a game," he said ironically.

"Enough of your antics, Igor. If you think you're getting back at me, bringing me to justice . . ."

"Justice! You don't have a clue, Comrade. I don't give a damn about justice."

"The reason I failed you is that I was certain you'd denounced me to Cees Draaisma."

"Me?!"

"After the first semester somebody complained to Cees that we hadn't done a thing in class, that it was a big waste of time, and that I forced you to go to cafés with me.

"You don't say!" he said in English, his scoffing language.

I had the feeling he wasn't the least bit surprised.

"Cees told me all about it."

"And you really think it was me?"

"Well, it was one of you. You or somebody else."

"So what?"

"So what! You lied about me, you informed against me, you didn't have the nerve to tell me to my face what was bothering you; no, you ran to Cees and told him behind my back!"

"So you decided to get back at us."

"I wasn't getting back at you. I was doing my job."

"But what if nobody did complain? What if Draaisma dreamed the whole thing up?"

"Why would he do a thing like that?"

"For the fun of it. Or to show how easy it was for him to manipulate you, manipulate all of us."

"I don't think so. It had the ring of truth, what he said. He seemed to have reports on each and every class."

"Know what I think, Comrade? I don't think Cees is the problem, and I don't think we're the problem; I think the problem is you. You were itching for it to happen. Even if we had complained, you could have ignored it, forgotten it. Or you could have dealt with it. We're all in this together, after all. You could have forgiven us. You could have pitied us shitheads. You could have talked it over with us. You had all kinds of options. See? And the one you chose was to wage an *angry little war* against the class."

"What are you talking about? I don't understand."

"Tell me, why did you give me an F?"

"I don't know," I said. It was the most honest response I could come up with.

"You know perfectly well, you fucking bitch," he said calmly, touching my knee, "only you're embarrassed to admit it."

"Don't you dare use that language with me! And remove these handcuffs immediately or I'll call the police."

"You're *pathetic,* Comrade."

"*Pathetic?*"

"How do you propose to dial the number?"

He had me there.

"What do want from me anyway?"

"You sound like you get your lines from some B movie. What do I want from you? I don't know what I want from you the way you don't know why you gave me an F. Let's just say I want to make you squirm a little. I want to hear what you sound like when you sound the alarm. I want to hear what's really going on."

"What's really going on?"

"Oh, I read you like a book. I know how scared you are. But there's something keeping you from taking off that Teacher mask of yours. I feel like I'm at a *fucking* course in *fucking* territorial defense."

"I've had enough of this. I'm going to scream." I couldn't believe how stupid I sounded.

"Scream and I'll give you such a slap . . ."

"You wouldn't dare," I said.

"Wanna bet?"

Before I could open my mouth, he slapped my face, slapped it hard. All the breath went out of me.

"You're out of your mind!" I managed to come out with.

"And you?"

"How dare you!" I said, catching my breath.

"I'm a daring kind of guy. And now that I've slapped off your mask, you can drop the airs and graces bit."

"Look, Igor, all I have to do is dial the office and report a grade change."

"You're being pathetic again, Comrade. I'm an A student. One F doesn't mean a thing."

He had me there. I had no means of defending myself. Nor the will to do so. I took a deep breath and said guardedly, "Forgive me, Igor. Forgive me. Please."

"I can't seem to get it out of you," he said calmly.

"Get what out of me?"

"What needs to be said."

"You can't and you won't, because I haven't got it! I've been trying for months now!"

I was trembling with fury. Once more I heard myself sounding like a student in a Croatian for foreigners course. I tried jerking my hand free, but yelped with pain.

Igor took in my protest as if watching a bad stage production. Then he dug a hand into his pocket and pulled out a roll of adhesive tape.

"Where do you keep your scissors?"

"On the shelf," I said through my tears.

Igor snipped off a piece of tape and placed it over my mouth with the skill of a pro.

"There! Now you've got what you were after: *a movie of the week.* You're a proud one, you are. You've got a high opinion of yourself: you know you're up shit creek, but you're sure you've got a paddle, you're sure you've got status, assets: a man (though he's run off to Japan), a flat (though it has strangers living in it), a library (though the books are yours no more), a Ph.D. (though a lot of good it does you). In some far-off corner of your brain you're sure life will go back to the way it was before. The life you're living now is just an outing, a little outing you thought you'd go on. All you have to do is snap your fingers and—hey, presto!—everything will be back to normal. *Am I right?* And even though you've spent months counting feet through the window, even though you've seen B movies galore, you've never pictured yourself in another scenario: standing in a shop window in the red-light district luring clients to your mini-room, mini-basin, and mini-towel, or humoring gaga geezers like Meliha, or scrubbing toilets like Selim.

"Has it ever occurred to you that your students might be better than you, better people? Well, has it? You're no insensitive lout, Comrade. Something of the sort may have occurred to you. But has it occurred to you that your students might know more than you? Except they've been schooled in humiliation and don't throw their weight around. Experience has taught them that things are relative. And things *are* relative. Until yesterday distances were measured in centimeters: you could be hit by a grenade. Sure you felt sorry for the people who suffered, who actually were hit. But—not that you'd ever admit it to yourself—somewhere in the recesses of your brain you think a grenade chooses where it lands. And if it does, there must be some fucking reason for it. Something keeps you from making connections, from grasping that your being our teacher is only a matter of chance. It could just as easily have been the other way round: you could have been sitting with us and, say, Meliha could have been the teacher. That grenade—it reduces us all to shit, human shit, but you seem to think you're a little less shitty than the rest of us and you've raised your momentary feeling of superiority into a law of nature.

"Tell me, has it occurred to you that all that time you may have been torturing us? Has it occurred to you that the students you forced to remember were yearning to forget? That they made up memories to indulge you the way the Papuans made up cannibalistic myths to indulge the anthropologists? Your students aren't like you. They love this country. Flat, wet, nondescript as it is, Holland has one unique feature: it's a country of forgetting, a country without pain. People turn into amphibians here. Of their own accord. They turn the color of sand; they blend in and die out. Like fucking amphibians. That's all they care about: dying out. The Dutch lowlands are one big blotter: it sucks up everything memories, pain, *all that crap.* . . ."

Igor paused. He seemed tired. He took down the Šenoa again from the shelf and leafed through it absentmindedly.

Suddenly I felt tears running down my cheeks. I couldn't make out what had caused them. Humiliation? Self-pity? The tragic nature of the situation I found myself in? Or its comic nature? Christ! I thought. I feel closer to this man at this moment than I've felt to anyone in my life, and I have no way of letting him know. And I wasn't referring to the fact that my lips were sealed with tape; they would have been just as sealed without it.

Igor must have read my mind. Turning to face me, he read out the following passage: " 'The barometer of your heart is falling, and your eyes are brimming with tears.' "

I was on the other side. We were separated by an invisible

wall of ice. Could he also tell that I had only one desire at that point, namely, to knock my head against that wall? I needed help. There was something wrong with my heart, but I was unable to determine how serious it was. I desperately needed a refuge, a warm lap to curl up in, somewhere to wait for the pain to pass, somewhere to come to, to return to myself.

"Pray tell, Professor," he said, theatrically tossing the book to the floor, "what am I to do with you? A minor literature like ours doesn't rate an opposition party. No, no, *don't worry*. I'm just sorry for you. You're a teacher of minor literatures, small literatures, and even they have shrunken as of late. But you go on dragging them behind you wherever you go. Time is passing, it's too late to change fields, you can't very well toss them out, can you? So what do you do? You save what you can. It's all gone to hell, boys and girls, but let's pick up the pieces, let's go through the rubble and play archaeology.

"Have you given any thought to what went to hell? Piles of books in Croatian and Serbian, in Slovenian and Macedonian, in languages nobody needs and about what? Teaching the 'people,' the 'folk' to read. Real literature doesn't teach people to read; it assumes they can read. The year *Madame Bovary* came out, Zagreb was a village of 16,675 inhabitants. Sixteen thousand six hundred and seventy-five! By the time our local assholes picked up their pens, all the European giants—Goethe, Stendhal, Balzac, Gogol, Dickens, Dostoevsky, Flaubert, Maupassant—were in place. The year *Crime and Punishment* came out, eighty percent of Croatians were illiterate.

"So *get real,* Comrade. Have a look around you. Your classroom is empty. Your students have passed you by. They've gone out into the world—they've got their own value systems; they read all kinds of languages (if they read, that is, and if reading means anything anymore)—while you're still back in the age that knew "no more glorious task than spreading light, culture, and knowledge among the people." The heart beating in your breast is the heart that beat in Šenoa's village schoolmistress Branka over a hundred years ago. What else do you know? You haven't even learned fucking Dutch! Just that puts you a giant step behind your students.

"And that memory game you forced on us! In a few years all that *nostalgia crap* is going to be a big moneymaker. The Slovenes were the first to cash in on it: they've got a CD with Tito's speeches on the market. Mark my words. Yugonostalgia will be coming out of our ears. And if you want to know what I remember most about our former homeland, what I remember is that the local motherfuckers wanted to put me in uniform and pack me off to war! To safeguard the achievements of their fucking country. What fucking country? The whole kit and caboodle was mine. You know the song: 'From Vardar in the South to the Triglav in the North . . .' "

Igor was falling to pieces—contradicting himself and gasping for breath—but so was I, and I saw no way of putting myself back together.

"I had no one to stand up for me. Nobody. I'd be a corpse today if I hadn't escaped. You didn't stand up for me, either. But we didn't need your fucking grades. Or your fucking literature for that matter. What we needed was a reasonable human being to put things in place. At first you seemed on the right track, you hemmed and hawed and wrung your hands. But you capitulated soon enough. You stopped halfway. Your course was about a culture that had totally compromised itself, and you neglected to mention that fact. Besides, you talked exclusively about the past: when you lectured on Andrić, you neglected to mention that the current cohort of culture butchers have chopped him in three and there's now a Croatian and a Bosnian and a Serbian Andrić;

when you lectured on literary history, you neglected to mention that the Sarajevo University Library was bombed out of existence and that even now books are being tossed into bonfires and dumps. There you have the real literary history of the Yugonation. Arson. You didn't lecture on the statistics and topography of destruction. No, you stuck to your syllabus. You didn't stand up for what you believed, not even here, where you are free to say what you please. You totally discredited yourself.

"At first, like I said, you seemed to get it. You said we were all sick and you were sick, too. But then you got scared and decided to save your skin. Like the only thing that mattered was your field, because that's what you were paid to teach. But what a miserable little field it is and how full of shit. Still, you thought if you were *a good girl* they'd give you the job for good and you'd be on cloud nine. How wrong you were. You hadn't counted on Draaisma, another pitiful character. But he's got one advantage over you: he's Dutch, he's defending his home turf, and he's worked like hell to get it. He's as superfluous as you and he knows it, but unlike you, he's got power. So he gave the job to people he has control over—his wife—or can outsmart—Laki.

"I pity you, Comrade. Grab the first *Dačer* you can get your hands on. Because this country, it's okay. It won't let you down. And one more thing. *You're a lucky bitch*. You're lucky I'm telling you all this. Because one of three things happens when you've been through what all of us have been through: you become a better person, you become a worse person, or, like Uroš, you put a bullet through your brain."

Igor broke off abruptly, and the room filled with a balmlike silence. His eyes were still on me.

"Well, I'll be damned! You're enjoying all this! You're a wild little beastie, you are." He ran a finger over my features, as if penning a message: "My sweet little Croatian teacher, sweet little Serbian teacher, sweet little Bosnian teacher. . . ."

I held my breath.

"What am I to do with you, Teacher? Tell me. You've withdrawn. You're hiding. You're a tortoise, under your shell. No one can get to you. You're peering out of an invisible burka."

Again he broke off. He put his hand in his pocket and took out a razor blade. I froze. He bent over me, grabbed my right hand, pressed it palm down into the chair arm, and made a slow, careful incision in the wrist. It was short and shallow. Then he made a second and a third.

I felt no pain, but tears streamed down my cheeks. Through the tears I could see thin spurts of blood running along my hand. The bloody slits in my wrist looked like a natural bracelet.

"Something to remember me by. Your watch on the left wrist and on the right—Igor, the teacher's pet. . . . Well, I'll be off. And by the way, the number of the police is one one two."

He picked up his backpack from the floor and headed for the door. But then he turned back and with a quick flick of the wrist pulled the tape off my mouth. I yelped.

"Shhh!" he said soothingly, placing his hand on my lips. Then he took his hand away, bent down, and gave me a delicate, childlike kiss, his lips gathering up my tears on the way. "You have another chance now to say your piece, Professor."

I stubbornly held my tongue.

Looking me straight in the eye, he said in a calm voice that was nearly a whisper, "What if I was the asshole who went and complained to Draaisma? I could have been. I hated your self-possession, your self-righteous feeling of indignation, your simulated uncertainties, your halfhearted participation in our lives. Yes, it could easily have been me. Because I too have turned terminator. The Schwarzenegger jaw—we all have it. Murderers, crooks, innocents, victims, survivors, refugees, the old folks at home and the new folks here—we've changed. The lot of us. It's the war that did it, that fucked us up. Nobody comes out of a war unscathed. Nobody who's sane. And you looked so shiny and bright. Like a porcelain teacup. Of course I wanted to break you, smash you, knock something out of you. A shred of sympathy, a flicker of compassion, anything. . . ."

Igor fixed me with his dark, slightly crossed eyes as if gauging my soul. I held my tongue.

After he had left and shut the door behind him, the room filled with a new, heavy silence. For a while I sat there numb, straining my ears; then suddenly I convulsed and spit out an invisible bullet, the one I'd been clenching between my teeth since it all began. And from my throat came a mighty scream, the scream Igor must have been trying to coax out of me the whole time. But by then he was too far off to hear it.

After Igor's departure an image of my first year in school flashed through my mind. The way our teacher punished pupils was not by standing them in the corner but by standing them behind the blackboard, blackboards resting as they did at the time on wooden stands. "Behind the blackboard" was thus a symbolic space of shame and humiliation.

In the depths of the image stood a girl the teacher had sent behind the blackboard. All we could see of her were her legs in white knee-socks and feet in black patent leather shoes. We would have completely forgotten about her had we not suddenly heard a faint sound that grew louder as we stopped talking and held our breaths: a thin stream of urine was trickling onto the wooden floor. We sat and stared at the golden puddle growing under her legs, then making its way along the floor toward our desks.

Enlarged and in slow motion the scene now played itself out before my eyes. The girl's body was still hidden by the blackboard; all I could see was the stream of urine splashing into myriad sparkling droplets. And then I realized I was urinating. I could feel the warm liquid trickling down my legs. I sat there for a while, all but comatose, listening to my heart beat. I held my breath and followed its rhythm. It might have belonged to a bird about to take wing.

Then more images came, slow, languid images from far, far off. The first to float to the surface was a familiar one, a small black-and-white picture from Mother's album. I must have been four or five when it was taken. I am standing on a barren piece of land looking straight at the camera. It is winter, but there is no snow. I am wearing a severe-looking double-breasted tweed overcoat, its collar and flaps trimmed with velveteen. One hand is in a pocket (the flap is sticking up a little), the other at my side. My face shows the trace of a smile. There is nothing behind me. There is nothing to either side. I am the only thing in the picture. I am a small human figure that has been catapulted into a clearing somewhere. As familiar as I am with the picture, I was struck for the first time by how clearly and unequivocally alone I am in it.

A sudden chill drew me out of my comatose state, and I pushed my way over to the phone. But once there I fell apart again and froze for a while. Then I somehow managed to get the receiver off the phone, dial 112 and grunt my address into the mouthpiece. When a policeman appeared at the door a while later and saw me handcuffed to the chair, saw the three stripes of congealed blood on my right wrist, and smelled the urine, I read something I could identify with in his glance. Something came together with something at that moment, and I finally made the connection: the policeman was observing me with the look I had used to observe the girl in the clearing.

Igor was right. I won't forget him. Nor will he forget me; of that I am certain. Because I could have kept his name from the policeman, but I didn't. What is more, I accused him of rape, and for breaking and entering and rape he would, I presume, get several years and a criminal record that would hound him the rest of his life. If I hadn't done it, he wouldn't have remembered me. I did it so he would. I had sown my seed. I was a teacher, wasn't I?

There is no such thing as mercy, no such thing as compassion; there is only forgetting; there is only humiliation and the pain of endless memory. That is the lesson we brought with us from the country we came from, and it is a lesson we have not forgotten. Screaming and shouting are like Pavlov's bell to us; we are deaf to everything else. Catching the scent of terror is child's play to us; nothing tickles our nostrils more.

The natural bracelet of the three small incisions on my right wrist and the acrid odor of urine were the invisible handcuffs that would bind us, me and my pupil. I saw my future self making a newly acquired gesture, a kind of tic I would long be unable to shake off. It consisted of bringing the mouth down to the wrist, slowly pressing the lips to the three thin stripes and kissing them—Igor's stamp, Igor's brand—then tracing them with the tip of the tongue, testing whether they were still there, and finally raising the wrist slowly and holding it up to the light so that the stripes, now moist with saliva, glistened like mother-of-pearl.

PART 5

CHAPTER 1

Humpty Dumpty sat on a wall.
Humpty Dumpty had a great fall.
All the King's horses and all the King's men
Couldn't put Humpty together again.

I was plagued by nightmares at the beginning of the war and again when Goran and I left Zagreb. They had the same structure and were connected with a house. The house always had two sides to it: a front and a back. The front I knew; the back I came to know as I dreamed. The back was a false bottom, leaping out at me like a jack-in-the-box and thumbing its nose. In the dream I would come across a door, a set of stairs, or a passageway that would lead me to a parallel part of the house whose existence I had never suspected, or else I would discover that the house was partly floating, like the proverbial castles in air. I would move a shelf away from a wall and find a large hole with a gale of a wind rushing through it or no wall at all, and I looked out to see the house dangling on a thin, frayed wire.

Parallel spaces in my dreams inevitably portended monstrous grimaces, malicious warnings. The dreams came like sudden gusts of wind. They were followed by periods of calm, then started up again with renewed force. But eventually they petered out and ceased altogether.

In time they wound together into a single skein, and I put them aside. All but one, that is, which I made it my business to remember. The house in that dream was something of a labyrinth. It had several levels and was made of a number of incongruous materials. The roof was so high it seemed more suitable to a church. Suddenly I noticed that the roof was swelling into the shape of something like a funnel, and before I knew it the roof burst and what should come down through the "funnel" but a stream of books. It began the size of a trickle of grain but ended up an avalanche, pages hurtling through an air thick with book dust. Goran wasn't there, but I could see Mother on the other side of the room staring up at the ceiling in amazement. I ran over to her and grabbed her by the hand, and the two of us ran out into the street just before it collapsed like a house of cards.

"The key!" Mother screamed. "Have you got the key?"

"No, I haven't," I said with a pang of guilt, yet perfectly aware of how ridiculous her concern was: what good is a key without a house?

"Well, now we haven't even got a key," she said in despair.

Geert and Ana's flat consisted of a living room, a bedroom, a tiny kitchen with a balcony, a narrow hallway, and a tiny bathroom. There was a television set and a pile of videos on a low table in the living room and a half-dead rubber plant next to the television set. There was a bookshelf with a few books against one wall and an old couch with a grimy, faded slipcover against the other. The wall above the couch was decorated with an upbeat but beaten-up Dušan Petrišić poster, a map of Belgrade in its Yugoslav heyday. On the table with the videos I found Ana's list of instructions: the numbers of the phone and gas companies, the location of the stopcock, and so on. The carpeting in the living room was mud-stained and threadbare, the wallpaper in tatters, the windows curtainless and cloudy. The blinds were covered with a thick layer of dust.

Without giving the matter much thought, I went out and bought a variety of detergents and all sorts of scrub brushes and sponges. I began with the bedroom. Everything that could be turned upside down I turned upside down. I washed the windows and door. I swabbed the wardrobe with alcohol to get rid of the stale odor. I gave the blinds an alcohol rub as well. I vacuumed everything, walls included. Then I hung my clothes in the wardrobe and made the beds with the freshly washed linen I'd brought with me. The bedroom was now tolerable. One room down.

Next I gathered up the rubbish. I threw out a pile of newspapers, all the leftover food, and some cracked dishes. I tore down the poster from the living room wall and emptied the bathroom of everything that wasn't cemented in place. I put it all into black plastic bags, which I put out by the front door. I would haul them downstairs in the morning. I then gave the bathroom a thorough going-over. I filled the medicine chest with my own cosmetics and adorned the sink with a porcelain soap-dish I'd picked up somewhere. Once the bathroom felt more or less presentable, I took a shower, fell dead-tired into bed, and slept the night through.

The next day I launched into the kitchen. I spent a great deal of time and energy removing stains from the cabinets, fridge, stove, tiles, windows, and door. Despite my aching wrists I proceeded to the living room. I vacuumed the walls, carpet, and couch and did my best to beat the unpleasant smell out of the latter two, after which I attacked them with a wire brush and cleaning fluid. Because the wallpaper was hopelessly filthy, I went out and bought some paintbrushes, a can of paint, and a ladder. I spent the next two days covering the wallpaper, which was luckily the kind that can be painted over, with a thin layer of white paint. The place was beginning to look better now, but the freshly painted walls only pointed up the grayish cast of the woodwork. So I sanded it all down and sealed it with a white oil-based paint. That took another two or three days.

Then I started shopping in earnest. I found a nice grayish-white bedspread, and once I'd draped it over the couch, put a lamp I'd purchased earlier on the table, filled a vase with fresh flowers, and hung a solidly framed poster of the Louis Hine black-and-white photo of workers perched high up on a beam during the construction of the Empire State Building and smoking away, the living room became livable. True, it was still very much a "student pad," but that didn't bother me in the least.

I stocked the kitchen cupboards with the basics and bought a new teapot and an elegant china teacup. Nor did I neglect the rubber plant. I took it out onto the balcony, replanted it in a bigger pot, mixing in enriched soil, pruned the dead branches, wiped the dust off the leaves, and brought it back into the living room. I looked through the collection of videos Geert and Ana had left behind, dusted them off and arranged them neatly in the bookshelf. I wiped the covers of their books with alcohol and put them back on the shelves next to the ones I had brought.

On a tour through the flat looking for other things in need of repair, I noticed that the wallpaper just above the door leading to the living room had buckled a bit. I took the ladder out of the closet where the gas and electricity meters were, and climbed up to finger the place in question. It burst like a balloon, scattering bits of plaster over the floor and revealing a concrete wall covered with postcards and magazine illustrations, now completely yellow. I broke off a piece to get a better look at it, and off came several layers of paint, which fell to the floor with a *thwack*. I stood facing a "frieze" of pornographic images, an amateur collage of homosexual fantasies, most likely the work of the tenant who had lived there before Geert and Ana. They showed dark-skinned boys with laurel wreaths on their heads either urinating, kissing, or embracing against a stylized Greco-Roman backdrop. The paper, which had turned the color of stale urine as it became one with the wall, made me retch.

I climbed down and sat on the couch, unable to move, listening to the silence. Suddenly I heard a popping sound and looked up, holding my breath, to see the wallpaper cracking open along the walls, making a series of wavy, eventually joining paths. I watched them crack, peel, reel, twist like springs until off they snapped, and dropped with a crisp, dry thud. I was surrounded by a wall of dust raised by an invisible wind. I threw a glance at the front door, but, no, the key was in the lock. In the meantime, the silence had returned. I looked down at my hands. They were red and swollen. The detergents had taken their toll: my hands were one big wound, the skin peeling off in tiny flakes to reveal the three bloody stripes.

It occurred to me that I hadn't looked out the window even once during the past few days. I didn't know what the weather was like or what time it was. I had completely lost my bearings. I just sat there holding an invisible low-life visa and peeling inside.

I realized I had to pick myself up and do something, anything. I had to combat the despair that had momentarily taken me over. I stood, pulled down the first video that came to hand, and popped it into the VCR. Then I went back to the couch, gave the spread enough of a shake to send the scraps of wallpaper that had alighted on it to the floor, and lay down.

At some point during the night I was awakened by the buzz of the television set. The snow on the screen seemed to have slipped into the room. I opened the window and let in the July air. The concrete square was shining in the moonlight and the neon BASIS sign on the building across the square. To the right I could just make out a corner of the modest local mosque's turquoise dome. The square had some squat, small-crowned chestnut trees and a few benches. There was a man sitting on a bench beneath a tree. He was wearing a turban. He seemed to be asleep.

Geert and Ana's flat was in one of those gray, crowded, cheaply constructed prefabs that encircle the city center like keys on a castellan's ring. Some people call them ghettos. This one was called "Little Casablanca." But I was not to learn that until later.

We are barbarians. The members of our tribe bear the invisible stamp of Columbus on their foreheads. We travel west and end up east; indeed, the farther west we go the farther east we get. Our tribe is cursed.

We settle on the outskirts of cities. We choose them so we can gather up our tents when the time comes and set off again, move farther west to get farther east. We live in gray, crowded, cheaply constructed prefabs that encircle the city center like keys on a castellan's ring. Some people call them ghettos.

All our settlements are the same. They can be recognized by the round metal satellite dishes sticking out from our balconies, the devices that enable us to feel the pulse of the people we have left behind. We, the losers, are still one with the mega-circulating lifeblood of the land we abandoned in hatred. Except the people there have no antennas; they have dogs. At twilight their dogs go out onto the balconies and bark their messages to one another. Their barking bounces back and forth against the concrete buildings like Ping-Pong balls. The echo drives them mad. They bark even louder.

We have children. We multiply dangerously. Kangaroos are said to have one of their young in tow, another in their pockets, a third in their wombs on the point of bursting out and a fourth, in the form of a barely fertilized egg, waiting to take its place. Our women are as big as kangaroos: they have their numerous offspring in tow like the keys on the ring of a castellan's wife. Our children have straight necks, dark complexions, dark hair, and black eyes; our children are clones, the males little men, the spit and image of their fathers; the females little women, the spit and image of their mothers.

Here we bring neatly packed food home from Basis and Aldi and Lidl and Dirk van de Broek; there we buy wholesale, in bulk. Our fish markets reek of fish, our butcher shops of blood. Our shops are dirty: we buy meat from large plastic barrels filled with brine. We finger everything, pick at it, poke at it, turn it over, listen to it, and then drag it from stall to stall. The bazaar is the very heart of our existence.

Our settlements are like oases: they satisfy our every need. They've got nursery schools and elementary schools and driving schools; they've got post offices and filling stations and telecom centers offering cheap rates to the home country; they've got dry cleaners and launderettes and beauty salons, where our people cut our people's hair; they've got coffee shops, where the young can get their hashish, and the other youth center, *Turkse Pizza;* and they've got our place of worship and two or three of our pubs for the men. We've got our pubs; they have theirs. The zones are sharply delineated. No tourists find their way to us, except when lost. As for the high life, the "canal people," they say they need a low-life visa. And what would they do here anyway? So they stick to their part of town and we to ours. Everyone feels safer that way, more at home.

We are barbarians. We are the false bottom of the perfect society, we are its thumb-nosing jack-in-the-box, its demimonde, its ugly underside—its parallel world. We wade through its shit, canine and human; we confront its rats in our early-morning and late-night peregrinations. The wind comes to us to blow litter through the air: the plastic bags we leave behind, the Mars, Kit-Kat, and Snickers wrappers our children drop. And every morning seagulls come to dine on rotting junk food, magpies to peck at Turkish pizza.

Our young men are wild and sullen, full of anger. At night they converge in the concrete wasteland like packs of stray dogs and let off steam till the wee hours. They chase one another across abandoned playgrounds, swinging on swings, jumping and shouting; they yank receivers out of public phone booths; they hurl stones at car windows; they steal whatever they can lay their hands on; they play soccer with empty beer cans that sound like machine guns; they ride their motorcycles like maniacs through the settlements. Nighttime is their time. We hide and tremble like mice: their caterwauling makes our blood run cold. The police give our zone a wide berth; they let the screams eat into us like acid. Our young men are quick with their knives: their knives are extensions of their hands. Our young men are champion spitters: their spittle marks their territory as dogs' urine marks theirs. And they always run together, in a pack, like village curs.

Our young women are quiet. That their very existence is an embarrassment to them shows clearly on their faces. Hair hidden under kerchiefs, eyes fixed on the ground, they slip through the city like shadows. If you happen to see one in a tram, she will be hunched over a prayer book chomping the sacred syllables like so many sunflower seeds. She will soon alight, looking neither right nor left, and scurry off, still mouthing the text, her lips in constant motion, like a camel's.

Our beetle-browed men congregate around turquoise-domed concrete mosques that look more like day-care centers than places of worship. In summer they squat against their mosque, scratching their backs on its walls and seeking relief from the heat (though there is no sun). They mill about, sniffing at one another, circling the mosque, hands behind backs, pausing, shifting their weight from one foot to the other, patting one another on the back, embracing when they meet, embracing when they part, and when on special holidays the mosque is full to overflowing they overflow onto the asphalt and kneel there facing east. Like a dog its bone, our men gnaw their mosque from dawn till dusk.

And when the sky comes down so low that it touches our heads, when the barometer sinks and the air is so humid we breathe through gills, then our bodies grow heavy and fall to the bottom, where there are no zones, where we crawl about on all fours, spent like fish after spawning. And only there, at rock bottom, do our scales graze one another, do our fins meet as we pass, do we press our gills to those of another.

We are barbarians. We have no writing; we leave our signatures on the wind: we utter sounds, we signal with our calls, our shouts, our screams, our spit. That is how we mark our territory. Our fingers drum on everything they touch: dustbins, windowpanes, pipes. We drum, therefore we are. We make rackets, rackets as painful as toothaches. We bawl at weddings and wail at funerals, our women's convulsive voices battering the concrete façades like tempests. We break glasses and go bang: firecrackers are our favorite toy. Sound is our alphabet, the noise we produce being the only proof that we exist, our bang the only trace we leave behind. We are like dogs: we bark. We bark at the lowering gray sky weighing down on our heads.

We are sleepers. The members of our tribe bear the invisible stamp of Columbus on their foreheads. We travel west and end up east; indeed, the farther west we go the farther east we get. Our tribe is cursed. Returning to the lands whence we came spells our death; remaining in the lands whither we have come spells defeat. Hence the endless repetition, in our dreams, of the departure sequence, the moment of departure being our only moment of triumph. Sometimes during our short walk home from the mosque we are overcome by sleepiness and find a bench beneath a tree doing its best to grow. The air is moist and warm, the neon moon full, the night sky navy blue. And so we fall asleep in the concrete oasis under the concrete tree and rerun the departure sequence for the umpteenth time. We take up our tents, hoist our bags on our back, and up comes a gale and churns the desert sand, and our silhouettes start to fade, and we vanish altogether in the thick curtain of sand.

I stood, pulled down the first video that came to hand, and popped it into the VCR. Then I went back to the couch, gave the spread enough of a shake to send the scraps of wallpaper that had alighted on it to the floor, and lay down. . . .

It was Philip Kaufman's adaptation of Kundera's *Unbearable Lightness of Being*. I had read the novel twice. Besides, I had my doubts about cinematic adaptations of literary works: even the best seemed unworthy of their models. The very first frames put me on my guard: Daniel Day-Lewis and Juliette Binoche may have looked more Czech than many Czechs, but Binoche was trying to speak English with a Czech accent and the only words she got right were *Anna Karenina*. I was also put off by the way the film poeticized everyday Communist reality: the effective shots of ugly naked bodies in a shroud of steam or old men playing chess in a swimming pool, the scenes of run-down Czech spas (which could well have been in Croatia) and Prague streets (so reminiscent of Zagreb). Perhaps my irritation resulted from the reflex reaction (What can *they* know about *us*?) that I had heard so many times and that was merely the arrogance of the colonized

and thus of no more consolation than the arrogance of the colo-
nizers. In that scheme of things the perfectly innocent Kaufman
became the colonizer of the territory that only I at that moment
had the right to inhabit.

But when the black-and-white documentary footage of the Russian
occupation of Czechoslovakia came on the screen, when I saw the
Russian tanks entering Prague, the scenes of protest and violence
in the streets culminating in the close-up of a Russian soldier
aiming his revolver at the onlookers, including Binoche, I was,
well, bowled over. That revolver was aimed at me. Binoche, who
had been skillfully inserted into the footage and was frantically
snapping pictures of the tanks, no longer got on my nerves. Not
only had the film suddenly become "authentic"; it had become
personal, my "personal story." Or so I felt, at least. And I felt the
tears running down my cheeks.

What was going on? I wondered. I was only six when the
Russians invaded Czechoslovakia, so there was no way I could
purely and simply identify with the story. I embarked on a round
of feverish calculations: if, as the liner notes told me, Kundera's
novel came out in 1984 and Kaufman's film was shot in 1987, then
the film dates from two years before the fall of the Berlin Wall
and four years before the outbreak of the war in Yugoslavia,
which means I could have seen it (though I did not) in Zagreb.
My head started swimming from the pointless calculations, and
before I knew it I had completely lost my way in time. I was like
those Japanese soldiers left behind in the Philippine jungles after
the War and who, when found, thought the War was still going
on. I'd jumbled up everything—time frames, camera frames—
and was incapable of sorting it out. What had taken place far in
the past now seemed recent, and the most recent events had
moved back in time. My only point of reference seemed to be

that dated video. I looked around like a shipwrecked sailor newly washed ashore. I was in a flat not my own in a city not my own in a country not my own, surrounded by crumbling walls and the smell of must. The remote control in my hand was still working, but the batteries in my internal control mechanism had gone dead: no amount of button pushing could get me going. I wondered when the things that had happened had found time to happen and what made me experience Kaufman's movie as if it were CNN's lead item for the day and the fragile Dayton Agreement, signed only two years previously, as if it were ancient history to which I could afford to be supremely indifferent.

The blow I had just received proved much more complicated than it had seemed at first. Words like "phantom limb syndrome" or "nostalgia" are arbitrary lexical labels meant to denote the complex emotional blow that comes of loss and the impossibility of return. They imply that it makes virtually no difference whether we make our peace with the loss or experience relief at being able to let go of the past or of the desire to return to it. Because the blow does not lose its intensity thereby. Nostalgia, if that is the word for it, is a brutal, insidious assailant who favors the ambush approach, who attacks when we least expect him and goes straight for the solar plexus. Nostalgia always wears a mask and, oh, irony of ironies, we are only its chance victim. Nostalgia makes its appearance in translation—most often a bad one—after a complicated journey not unlike the children's game "telephone." The words the first player whispers into the ear next to him pass through a whole chain of ears until it emerges from the mouth of the last player like a rabbit out of a magician's hat.

The blow that had recently hit me in the solar plexus had undergone a long and complicated journey, passing through any number of mediators and media until, mediated for the umpteenth time, it turned up in the form of—Juliette Binoche. Binoche was the last in the line of transmitters, the one who translated my personal pain into my language. At the perfect moment. Because at a different time her translation might have been gibberish. At that and only that moment Kaufman's images, much like the ideal Coca-Cola commercial, were able to launch a sudden subliminal attack on me, and I totally fell apart.

Even though I felt the only story I had a proper copyright on was the "Yugoslav story," at that moment all stories were mine. I wept in my innermost being over the imaginary tangled web that bore the arbitrary label of Eastern, Central, East-Central, Southeastern Europe, the other Europe. I couldn't keep them straight: the millions of Russians who had disappeared into Stalin's camps, the millions who had perished in the Second World War, but also the ones who had occupied the Czechs and the Czechs who were occupied by the Russians and the Hungarians (they too occupied by the Russians) and the Bulgarians who fed the Russians and the Poles and the Romanians and the former Yugoslavs, who basically occupied themselves. I was beating my head against the wall of a generalized human loss. Like a Balkan keener I wailed my agony over one and all, only my agony was mute. I grieved for the Zagreb, Sarajevo, Belgrade, Budapest, Sofia, Bucharest, and Skopje facades that were coming down. I was touched by the endearingly bad taste of a chocolate wrapper of my youth (to say nothing of the literal bad taste of the chocolate), I bemoaned the swatch of a melody that happened to ring in my ear, a face that emerged at random from the darkness, a sound, a tone of voice, a line of verse, a slogan, smell, or scene. There I sat, staring into the landscape of human loss and weeping my heart out. I even shed a tear for Kaufman's trick shots, which had after all brought my feelings to a head, and another for my celluloid Binoche.

Then I thought of my students. They would be moved by the same landscape. The problem was, their metamorphosis had only the scantest chance of success: they were a second too late, a fraction of a second. No, their metamorphosis would end in failure. I could sense it in their internalized stoop, in the hint of gloom in their eyes, the invisible slap on their faces, the lump of vague resentment in their throats.

Any minute now, any second, a new, completely different tribe will arise from the post-Communist underbrush bearing doctoral dissertations with telling titles like "Understanding the Past as a Means of Looking Ahead." They will be the children of Tomáš and Tereza, who returned to Czechoslovakia only to die there, because returning spells death and remaining spells defeat. They will be the orphans of Tomáš and Tereza. They will set out on their run like salmon, but other times mean other streams and other fellow travelers, people who really are "looking ahead" and who will no longer "understand the past" or at least not in the same way. And these new team players from the "gray backwaters" of Mongolia, Romania, Slovakia, Hungary, Croatia, Serbia, Albania, Bulgaria, Belarus, Moldavia, Latvia, and Lithuania, these transition mutants will storm European and American universities and finally learn what needs learning. They will form a vibrant young contingent of specialists, organizers, operators and, above all, managers, experts in business management, political management, ecological management, cultural management, disaster management—the management of life. They will be a genus that propagates itself with inhuman rapidity, as if propagation were their sole aim in life. They are the type that always lands on its feet, that has no qualms about living off the misfortunes of the people they help, because even misfortune needs to be managed: misfortune without management is merely failure. They are the people who will look after the disabled in Bulgaria, Bosnia, Belarus, Moldavia, and Romania; of the orphans in Bosnia, Georgia, Tajikistan, Kazakhstan, Chechnya, Kosovo, Azerbaijan, and Armenia; of the minorities in Europe and the Roma everywhere; of sex professionals and victims of the white, black, and yellow slave trade; of refugees, emigrants, immigrants, and migrants; of the homeless. They are mutants who will be as efficient as laboratory viruses in spreading, spreading their nets and networks, their umbrellas and umbrella organizations, their centers, their links. They will become the heads of audiovisual and telecommunications departments, the net and web people. They will be the self-confident designers of their own careers and of the lives of others. They will be deep thinkers, voracious readers, and consummate stylists. They will have multiple identities: they will be cosmopolitan, global, multicultural, nationalistic, ethnic, and diasporic all in one. They will wear any number of hats and be flexible in the extreme, ever ready to define and refine themselves, reflect and deflect themselves, invent and reinvent themselves, construct and deconstruct themselves. They will be the champions of democracy in these transitional times, and since everything is and has always been in a state of flux the words *mobility* and *fluidity* will be like chewing gum in their mouths. They will be progressive and aggressively young, the well-paid commissars of *European integration and enlargement,* the harbingers of the new world order, the creators of *unique postnational political units,* of *new national and postnational constellations,* advocates of *globalization as opposed to localization* and vice versa, advocates, zealous advocates of whatever happens to be in need of advocating. Born in the Ukrainian hinterland, they will study medieval history in Kiev, English business terminology in Birmingham, and write dissertations on "What Medieval History and Business Terminology Have in Common." They will flock from Vilnius to Warwick to learn about micro- and macroeconomics, to specialize in *good governance and sustainable peace in war-torn societies*. They will come from Voronezh, Kaunas, Timişoara and Pécs to work for NGOs, the EU, the UNHCR. They will come from Ulan Bator with MBAs to study *modeling policy instruments*. They will come from Yerevan, from Alma Ata, from Veliko Tŭrnovo, from Tashkent and Varna and Minsk to become *the leaders and future elite in a unified Europe*. They will come from Iaşi in Romania and Ruse in Bulgaria and Tetov in Macedonia with doctorates in pastoral Orthodox theology in their pockets, spend a few years in Fribourg studying international relations, join think tanks in Salonika, Boston, and Prague, and hold a series of handsomely remunerated *briefing sessions* in a Romanian, Bulgarian, or Lithuanian institute on the topic of Euro-Atlantic integration and the politics of defense, flaunting their rampant bastardization. They will be linguistically gifted, speaking several languages and creating a Eurospeak of their own, peppering it with personal coinages. They will always write the word *Enlargement* with a capital *E,* because for them it heralds a new era, a new humanism, Renaissance, and Enlightenment rolled into one. Their buzzwords will be *management, negotiation technology, income, profit, investment, expenses, hidden communication,* and the like. Quick to position themselves, forever with an eye to the main chance, resilient as the proverbial cat with nine lives, they will be *hardworking, communicative, loyal, discreet, tolerant, friendly,* and *skillful in coping with stressful situations*. They will show a special interest in *diplomatic privileges*. They will come from Samara after short stints in Coca-Cola Samara and Samara Light and Power and enroll in the Fletcher School of Law and Diplomacy and the Mediterranean Academy of Diplomatic Studies. They will spice up their applications with phrases like *Challenge is my propeller* and *Perfection is my ulti-*

mate goal and jargon like *the contemporary self, the bastardization of our age, postcolonialism, marketization, recruiting tactics, sensitivity training,* and *contacts.*

But on their way they will forget that the *very* flexibility, mobility, and fluidity that catapulted them to the surface leave a nameless mass of slaves down below. All through the gray backwaters people will be eking out precarious livings by manufacturing the goods the West European magnates call for. They will be rummaging in dustbins for food, going on benders, giving birth to homeless children who will give birth to more homeless children. They will sell their sperm, their kidneys; they will sell any organ that will fetch a price on the global black market. They will rent out fresh East European sexual organs to the weary ones of Enlarged Europe. They may also help out their brothers, lay Croatian customers, say, traveling to Bulgaria (where human flesh is cheaper). And some of them will travel all the way to the shores of Western Europe, where the more fortunate will pick asparagus in Germany and tulips in Holland and the less fortunate will scrub toilets.

My students appear to have missed the boat, as have I, for that matter, but only by a second. We stood there with our mouths open for a second too long and missed our chance to enter the new age. All we can do now is run our legs off to keep in place. The loser bug has made its way into our hearts and weakened the muscles there.

I was sitting in the room surrounded by peeling walls and the smell of old dust. It suited me just fine: it belonged to somebody else and went well with my newly acquired low-life visa and several pieces of luggage I might just as well have left to rot in a public locker somewhere. If I had done so and if the authorities had traced the luggage to me, I would have been hard put to tell them what was in it. The contents were untranslatable. So there

I sat surrounded by peeling walls with a profession that was likewise untranslatable and a country that had come apart at the seams and a native language that had turned into three languages like a dragon with a forked tongue. I sat there with a feeling of guilt whose source I couldn't put my finger on and a feeling of pain whose source I couldn't put my finger on.

I pressed "off" and "eject" on the remote, took the cassette out of the VCR, and put it back neatly on the shelf. I decided that my best option was to go on staking out my territory, set up a day-to-day routine, get things done. Tomorrow, I thought, I'd start by picking up a newspaper to check on the date (I wasn't sure just how much time I'd spent in the cell I'd locked myself up in) and locating the nearest launderette. Then I had to clean up the rest of the mess and buy new wallpaper for the places where it had buckled and come off. But first I'd need to get rid of the ugly stains on the walls. This time I'd sand the walls and fill the cracks with putty before hanging the wallpaper. I might even just paint it—white, of course.

I went over to the window and opened it. The concrete square was lit by the pale glow of the streetlamps and the bright letters of the BASIS sign on the other side. There was a hot, heavy, subtropical humidity in the air. All the way to the right I could see a piece of the turquoise dome atop the small concrete mosque. The crowns of the chestnut trees had a muted luminosity of their own, and the metal satellite dishes on the nearby balconies shone white through the darkness. It was unusually quiet. I was soothed by the sight. Perhaps I had come home after all, I thought.

And then out of the darkness into the semidarkness of the concrete there emerged the figure of a man. He made his way slowly and with difficulty, as if wading through the ocean. Suddenly he flicked something that looked like a cigarette butt to the ground, and there was a sharp retort. It was a firecracker. Not realizing that he was being observed, the passing stranger had left his mark upon the night: he had sent a message with no content only to vanish into the dark. As he disappeared, he seemed to be walking at a slight angle, like a dog.

The cyclone had set the house down, very gently—for a cyclone—in the midst of a country of marvelous beauty. There were lovely patches of green sward all about, with stately trees bearing rich and luscious fruits. Banks of gorgeous flowers were on every hand, and birds with rare and brilliant plumage sang and fluttered in the trees and bushes. A little way off was a small brook, rushing and sparkling along between green banks, and murmuring in a voice very grateful to a little girl who had lived so long in the dry, gray prairies.

L. Frank Baum, *The Wonderful Wizard of Oz*

I left the flat and headed toward the metro station. I was almost there when I felt a blow on my back, a blow so powerful and unexpected that it knocked the breath out of me. A second or two later I felt a determined tug at my bag, which was hanging from my shoulder. My shoulder blade kept the strap from slipping off, and I turned, pulling back the bag, to see three small boys with satchels on their backs. They were coming home from school. They could not have been more than ten. One of them, I saw, had a toy pocketknife in his hand. He lowered his eyes and dropped it. All three had the dark, sullen look of grown men. I can't tell how long we all stood there motionless. Two or three seconds at most. Clearly none of us knew how to deal with the situation. But then the strongest of the three took over and, opening his mouth wide and aiming his black pupils at my face, he let out a long, piercing cry full of hate. The hate was as unexpected and powerful as an electric shock. It came from some unknown depths, some unknown darkness; it came from light-years away to crash before me, bare and sharp as a knife and completely divorced from the situation and the boy, whose lungs, throat, and mouth served merely as a chance medium.

The boys turned and fled. They had an awkward, childlike, flat-footed way of running, and their satchels bounced up and down on their backs. Once they felt they were at a safe distance, they stopped and turned. The sight of me still standing there rooted to the spot and staring after them elicited several mocking gestures on their part, after which they burst into high-pitched giggles. Their first attempt at theft may have been a failure, but this part was great fun. I stood there watching them until they moved on.

I opened my hand to find I was holding the knife. I couldn't remember having bent to pick it up. Staring at it, I realized the incident that had just played itself out was both moving and dreadful. The boy's hate-driven scream still echoed in my ears.

It was late afternoon. The dusk was magnificent, the sun pouring its warm terra-cotta glow over everything. The pain had subsided, and I set off, still clutching the knife, but no longer clear as to where I was headed. I used deep breathing to suppress the incident, which could have happened to anybody, in any part of the city, anywhere. I thought of myself living in the largest dollhouse in the world, where everything is simulation, nothing is real. And if nothing is real, then there's nothing to be afraid of,

I thought, and felt a certain spring come into my step. It was almost as if I were walking on air.

Madurodam unraveled before me like a skein of wool. I couldn't get over the fact that everything looked new: the bonsai imitating mighty oaks, the patches of grass imitating luxuriant lawns. Everything was suddenly clear as crystal, plain as the nose on my face. The Madurodamplein was rice-paper thin. A bluish horizon glowed in the distance. Looked at thus, the heart of Amsterdam had the form of a partially bisected cobweb. First came Magere Brug, whose filigree made me think of a dragonfly, then the De Waag Chinese fish market with its wriggling catch, then the Waterlooplein flea market. The scenes flashed by before me, fragile, lacelike, limpid like the caps on the girls' heads in the painting by Nicolaas van der Waay. I saw canals overhung with shady trees; I saw the façades of the houses along the canals—the Herengracht, the Keizersgracht, the Prinsengracht, and Singel in neat rows like pearls; I saw Mint Tower, the flower market, and Artis and took in the heavy, warm, intoxicating sight of the Botanical Museum. The entire city lay before me, a city of sky, glass, and water. And it was my home.

In front of the small Anne Frank Museum I saw an earthworm of a line. Inside I saw myself standing in front of a monitor absorbed in its video quiz: *1. Whom did Anne first share her room with? 2. Whom did she have to share it with later on? 3. What did Anne do to liven up her room? 4. Who built the bookcase? 5. From which country did the Frank family flee? 6. Were all Anne's girlfriends refugees?*

I suddenly realized that the house at Prinsengracht 163 bore a distinct resemblance to the houses that obsessed me in my nightmares, and it was with a sense of relief that I mounted the virtual stairs, opened and closed the virtual doors, and left the house simply by pressing the Esc key. I no longer had anything to fear: escape was always an option.

I pictured a Hague Tribunal the size of a matchbox, with tiny judges in tiny gowns, tiny defendants and witnesses, tiny counsels for the defense and the prosecution, miniature surrogates simulating a life in which right and wrong exist. In actuality, there are no right people and wrong people, no good people and bad people; there is only the mechanics of it all, the operation. And the only thing that counts is action; action is all. For the windmills to turn, as small and lively as the city's sparrows; for the bridges to go up and down, for boats to buzz along the canals like remote-controlled flies; for tiny prostitutes in the red-light district to open and close the curtains of their displays, as neat and meticulous as those old-fashioned barometers; for tiny mounted policemen to make their rounds on horses no bigger than white mice. And as long as the curtains open and close, as long as the windmills turn, as long as the bonsai grow, as long as the blood flows through our filigree veins and into our filigree hearts, everything is just fine. The language of Madurodam has no words for fatality, destiny, or God. God is the mechanics; fatality is a breakdown. Now that I have settled down here in Madurodam, be it of my own free will or not, this is something I must understand.

1. What was the name of the country in the south of Europe that fell apart in 1991? a) Yugoslovakia, b) Yugoslavia, c) Slovenakia. 2. What was the name of the inhabitants of that country? a) The Yugoslavs, b) the Mungoslavs, c) the Slavoyugs. 3. Where do these people, whose country has been disappeared, live now? a) They are no longer alive, b) They are barely alive, c) They have moved to another country. 4. What should people who have moved to another country do? a) They should integrate, b) They should disintegrate, c) They should move to yet another country.

I must understand that simulation is all and if simulation is all I am not guilty; that here in Madurodam, under the bright skies of Madurodam, I am guilty of nothing; that it is all a matter of perspective, that things are big if we experience them as big and small if we experience them as small; that for us, the inhabitants of Madurodam, the magpies that alight on our rooftops are more dangerous, are in-com-pa-rab-ly more dangerous than the boy's sudden, inexplicable, hate-saturated scream that had just caused me a pain disproportionate to its significance.

It was late afternoon. The sunset was magnificent, the sun pouring its warm terra-cotta glow over everything. I was walking toward the woods, my feet scarcely touching the ground. It was unusually quiet: all I could hear was the occasional *whoosh* of a passing cyclist. I saw the kerchiefed women sitting on the grass like mother hens, their broods all around them. My nostrils swelled with the scent of newly mown grass. I entered the woods. It was so sparse I could see the blueness of the lake through the trees. Although it was August, autumn was in the air. I sucked that air into my lungs greedily as I walked. I can't say for sure how long I walked and how long it took me to reach the clearing. . . .

. . . in the wood that was covered with luxuriant patches of wildflowers; an extraordinarily limpid brooklet frisked through its center; the sun's gold pierced the densely interwoven branches of the surrounding oaks. Sitting on a stump near the pond was a healthy, robust girl with black eyes. Her copious hair was gathered at the neck, a summer shift of rose muslin drifted along her well-proportioned body, a small, simple cross hung on a black ribbon round her neck, and before her on the grass lay a hat and a songbook. Sitting opposite her was a flock of the sweet village children, all of whom, lads and lasses both, boasted such lively, gay faces and bright eyes, such clean, white garments that it was a pleasure to gaze upon them. Many of the lasses had woven wreaths of wildflowers for their heads. Raising her hand, the young miss beat out the rhythm of a song for her charges, who attended, rapt, to her index finger until her tiny mouth opened and the most beautiful sound emerged. It was truly a glorious sight: the young, festive faces, the lads rocking their heads animatedly in time to the song, the lasses, more subdued, holding their backs straight as candles, and in their midst that intelligent face glowing with a smile of satisfaction, those sharp, black eyes keeping watch over each lamb in her care. Not far from the schoolmistress sat two lasses weaving a large wreath of green leaves. Once they had finished, they rose, tiptoed over to her, and placed the wreath on her head. When the song was over, the children swarmed round their teacher like bees, shouting as heartily as their voices would allow. The schoolmistress rose, placed her hat on her head, and made her way out of the wood through the crowd of cheering children like a fairy in a fairy tale.

EPILOGUE

Life is sometimes so confusing that you can't be certain what came first and what came later. By the same token I don't know whether I'm telling this story to get to the end or the beginning of things. Since living abroad, I have experienced my native language—which, as the Croatian poet's ecstatic verse would have it,

> Rustles, rings, resounds, and rumbles
> Thunders, roars, reverberates—

as a stammer, a curse, a malediction or as babble, drab phrase mongering devoid of meaning. Which is why I sometimes feel that here, surrounded by Dutch and communicating in English, I am learning my native language from scratch. It's not easy. I swallow words, regurgitate vowels and consonants. It's a losing battle: I fail to convey what I want to say, and what I do say sounds empty. I'll come out with a word, but can't sense its substance, or I'll sense a certain substance, but can't find the word for it. I keep wondering whether a language thus maimed, a language that has never learned to depict reality, complex as the inner experience of that reality may be, is capable of doing anything at all, telling stories, for instance.

Life has been good to me. I've learned to leave my curtains open. I'm even trying to consider it a virtue. I've enrolled in a Dutch course. Like my classmates, I overuse the personal pronoun *ik*. For beginnings the world begins with *ik: Ik ben Tanja. Ik kom uit vormalige Joegoslavië. Ik loop, ik zie, ik leef, ik praat, ik adem, ik hoor, ik schreeuw* . . . For the time being *ik* doesn't commit me to anything: *ik* is like a children's game, it's like hide-and-seek. People say it's easiest to hide out in the open. In the Dutch mountains. Behind that tough little *i* and *k*.

True, my nightmares have started up again. Now I dream of words, not houses. In the dream I speak an unchecked, uncontrollable language, a language with a false bottom, whose words leap out like a jack-in-the-box and thumb their nose at me. They are usually monologues reflecting my fickle moods. I go through them with a fine-toothed comb. They are long and painful, a never-ending list of complaints. I am often awakened by a painful doglike whimper, my own. In the dream I populate the space around me with words. They burgeon and wind round me like lianas, they spring up like ferns, climb like creepers, open wide like water lilies, overrun me like wild orchids. Their luxuriant jungle sentences leave me breathless. In the morning, ravaged, I can't tell whether to construe their lexical exuberance as punishment or absolution.

But life has been good to me. Paul and Kim, the American couple whose children I take care of four days a week, pay me more than a decent wage. I've become an expert in nursery rhymes and counting rhymes: ours, the English ones, and even a few in

Dutch. The children know *En ten tini, sava raka tini, sava raka tika taka, bija baja buf.* And *Eci peci pec, ti si mali zec, a ja mala vjeverica, eci peci pec.* They know *Rub-a-dub-dub, three men in a tub: the butcher, the baker, the candlestick maker.* And *Amsterdam, die grote stadt. Die is gebouwd op palen. Als die stadt eens ommeviel, wie zou dat betalen.* . . . . Paul and Kim never fail to introduce me to their friends and relatives: "This is Tanja, our babysitter. She's wonderful with children. She really has a way with them. . . ."

My mother is doing fine too, if "fine" is the word for it. She perks up whenever I phone. She tells on life the way children tell on one another: she pulls out her list of complaints and goes on about her diabetes (which she calls "the sugar curse"), her arthritis, the high cost of living. . . . She never asks about me: I'm just there to register the complaints. I've made peace with my role and grown used to our one-way dialogues. I've learned not to let it hurt too much.

Goran's father is no longer with us. "They might as well have stuck him in a garbage bag!" said Olga, sobbing into the receiver. "A garbage bag!" He'd fallen into a coma, so she called for an ambulance, but the paramedics couldn't get the stretcher into the elevator, so they had to wrap him in a blanket and carry him down all ten flights. He died in the hospital a few days later. She told me all about it when I phoned with my condolences. "Though it had to end somewhere," she added in an odd voice, thereby putting a sad yet apathetic end to the incident.

Ana survived her return to Belgrade by less than two years: she was with the Belgrade Television team that perished in the NATO bombing of the city. I've kept the letter she sent me several months after her departure. Along with a short note saying she had found a job and was doing fine, she enclosed a short composition entitled "Depot," her late contribution to our imaginary museum of everyday life in Yugoslavia. It was a melancholy description of the place where the Belgrade tram lines come to rest, a description of the sounds, the sultry summer sunset, the smell of the dust-filled air. "Put it into our plastic tote, the one with the red, white, and blue stripes," she wrote. I was touched by the sweet folly of the gesture. Geert decided to remain in Belgrade. I have no idea what he's doing or how he earns his keep. He phones me now and then, and I can tell from his voice that I, a foreigner, am his only link to "home." I am still at his address.

As for the rest of them, they seem to be holding their own. Ante still plays his accordion all over town. He's at the Noordermarkt every Saturday. People toss their coins into a cap given to him by the fellow from Virovitica who has the hat stall there. All "our people" know him. Nevena has married one of "our" boys and has a daughter by him. She's working at the Mercatorplein branch of the Rabo Bank. Meliha is in Sarajevo. She's managed to reclaim the family flat and evict the people who had been living there illegally. Meliha's parents will have nothing to do with the city: they haven't been back once since moving here. Meliha is living with her *Dačer,* who has set up an NGO for "vulnerable people." Mario has left the university and found work in computer graphics. He has a baby, too, a boy. Boban has joined a local Buddhist sect, shaved his head, turned vegan, and got himself on welfare. Only Johanneke has stuck it out at the university. Her elder daughter has run away. She's in Bosnia with her father. Johanneke is devastated. Selim has gone super Muslim, hanging out with the Vondel Park weirdos, grumbling about how "us Bosnians gotta kick the shit out of them Serb bastards and then the Croats and then the whole Euro crowd, Yanks included." Zole, who came to class only once or twice, has supposedly split for Canada, claiming to be a "double victim"—of Milošević and of the NATO bombs. But a more likely version is that he got in with the local Serb mafia and split to save his skin.

I had this all from Darko when I ran into him on a deserted beach near Wassenaar one day. It was surreal. I barely recognized him: He had a bronze tan and light blond hair, and sported a pair of chic sunglasses and a Walkman. And he was on a horse. He looked like a Calvin Klein model or, rather, a fragile version of same. He was taking riding lessons at the Wassenaar Equestrian Club, he told me. He had a friend, a successful American businessman, and hung out with the gay crowd. Except now he'd left the low life—which he'd always been open about—for a house in Reguliersgracht: Thanks to the friend who'd blown a cool million on it. That's right—a million dollars, two million *guće*. . . .

"I've discovered I love riding," he said. And giving me a soulful look, he added, "Sign up for a course, any course—yoga, salsa, whatever—I tell everybody. As long as it's physical, you get a lot out of it."

"I'm taking Dutch," I said.

"Good for you!" he said, as if talking to somebody somewhere else.

Just then I caught my reflection in his sunglasses and a chill ran up my spine: there were two faces glinting in the lenses, and neither was mine.

But most incredible of all was Igor's story. He'd gone off the deep end, people said. First he got a job as a translator at the Tribunal, where he wasn't the only member of our gang to be thus employed, by the way. But he got himself fired when he stopped showing up for work. Then one day he was found—found himself might be closer to the truth—at some airport or other in Calcutta, Kuala Lumpur, or Singapore. They said he was suffering from a post-traumatic syndrome with a great name, the musical name of "fugue": dissociative fugue, to be exact. These fugues are apparently brought on by a sudden trip. They last anywhere from a few days to a few months and trigger a total blackout, during which the "fugued out" have to manufacture an identity: they have no idea who they are or where they're from. And when they go back to their former lives, they have no idea what they went through in their fugued-out condition. It is a completely crazy lost-and-found disorder nobody'd ever heard of before. Some psychiatrists claim that the fugues don't just happen, that they're set off by drink. Maybe so, but Igor didn't remember having been a drinker. Nobody knew where he was or how he was making ends meet. He might even have gone home. As for the others, they'd gone their separate ways. They'd lost touch.

"By the way," Darko said in a voice a bit too cheery, "I've made another discovery."

"Namely?"

"Opera!" he said, pointing to the Walkman. "I'm wild about Verdi."

He paused and slumped ever so slightly, a fine shadow crossing his delicate, pretty-boy face.

"That time with Uroš . . ." he said haltingly, as if spitting sand from his mouth, "after the dinner, when we celebrated your birthday, remember?"

"I remember," I said.

"Well, I walked him home, and we . . . horsed around a little. . . . Uroš wasn't gay . . . But we were drunk. . . ."

"Why are you telling me this?"

He shrugged his shoulders.

"Don't know. . . . It's been bothering me forever. . . ."

As far as the Hague Tribunal is concerned, the files are piling up, the mounds of paper growing; the videotapes of the proceedings could cover the length and breadth of the land that is no longer. Every loss seems to have been taken care of in real, ironic, or grotesque terms—yet taken care of nonetheless. Wounds have healed properly for some, poorly for others—yet healed they have. Even the scars are fading. Everyone is somewhere, some doing what they do best, others doing the best they can. Life has dealt better cards to some than others, but everyone has found some kind of niche. The dead and disappeared have yet to be counted, many of the perpetrators are still at large, much rubble has yet to be cleared, many mines defused, but the dust has settled. Life goes on and for the present at least is good to everyone.

One day the Tribunal will land the biggest culprit of them all, and I will go have a look at him. He will be wearing a gray suit, white shirt, and bright red tie. The color of the tie will be identical to that of a judge's robe. The defendant will sit in his glass cage, his jaw clenched and his mouth in the shape of an upside-down U. The clock will show the time, but it will not be the time of the world outside the courtroom. I will be shocked to discover that in the few intervening years I have forgotten everything, that I can scarcely bring up the names of the people who so played with our lives. I will have the feeling it is a hundred years since the war broke out, not nine or ten. I will confront my forgetting head on and with a profound sense of horror. The man in the red tie will speak a language I no longer understand. I will remember even the following detail: leafing through the papers in front of him, the accused will lick his fingers like a village shopkeeper; he will raise his head, as if to sniff the air around him, and squint into the courtroom; at that moment the eyes behind the glass and mine will meet; the eyes will be dark, dull, void of expression; his tightly clenched jaw and dull stare will remind me of a polar bear; then he will lift his paw, brush the invisible flies away from his nose, and go back to staring blankly in front of him.

Sometimes I think of Uroš and think he made the right choice. He took along his pencils and pads and velvet yarmulkes, one for each day of the week. He brushes his teeth and, circumstances permitting, turns to face the sacred Kotel ha-Ma'aravi wall. Sweating like an accountant, he writes out his grievances and prayers on scraps of paper, which he rolls into small tubes, and stuffs them into the cracks between the blocks of stone.

We've come out of everything we went through in one of three ways, says Igor: The better for it, the worse for it, or, like Uroš, with a bullet in the skull. I don't know where I stand, except that I managed to dodge the bullet.

And speaking of Igor, I didn't let on to Darko that I knew more about his circumstances than what he'd told me that day on the beach. For one thing, the statement I gave to the police never reached him. The cop who came to my place must have felt he'd done enough for me by removing the handcuffs. And right he was, too. I underestimated his acumen.

Igor is currently working with some Irish builders. The Irish are good with their hands, skilled carpenters. They renovate houses and flats: tear down walls and build them up again, lug out all the junk that has piled up over the years—do whatever is called for. Not that Amsterdam isn't full of "our people," but Igor steers clear of them. Igor has taken to this hard manual labor quite recently. He puts everything he's got into it, as if it were a penance of sorts. Maybe he's driven by the insane notion that by the sweat of his brow he is restoring a certain equilibrium, that for every wall he builds here one will rise out of the ruins there, in the villages of Bosnia or Croatia or wherever it may be needed.

Life has been good to us. Igor leaves early and comes home early. He heads straight for the shower, washes off the dirt, puts on clean clothes, rolls up his shirtsleeves, and takes his seat at the table. I serve a freshly prepared meal. We eat slowly and, oddly enough, speak little. Our words are as dry as sand. I like their dryness. Maybe we're becoming Dutch. The Dutch are said to speak only when they have something to say.

After dinner I curl up next to him, breathe in his smell, breathe through his skin like a fish through its gills. I set my pulse to his, I course through his veins. I pull back for an instant to look at him, as if unable to believe he's here . . . I notice a smudge of paint left on his cheek and lick at it, remove it with my saliva. I pull at his lip with my teeth, push my tongue into his mouth and suck out the oxygen crucial to my survival, then deliver the oxygen crucial to his. We both feel an intoxicating blast as the present invades our every last vein, and for a time we inhale the pure extract of nothing to remember and nothing to forget.

Occasionally my angst gains the upper hand. When it does, I grab my bag, fling a coat over my shoulders, and race out of the apartment. Igor has stopped offering to go with me; he leaves me to my own devices, knowing where I'm off to. It's usually the seaside, one of those long sandy beaches. I love the deserted Dutch beaches in late autumn and winter. I stand there gazing at the gray sea and gray sky, stand there riveted, facing an imaginary wall. Then I open my mouth and let out the words, slowly at first, then faster, faster and louder. I flicker my tongue like a fairy tale dragon, and it forks into Croatian, Serbian, Bosnian, Slovenian, Macedonian. . . . Facing the invisible wall, I thrust my head rhythmically into the wind and speak. I do not believe in God; I know no prayer. Enveloped in the wind, imprinted onto the landscape as into a lantern-slide panorama, I, the Teacher, the pride of my generation, speak what I have to speak, speak my Balkan litany. I shatter the glass with my voice like Oskar Matzerath. I secrete the words from my mouth like ink from a cuttlefish. I post my sounds to the nameless like a message in a bottle. Having cast them to the winds, I see them flying through the air. I watch them curl into tiny tubes, loop the loop and nosedive into the wall of water, where they dissolve instantly, like Alka-Seltzer.

May you be cursed in this world and the next.
May you not live to see the sun rise.
May the vultures get you.
May you vanish from the earth.
May you walk a thorn field barefoot.
May God make you thinner than a thread and blacker than a
     pot.
May you reap wormwood where you sow basil.
May the Devil torment you.
May the Devil lap your soup.
May ravens caw at you.
May thunder and lightning strike you.
May lightning strike you and split you down the
     middle.
May you wander blind over the earth.
May a serpent bite you in the heart.
May you suffer like a worm under bark.
May your heart quarter and burst.
May you never more see the light of day.
May all abandon you.
May you lose all but your name.

May your seed be obliterated.

May your life be bleak and barren.

May a serpent wind round your waist.

May a serpent swallow you whole.

May the sun burn you alive.

May your sugar be bitter.

May you choke on bread and salt.

May the sea cast up your bones.

May grass sprout through your bones.

May you turn to dust and ashes.

May your mouth utter never a word.

May you be damned.

May a live wound devour you.

May the waters close up over you.

May your name be forgotten.

May you never see the sun.

May you rust over.

May you be murdered every day of the year.

May your roots dry up.

May you lick ashes.

May your heart turn to stone.

May you die in darkness.

May your soul fall out.

May you never eat your fill.

May your joys lament.

May you drift without end.

May you go deaf.

May you go dumb.

May the earth push up your bones.

May you be devoured by worms.

May you lose your soul and nails.

May you never again see your house.

May you lack bread when you have salt.

May you turn to wood and stone.
May your star go out.
May you take to the road.
May your days be black.
May your tongue go mute.
May you leave your bones behind. . . .

And when my vocal cords give out, when my forehead goes numb from the wind, I abandon the beach calm and collected, leaving no trace. The Dutch horizontals are good; they are like the school blotters of yesteryear: they absorb everything.